"Didn't you know how important a child would be to me?"

Adam shouted, surprised at his own sudden rise of anger. "How could you not know that?" he persisted. "Children are everything to the Amish. There is no purpose in our lives—not for a man or a woman—without children."

"I knew, Adam. Probably better than anyone who isn't one of you. Your way of life was mine as long as I could get away with it."

"And you still denied me my child!"

"Yes. I did what I thought was best."

"What *you* thought. You had no time, no need to ask the baby's father."

"My baby's father was lost to me."

"Your baby's father was in *hell*!" he hissed at her.

Dear Reader,

Each and every month, to meet your sophisticated standards, to satisfy your taste for substantial, memorable, emotion-packed stories of life and love, of dreams and possibilities, Silhouette brings you six extremely **Special Editions**.

Now these exclusive editions are wearing a brand-new wrapper, a more sophisticated look—our way of marking Silhouette **Special Editions'** continually renewed commitment to bring you the very best, the brightest and the most up-to-date in romance writing.

Reach for all six freshly packaged Silhouette **Special Editions** each month—the insides are every bit as delicious as the outsides—and savor a bounty of meaty, soul-satisfying romantic novels by authors who are already your favorites and those who are about to become so.

And don't forget the two Silhouette *Classics* at your bookseller's every month—the most beloved Silhouette **Special Editions** and Silhouette *Intimate Moments* of yesteryear, reissued by popular demand.

Today's bestsellers, tomorrow's *Classics*—that's Silhouette **Special Edition**. And now, we're looking more special than ever!

From all the authors and editors of Silhouette **Special Edition**,

Warmest wishes,

Leslie Kazanjian,
Senior Editor

CHERYL REAVIS
A Crime of the Heart

Silhouette Special Edition

Published by Silhouette Books New York

America's Publisher of Contemporary Romance

For Linda Buechting and Dawn Poore,
who supported this book in
thought and deed: Many thanks.

For M.C., my Mennonite friend,
whom I remember fondly.

And for D.B., who shared with me
the Pennsylvania Experience: Be strong.

SILHOUETTE BOOKS
300 East 42nd St., New York, N.Y. 10017

Copyright © 1988 by Cheryl Reavis

All rights reserved. Except for use in any review,
the reproduction or utilization of this work in
whole or in part in any form by any electronic,
mechanical or other means, now known or
hereafter invented, including xerography,
photocopying and recording, or in any information
storage or retrieval system, is forbidden without
the permission of Silhouette Books, 300 E. 42nd St.,
New York, N.Y. 10017

ISBN: 0-373-09487-6

First Silhouette Books printing November 1988

All the characters in this book are fictitious. Any
resemblance to actual persons, living or dead, is
purely coincidental.

®: Trademark used under license and
registered in the United States Patent and
Trademark Office and in other countries.

Printed in the U.S.A.

Acknowledgments

Thanks to Richard W. Reavis, who baby-sat a printer and tore pages into the wee hours.

And to the gentlemen of MBI Business Centers in Charlotte, North Carolina, who take great pains to treat a writer with malfunctioning softwear kindly.

CHERYL REAVIS,

public health nurse and award-winning romance novelist who also writes under the name of *Cinda Richards,* says she is a writer of emotions. "I want to feel all the joys and the sorrows and everything in between. Then, with just the right word, the right turn of phrase, I hope to take the reader by the hand and make her feel them, too." Cheryl currently makes her home in North Carolina with her husband and teenage son.

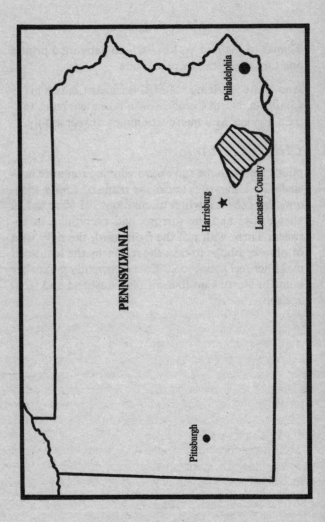

Author's Note

I was nineteen years old when I first heard about the Plain People. It was a snowy afternoon, and I was attending a lecture on coping mechanisms. At one point the lecturer cited Amish girls as an example. Since they were forbidden makeup and jewelry of any kind, young Amish girls, he maintained, sometimes satisfied their basic human need for adornment by wearing eyeglasses—whether they needed them or not. Fascinating! And what a tribute to the indomitable spirit of women.

Thus began my long interest in this remarkable group of people, who, by their own choice, remain firmly entrenched in another century. Finally, nearly twenty-five years later, I was ready to begin that wonderful writer's game of "What if..."

Chapter One

He hadn't thought it would hurt so much to see her again. He had expected, at the very most, anger. He had never really believed she would come back here, he hadn't *wanted* her to come back here, and yet here she stood, the long dark hair he remembered cropped off short in a way he supposed was fashionable.

"Adam Sauder," she said quietly, extending her hand to him as if they were old friends and not old lovers.

He hesitated a moment, then took it, because he thought it hadn't occurred to her that she might find him in the shambles of what was once her mother's kitchen on her first day back, and because he thought she wasn't quite well. She was very pale, and her hand—the same small hand he remembered—felt cold and trembly in his. He stared into her eyes, lovely hazel eyes that wanted to dart away but didn't.

He gave a small shrug and let go of her hand. "I don't know what to call you."

She smiled. "Quinn," she said dryly, teasing him as if she had the right to do that.

He didn't return the smile. "I heard you were married." He sensed Holland Wakefield, the contractor she'd hired to undo the damage the previous owner of the house had done, shuffling nervously in the background.

Holland, like everyone else, knew the old scandal about Quinn Tyler and the Amishman, Adam Sauder—or thought he did. But it had been a long time ago, and Holland had needed a good, dependable carpenter to work part-time on the interior of this house. A family as big as old Jacob Sauder's could always use the extra money, and, until this minute, Holland had obviously forgotten Quinn's connection to this particular carpenter. Adam had realized that the afternoon Holland had come to the Sauder farm to hire him. He had left his father and brothers in the midst of their spring planting and taken the job anyway.

"No," Quinn said. "We . . . we didn't have the wedding."

"The 'English' have strange customs," he said, not meeting her eyes now. He picked up a hammer and went back to his work.

Quinn heard quite plainly what he didn't say: *Like almost getting married. Like giving away my son.*

So that was how it was going to be, she thought. He was unforgiving—as unforgiving as old Jacob himself.

She gave a soft sigh. No doubt she was being unfair to Adam's father. Jacob Sauder had only wanted Adam to remain in the way of life he loved and believed in. In the end, she had wanted that, as well. And yet Adam was clean shaven. He was wearing the usual Amish clothes—black "barn door" trousers with suspenders and a blue shirt that gave more color to his pale blue eyes. His hair, light brown and sun streaked from the time he spent outdoors, was cut in the acceptable Amish fashion—a bit long, with bangs that wanted to fall into a center part. Yet he didn't have the untrimmed whiskers that were, among other things, the symbol of a married man.

She hadn't considered that he wouldn't have married, and she tried to ignore the fact that, selfish or not, it gave her a definite sense of relief. She had hoped to have some time to get used to being home again before she faced him; she certainly hadn't wanted to come back and immediately hear about what a good wife he had. Or about his children. His *other* children.

But you wanted him to be happy, Quinn. It takes that to make an Amishman happy—a good wife and children.

"I'm sorry, Holland, what?" she said, belatedly realizing that the man was addressing her. She tried to drag her eyes away from Adam's strong back as he pulled nails out of damaged boards in the far wall. Adam was tall and rawboned like his father and, at the moment, just as reproachful. She remembered only too well Jacob Sauder's reproach. No matter how much she tried to forget it or how painful it was, the memory still came to her: old Jacob, standing on the porch in the dark with her.

"Don't take away my son, Quinn Tyler."

"I said, how much in a hurry are you to move in?" Holland repositioned his green ball cap with the Hurst and Hahn Lumber Company emblem on it, clearly recognizing an awkward situation once he was knee-deep in it.

"I'm moving in today."

"Honey, you can't do that. It's not near ready to—"

"The plumbing works?"

"Well, yes, but—"

"The fireplace in the front bedroom upstairs?"

"I had the boy sweep all the chimneys last week."

"The electricity's on, and I've got a hot plate. That's all I need." She looked around the big kitchen, remembering what it had looked like when she was growing up, when her mother was alive. It was unbelievable what selfish, careless strangers could do. The room had been stripped of everything that could be taken—cabinet doors, light fixtures, molding, built-in appliances, and, in some instances, the cabinets themselves. She had lost this house once herself, yet she hadn't wanted to destroy it upon leaving. It was going to take a lot of work to set this place right again.

She glanced back at Adam, but he worked on in that quiet yet condemning way he had. But for that, she might have thought he believed himself to be alone. She walked outside with Holland, who was visibly trying to work up to something.

"Holland, what?" she asked to help him along. She had always been straightforward, and she hated to see anyone suffer as much as he was in trying to decide whether or not he should speak his mind.

"Quinn, I forgot about Adam and...things. If you don't want him here, I can—"

"Holland, it's all right. I don't mind him being here."

She had never seen a man look so relieved.

"You sure? I mean, I know you've been sick and all."

"I'm sure." She made herself smile. "I don't mind."

"Well, good, then. You know you'll get honest work from him. He's a fine carpenter. He won't do anything halfway. I'll be by tomorrow, and we'll see about some of the work upstairs."

She nodded and watched him get into his truck and go. Business must be good, she thought idly, waving as he backed around. The truck was new. She stood for a while on the porch steps, staring at the meticulously cultivated field that led to a line of budding trees in the distance. The field had once belonged to her father. Eighty acres of fine farmland, and she'd only been able to get back the house and ten by paying considerably more than the market value. The rest of land had been auctioned off piecemeal, bought up by her

Amish and Mennonite neighbors from the man who had acquired her father's farm and run the entire place into wrack and ruin. She walked down the rickety steps and out into the yard, turning back to look at the now neglected farmhouse she'd been born in.

She was glad her father hadn't lived to see the broken windowpanes, the desperate need for paint. The porch was rotting, and the four-in-one apple tree her mother had planted in the backyard had been chopped down to make room to park a car or a truck. She could still see the spots where the oil had leaked, and the grass no longer grew in the ruts. There were dozens of other places to park a vehicle that would not have required savaging such a grand and practical old tree. It had been quite a wonder, blooming in sections and bearing four different kinds of apples in a growing season. The man couldn't have been much of a farmer not to have seen its worth, nor to have followed the practice here of putting back whatever one took away. Adam, his father, her father—all would have replanted a cut tree.

She looked out across the fields again. This was her favorite season, spring, the time of new life and tender green. The sun was warm, and the wind gently lifted her hair.

Please... she thought, without really knowing what it was she wanted. A quiet life? To make peace with Adam?

She took a deep breath and turned to go back into the house. She hadn't eaten, and she resisted the urge to place her hand against the small circle of not-quite pain in her midsection. She had convinced herself that she had to come back to rural living for her health, to finally rid herself of the curse of the upwardly mobile—an old-fashioned, stress-induced stomach ulcer that had come with her job as head accountant for a brokerage firm in Philadelphia. And here was Adam Sauder, working silently in her kitchen.

"Adam, how much longer will you be here?" she asked as she opened the back door.

If he heard her, he gave no indication.

"Adam?"

He continued pulling nails, his broad back turned toward her, still unforgiving, unapproachable.

"What is this, the *Meidung*?" she asked, and he looked around sharply. "I didn't think you ever bothered shunning outsiders."

He pulled another nail. "You haven't changed, Quinn. You still make fun of us."

"That's not true. I've never done that."

He glanced over his shoulder at her. She was frowning, and she was still Quinn, regardless of their years apart, regardless of her "worldly" haircut. It was an old argument, one they'd begun when he was eight and she was six, and one they'd been destined to repeat over the years whenever he'd tried to make her understand the unbreachable differences between her life and his. He'd felt sorry for her then, when they were children and she couldn't comprehend that, no matter how hard she tried, no matter how good she was or how much she wanted it, she couldn't be Amish. She had loved his way of life, and she'd thought that he could somehow give her Amishness. But he couldn't make her Amish like him, and he'd had but one defense against her wanting and her disappointment. He had but one defense now—to deliberately make her angry.

"No?" he asked without looking at her. "That isn't what I remember."

"No," she said firmly. "And you know it."

He went on pulling nails. He hadn't fooled her. He'd never been able to fool her. She had always been able to tell what he was thinking. When he was sixteen and forced to quit school like all Amish children, when he was a barefoot boy plowing with a team of mules, she'd come to him in the fields time after time, secretly bringing him the books he wasn't supposed to want or need. He'd been unkind to her then, pretending that he had no interest in the "English" or their books, never expressing the gratitude that had filled his heart to bursting. But she had understood, and she'd lent him her books anyway, staying for a while to talk to him, walking with him as he cajoled the mules along, because she knew that he had to keep plowing, knew that he couldn't be idle.

But she hadn't known how upsetting her presence had been. He had loved her even then—he couldn't remember when he *hadn't* loved her. He had wanted only two things in his life. He'd wanted to know about the world, and he'd wanted Quinn Tyler, and his father had looked into his eyes and seen the longing for them both.

"What will your father say if he sees you out here with me?" he'd complained to her once, knowing it wasn't *her* father that worried him.

"He'd say, Adam, 'There's Quinn walking along with Adam while he plows.' *Your* father would think I was trying lead you into 'worldy wisdom and high-mindedness.'"

"Don't, Quinn! You always make fun of us!"

He'd hurt her with that accusation then, just as he'd hurt her with it now. She had never been any good at hiding whatever she was feeling from him, either. Even now he could see her struggle to keep her anger in check.

"Look, Adam. I'm going into town to buy some groceries. I don't know when the moving people are coming. If I'm not back before you go, just leave the door open for them, all right?"

He didn't answer.

"Fine," she said, snatching up her purse. "Lord!" she said under her breath on the way out. She pressed the circle in her midsection that was now a burning ache. She'd gone too long without eating, and she shouldn't have let herself get so angry. No, that wasn't right, either. According to her instructor in stress management, she should have done just that. She should have gotten angry and gotten it over with. She should have told Adam Sauder exactly what a jackass she thought he was being, so that she wouldn't be saddled with all this repressed emotion, and supposedly she'd feel better.

Except that whatever rudeness Adam Sauder showed her, she deserved. She sat behind the wheel of her car for a moment, then searched her purse for antacid tablets, popping two of them into her mouth and resting her head on the steering wheel. Her hands were shaking. She had to do better than this. She didn't know why Adam was here anyway. He'd known she was coming. She could tell the minute she walked into the kitchen that he hadn't been in the least surprised.

Adam. Her first lover. The father of her only child, a child she'd given away in adoption because he couldn't marry her without losing everything. Another memory surfaced, one of being sated from their lovemaking and wet with dew, and trying to creep into this very house. Her father—and his—had been waiting for her on the dark porch.

"I love Adam!" she'd told them defiantly.

"Yes," old Jacob had agreed, his voice tired and sad. "I see that from the time you are children. I see when you are a little girl that you love him as your brother because you don't have one of your own. I see you make him your hero and your friend. Now you would make him a husband you cannot have—"

"No! I *can* have him. We *can* be together!"

"Yes. You can be together—if he will never see his family again. If he will leave us, his home, the land that is to be his. Tell me this, Quinn Tyler. Our Adam is headstrong. He wants the books and the schooling. He wants to know, always to know worldly things. But is he unhappy to be what he is? Does he hate the land? Does he hate us?"

"No, of course not. He loves all of you. He loves being Amish."

"Yes! He loves that, and he thinks he loves you. But he can't have both. He will stay with us or he will leave—whatever *you* ask of him. Our children are raised up in the way they should go, Quinn Tyler, so that they should never depart from it. The shunning is a terrible thing for us. You know that, and you must be the one to decide which of these loves of his will hurt him more."

"I can't do that."

"You can, Quinn Tyler. You and you alone. I ask you now. Don't take my son! You say you love him. Do you love him enough to let him go?"

In the end, the answer to that had been yes. She had loved Adam Sauder with all her heart, but he was an Amishman, and he cared about his way of life as much as he cared about her. She hadn't known about the baby then, and by the time she did, her father was dying.

Like all farmers, John Tyler had been in debt, and his medical bills cost him the farm and everything else he owned. They had had to sell everything and take a small apartment near the hospital in Philadelphia so that her father could get the treatments he needed without the exorbitant expense of trips into the city and a hospital stay. It was there that Quinn learned the true meaning of the cliché, "mercifully quick." Her mother's death had been that, a stroke one quiet Saturday evening while she hemmed dish towels for the church bazaar; she hadn't lasted the night. But Quinn's father—she would never forget his bravery upon being plunged so abruptly into a disease whose cure was all but deadly, and, when he was still so bewildered by the loss of his wife.

He had been too ill to attend the auction of the property, too ashamed of having precipitated the sale, regardless of whether or not it was his fault. Quinn had taken care of it, stoically witnessing the final loss of purpose in her father's life. But, through it all, she had let herself be comforted by the knowledge that Adam Sauder loved her.

Then her father died; in a span of eighteen months she had lost both parents. She had been nineteen years old, not out of college, bankrupt—and pregnant. She could have let Adam choose between her and living Amish, but she didn't. There was the fact of her pregnancy, and his knowing about that would have left him no choice at all. He would have taken care of her—she knew that—and he would have lost everything else he loved. And not because he had made the decision himself, but because her circumstances had forced him into it. He would have been shunned, excommunicated from his family, his faith, forever. She hadn't trailed along after him for most of her life without knowing what pain that would cause him. Regardless of his passion for books and his insatiable curiosity about "worldly" things, he was Amish. It was one of the things she'd admired so about him, his reverence for this simple way of life and for the land, a reverence she herself had had. She had known in her heart which love would hurt him more, even without old Jacob's admonishments, and she had made the choice for him.

She hadn't kept their baby; she hadn't intended that he should ever know about him. And she had stayed away from here, because she had had to take away from Adam all possibility of a choice. She had known as no one else could that he would never have stayed Amish if she had kept his child. Dear God, the price she'd paid to give Adam Sauder a chance for a happy life—and he hadn't taken it. He wasn't happy; he hadn't married and had children....

"Quinn?" Adam said at the car window, and she jumped.

"You are...all right?" The eyes she turned to his were so filled with pain that he nearly reached out to her.

But then she looked away.

"I'm fine," she said coldly. And she started the car and drove off.

who hurriedly dressed, dragging on his shirt with fumbling fingers that refused to cooperate. She watched him from the bed, the sheet bunched over her breasts.

"Oh, damn," she cried, and she turned her face aside and wept.

Chapter Two

The short trip into town took longer than she expected. She was caught in a string of vehicles behind an Amish horse and buggy, and it was a long time before she could pass, a long time to creep along and think about Adam Sauder. She went around the buggy carefully when she had the chance, unable to keep from smiling and waving at the small face that grinned at her out the back window. Life here hadn't changed, only she had.

She bought groceries first, then a cooler and some ice to keep the few perishables she had purchased from spoiling in case the moving van came late. In every store she searched the faces around her for someone she knew. She saw no one, and it occurred to her that she was truly a stranger here now. There was almost no one left whom she could approach and say, "It's me, Quinn."

Her parents were dead. She had no siblings, no relatives. Yes, she did have a relative. She had a child, a son who was ten years old now. She had gone to great pains to see that he would have a good life, handling his adoption privately through Edison Clark, a local lawyer she'd known all her life. She had reviewed the statistics of the nameless couples he gave her with the same relentless intensity with which she approached anything that mattered to her. She hadn't known their names, but she had known everything else about them. She made sure of that, sending Edison back to the couples with additional questions before she finally made up her mind.

She had known exactly what she wanted for her baby: she wanted her son or daughter to grow up, not necessarily rich or successful by today's standards, but a decent human being. Recognizing the kind of man and woman she thought could provide that, even with Edison's kind advice, had been no easy task.

She sighed and turned into the Dairy Queen for a milk shake to soothe her burning stomach. Edison was helping her now, too. She would do accounting for his office, and she would be able to stay at home to do it. Surely that would help, being able to do something she was good at, in her own time, instead of being embroiled in the killingly hectic world of high finance. She hoped to add other small businesses to her list of clients, enough to keep her busy and solvent. Perhaps she might even be able to buy back more of the Tyler land.

She watched a group of little boys pile out of a van and rush inside the Dairy Queen while she waited for her milk shake. What do ten-year-old boys do? she wondered. Little League? Cub Scouts? She knew what ten-year-old Amish boys did. They worked. A child as young as five had his 'job' to do. But it was a good thing for children, she believed, to be responsible for something necessary for the welfare of the whole family, even at so young an age. Adam Sauder was proof of that.

The Adam she remembered was hardworking and honorable and kind, strong and yet gentle. She had never, in all her years away, really met a man she admired more, not even the man she'd almost married. Marriage would have been a mistake, because she had hopelessly confused her dreams with reality. She had wanted to be happy with another man, needed to be happy, but she had loved Adam Sauder.

On the drive back, she passed the one-room Amish schoolhouse, a white wooden building with an open steeple and a front porch, where her mother had taught for so many years. On impulse she backed up, stopped the car and got out to walk around the school yard under the trees. It still had a hand water pump in the yard, and outhouses with symbols cut in the doors—a crescent for girls, a star for boys. Her mother had been "worldly" but an acceptable teacher because the Amish had no educated teachers of their own and because she had been their neighbor John Tyler's wife.

Quinn could still remember how hard her mother had worked to instill as much knowledge as she could in the short time an Amish child was allowed to attend school, rising to the challenge of many different learning levels in one classroom and the barriers of culture and language. Most of the young children spoke only their "at home" German dialect when they started school, and she remembered well her mother returning home, exhausted from a day of pantomiming classroom instructions.

Quinn had wanted so desperately to go to school here— but to be with Adam, not because her mother was the reverently titled "Teacher." Even then he'd been a focal point in her life. She couldn't remember *not* feeling the warmth of knowing that they somehow belonged together, regardless of his being Amish and her, "English."

It was still there, that thread of belonging. She had felt it the moment she looked at him today. And he had felt it, as well. His silence, his aloofness told her that. She had always known him so well—still knew him so well.

Oh, Adam, somehow we're going to have to talk.

"You'd better get yourself together, Quinn," she said out loud, getting back into her car. She couldn't talk to Adam. What she had done was irrevocable, and to his mind, clearly unforgivable. There was nothing she could say, and there was no point in talking now.

She met another horse and buggy on the way home, one driven by an Amishman she thought was Adam's father. Their eyes met briefly as they passed, but he gave no sign of recognition. She didn't look the same, of course, but he did. Her heart began to pound as she drove past, even though she had no reason to be afraid of him now; she had done exactly what he'd wanted her to do that last summer night on the porch.

She hadn't been afraid the first time he had come to the farm to talk to her about Adam. She had been innocent then. She and Adam were only friends, not lovers, and perhaps they would have stayed friends, but for him. She had lived with the Amish community at her doorstep all her life, and she had understood Jacob Sauder's fear, understood that he believed she was willfully taking away his son. But understanding didn't prepare her for the beating he'd inflicted on Adam. She had known that the Amish were strict disciplinarians. Her mother taught in their school. There were never any problems with rowdiness or disrespect.

But Adam had been old enough to be beyond corporal punishment—she'd thought. Her heart contracted with the memory of that night he'd come to her, ashamed of what had happened to him but needing her desperately. She hadn't realized at first that he'd been hurt physically, seeing only the emotional pain, only him, standing in the rain on her back doorstep. He wouldn't come inside, and he wouldn't answer her questions. And when she reached out to touch him, he had pushed her hand away.

"What is it?" she kept saying, her alarm growing. And when he abruptly turned to go, she went out into the rain after him, hanging on to his arm to slow him down, finally throwing herself bodily at him to make him stop. He'd held her so tightly, the rain beating down on them both.

"I shouldn't have come here," he whispered. "I have to go, Quinn. If I don't, it'll be too late for us both...."

She remembered. The wet, green, damp earth smell of spring rain, the fierceness of her need to take away whatever it was that was hurting him so. They had never kissed before, but now her mouth sought his, knowing he wouldn't resist her. It was she who had led the way into the dry darkness of the barn. Their bed had been a rough army blanket her father kept in his truck, spread on a pile of hay in the loft. And there, in the torment of the impossibility of their love, they had bound themselves to each other forever.

"Get yourself together, Quinn!" she admonished herself again. "And keep your mind on your driving." It served no purpose to remember, to feel the pain of her loss again. If she'd learned nothing else in the years of her exile, she'd learned that. She drove the rest of the way, hoping that Adam had chores at home he needed to do and would no longer be there.

He was still working in the kitchen, and whatever had made him express concern about her earlier, he now had firmly in check. She made no further attempts to talk to him, filling the cooler with ice and the milk and cheese and cold cuts she'd bought and leaving it on the screened-in back porch. She made several trips to the car, lugging in a vacuum cleaner she'd brought with her, and a radio. She took them both upstairs, turning the radio on loud so she could hear it while she vacuumed the bedroom—her old bedroom, the one with the window that faced the Sauder farm.

When she looked out, she could see the rooftops glistening in the sun, just as she had when she was young.

Don't! she chided herself. *Keep working. Don't think about it.*

This room was in much better shape than the kitchen. She vacuumed everything, then mopped the floor and washed the windows. She'd be all right here. She had to be all right here. But she was so aware of Adam's presence in the house she could hardly bear it.

The movers came, and she had no choice but to go downstairs again. She didn't have that much to move, thankfully, just enough for one small truck. She'd been able to salvage only a few pieces of her parents' furniture when the farm was sold—family antiques, a bed with a five-foot headboard and carved oak leaves, a few random tables and an armoire. And she'd lived in a Philadelphia apartment small enough for her not to have acquired much more—a refrigerator, a chintz sofa, a big oak library table, which she planned to use as a computer desk for her accounting work, and an elegantly carved and upholstered rocking chair.

She could sense Adam's covert watchfulness, his interest in the things she was bringing home with her, but she kept working, supervising the placement of her belongings. She wasn't able to get the refrigerator into the kitchen, and the boxes of dishes and small appliances had to be stacked in the wide front hall, as well, until the carpentry work was finished. The movers, clearly not used to Plain People, stared at Adam and his Amish clothes with a curiosity that bordered on rudeness. But they—and she, for that matter—might as well have not been there for all the notice he gave.

By late afternoon she was technically moved in, and she was once again alone in the house with Adam. Or so she thought. She looked up from unpacking her clothes and bed linens to see a young Amish boy standing in the doorway. It had always been difficult to guess who was actually related to whom among the Amish, but this boy was definitely a Sauder. He had darker hair and eyes than Adam's, but the same basic nose, eyebrows and chin.

"Hello," she said. She knew he was here for a purpose, and she knew also that he would be typically curious about this "English" house.

He gave her a shy smile, then looked carefully around the room, his gaze falling on a long purple satin evening dress hanging on the closet door. The dress was expensive, a designer original; it was one of the few times she'd ever indulged herself. The boy seemed to find the sequined bodice and sleeves most interesting, but after a moment he remembered the reason for his trip upstairs.

"Adam says the sky wants rain. And your car is...opened," he said, his English sounding as if it were a literal translation of German. She had almost forgotten that peculiarity of the dialect, and she tried not to smile.

"I guess I'd better close it then, hadn't I?"

He was staring at the purple dress again. "What for dress do you have?"

"That? That's an evening dress. English girls wear dresses like that sometimes when they go to a special party. I used to wear it when I lived in Philadelphia. It's..." She tried to think of the way he might phrase it. "It's just for fancy," she decided.

He gave a small sigh. "Not plain," he said to underscore her definition, but it was merely an observation, not a recrimination.

"Do you want to see what makes it sparkle?"

He looked up at her and grinned.

She took the dress down from the closet door and unzipped the protective plastic bag. "See? The little round things here—those are sequins. They sew them on close together, and then when the light shines—"

"Daniel!" Adam said from the doorway, making them both jump. "Did you do what I told you?"

The boy nodded, looking from one adult to the other.

"Then come away from here. You know better."

"I was only showing him the sequins on the dress, Adam," Quinn said, knowing better herself but trying to intervene anyway.

"The less he knows of the English, the better off he will be."

"Dear God, you've grown up to be just like Jacob."

"What I am," he said sarcastically, "*Jacob* had no hand in." He turned to go, stopping at the head of the stairs. "I won't be back here. You will have to get Holland to find another carpenter."

"No, I didn't think you would," she answered, following him into the upstairs hallway. "Adam!" she called when he reached the bottom of the stairs. He looked up at her. "I saw Jacob on the road when I went into town today."

He didn't reply. The only response she got from him was the slamming of the front door.

"English girls wear shiny dresses to parties," Daniel said as they walked home over the damp, fertile earth in the plowed north field. The sky was growing darker, and Adam could smell the coming rain. He kept walking, knowing that Daniel was having to take big steps over the furrows to keep up, knowing how impressed his little brother was with his first encounter with Quinn Tyler and how badly he wanted to talk about her.

"The English—what is her name, Adam?"

"What her name is or anything else about her, you don't need to know," Adam snapped, walking faster to stay ahead of any more questions.

"Adam! Adam, wait," Daniel called behind him. "Anymore, I won't be a bad boy, Adam. I'll be quiet for you."

"I'll be quiet for you." When had he learned that he had to make concessions to be allowed to stay in Adam's company? He had no right to take his foul mood out on Daniel, yet how many times had he done it without even realizing it?

"Daniel, come on," he said, waiting for him to catch up. The boy could hardly be accused of being too boisterous, of being anything but persistent. Compared to some of the others of the Sauder clan—to Eli and Mary and Anna—one hardly knew Daniel was around at all. He had always been the quiet one, and, if Adam admitted it, his favorite of all his brothers and sisters. Daniel watched and listened and loved without reservation—everything, everyone. He had such a gentle way about him, with animals, with people. Adam gave a sharp sigh and began walking again, more slowly this time. "Her name is Quinn," he said after a while. "Quinn Tyler."

"Quinn," Daniel repeated, as if testing the feel of it. "Quinn! She... smells like pretty flowers. Like clover and like... roses. Will Quinn wear her shiny dress here, Adam? It's just for fancy, not just for so."

"Daniel, I don't know. If she does, you won't see it."

"You could take me to her house there and I could see it," he said hopefully. "In the buggy," he added, because he truly loved a buggy ride.

"No. I couldn't. And anyplace she'd wear a dress like that, we wouldn't want to go."

"Philadelphia."

"What?"

"She wears her shiny dress in Philadelphia. Could we go to Philadelphia again? On the train?"

"Sometime we will go to Philadelphia—to the zoo, not to see any shiny purple dresses." With that, he scooped Daniel up under his arm, striding along with his box of carpenter's tools and a dangling, giggling little brother. He had no reason to be in such a bad mood. He had seen Quinn again, and his curiosity was satisfied. She *had* changed, as he'd expected. She was different now.

And yet she was the same.

He pushed the thought away. It didn't matter that she was the same, that she looked and talked and smelled like Quinn, or that he remembered everything.

Everything.

He knew the feel of her body, how she would taste, what it was like to lie with her in the dark and hear her say his name. He closed his eyes with the pain of it.

"She wants to cry," Daniel said from his nearly upside-down position.

"What?"

"She wants to cry," he repeated as Adam put him down.

"Who wants to cry?"

"Quinn Tyler wants to cry."

"Daniel . . ." Adam said in exasperation. He didn't want to talk about Quinn anymore.

"But she can't. Why can't she?"

"Daniel, you talk too much. Get along now. You have chores to do before we eat. Go!" He watched his youngest brother run ahead, his brother who was the same age as his own lost son. He smiled a bit as Daniel turned and waved. If he said Quinn wanted to cry, then she did. Daniel would know that about her without her telling him, just because he was Daniel.

He looked back over his shoulder at the Tyler house. He still believed something was wrong with her, something that caused her to look so pale and tired, something that caused Daniel's conclusion. But it was no business of his. None. He regretted his foolish trip out to her car to see if she was all right. She had made it clear that whether she was or not, she wanted no help from him. And he regretted the petulance that had made him say he wouldn't be back. He'd given

Holland Wakefield his word; he had to go back. He had no choice about it.

"Stupid," he said under his breath.

The wind was picking up, and the first drops of the spring shower began to fall. In his mind's eye he saw her suddenly in that upstairs bedroom. The house would grow cold with the coming of the rain, and she'd need to make a fire. He could see her in that room with the firelight, and the rain against the windows, and the big bed. He'd never shared a bed with her, not in all the times they were together.

He looked around at the honking of unsettled geese. His father was bringing in the mules from the field.

"Adam!" he yelled. "You have nothing better to do than to stand in the rain and let your grandfather's tools rust?"

The truth of the matter was that he'd hardly noticed the rain at all. He gave his father a wave of acknowledgment and walked toward the barn, relieved that the old man had the mules and wouldn't be able to catch up with him immediately. He had planned to tell him that Quinn was back here. It would have been better if he'd been able to do it before Jacob saw her on the road. He had no fear of his father; he was thirty-two years old. It was just that he wasn't prepared to be questioned. Not when he had no answers, not even for himself.

He looked back. His father had stopped Daniel and was now gesturing in the direction of the Tyler farm. Adam made his way through the dark barn to the small workshop on the far side facing the house, savoring as he always did the smells of hay and dusty grain, new sawdust and warm animals, and the sweet smell of aged and weathered wood. He set the carpenter's helper on the rough table in the workshop, taking each tool out and drying it carefully with one of the neatly folded rags kept for that purpose. He was the third generation of Sauder men to use these tools, and he always wiped them carefully after he'd finished with them, even when he hadn't been caught standing out in the rain like a fool.

The wind changed, and the rain drummed against the windowpane. He could hear his brothers' voices in the animal stalls on the other side of the wall—Eli's and Aaron's and David's. And his father's. He waited. For his brothers to go into the house, for his father to stay.

Daniel's calico cat jumped onto the workbench, rubbing against his hand and arm for his attention.

"Daniel's looking for you, old lady," he said softly. "Shame on you, hiding your babies from him." As he stroked the cat's head, he knew that his father had come into the workshop. But he went back to drying the tools, putting each one away in its proper place. He had such a sense of déjà vu suddenly, of another confrontation in this barn. He'd been twenty-one then, the oldest son, new to manhood, expected to marry one of his own kind, and hopelessly in love with Quinn Tyler.

"I haven't done anything!"

"Not yet, Adam! Not yet!"

"Did you get the corn in, Pop?" he asked, pushing the memory aside. They stood eye to eye, alike in physique and totally different in opinion. Jacob Sauder was a hard man, though no harder on his sons than he was on himself. He was an elder in the church, and when Adam was a child, he had been certain that God himself must look like Jacob Sauder. He was well aware of the fact that he had disappointed the old man deeply, just as he was well aware that it couldn't be helped. His father had had great expectations, and he had never taken into account his son's humanness.

"I don't come in here to talk about the corn," Jacob Sauder said. "You go to *her* house, Adam. You don't say she is back. You know she is there, and still you go?"

"Yes," he said quietly. "If it's Quinn you're asking about." The rain beat against the window, and the cat meticulously washed her fur. He set the empty carpenter's helper to one side.

"Ach! Adam! What are you doing there?"

"Kitchen cabinets."

"You make jokes? This woman—this *English* who will lead you astray is here again, and it is something for joking?"

"Quinn never led me anywhere I didn't want to go."

"Is that something to make you proud? To make *me* proud—this sin of yours?"

"I don't want to talk about this, Pop. I have paid for what you call my 'sin.' I am a good son."

"You aren't one of us, Adam! You don't marry! You stay here, but you don't do your duty!"

"I've told you. There is no one here I want to marry."

"There are other places for you to look."

"No," he said, moving toward the door. He stopped in the doorway and looked back. "You're my father. I'm here, and I do everything I can for you, for the family. The one thing I can do for myself, I don't do unless *I* want it." He stepped out into the rain.

"Adam! You don't go back there!" Jacob Sauder yelled after him. "You don't go back into the English woman's house!"

He kept walking, ignoring the rain, ignoring the man he was supposed to honor. He fought to keep his resentment at bay, but his father wasn't going to leave it alone. He wasn't a boy now. He was a man, a man who'd let go of Quinn, let go of everything that mattered to him, to stay Amish.

Actually, it was Quinn who'd done the letting go. She'd left him here with nothing but his anger, an anger he'd lived with for years yet couldn't find when he saw her again today. He hadn't married because of her; he was spending his life alone because of her, and still, *still* he'd wanted to see her.

No. No, it wasn't just because of Quinn's leaving that he was alone. It was because his people didn't recognize the need for love in making a marriage. For them, marriage was based on mutual respect and a common goal: children—children to raise strong in the faith and in their love of living Plain. He hadn't married, because he had known something special with Quinn, and not just some recalcitrant emotion that happened because of his budding manhood and her proximity. She had been a part of him for all of his life; they were not separate entities. They were, and always had been, two halves of a whole. But for the accident of her birth, she would have been more Amish than he. She would have been a good wife, a good mother; she would have been a joy to their children and to him. His father, his family, all of them had to know that no one could take her place. No one. He had loved her when they were four and six and standing at their fathers' knees at the livestock auctions. He had loved her when he was twenty-one and had given her a child.

And he loved her now.

Oh, Quinn!

His father caught up with him on the slate walkway that led to the house. "Do you hear me, Adam? You don't shame this family again!"

"I have given Holland Wakefield my handshake that I will do the job for him," he said without stopping. "Is there less shame in breaking my word than in your suspicions about what I *might* do?"

"My suspicions? Am I wrong to be suspicious when you don't say she is here again? When you know she is back, and I have to see her on the road?"

"Enough, Pop!" Adam cried, jerking his arm free when his father would have detained him.

"Adam!"

He kept going, running the last few steps to the house to get in out of the rain. He hung his straw hat on one of the pegs by the back door. The kitchen was warm and filled with good smells. It should have been filled with conversation and laughter, as well, but there was only silence as the family waited to take their seats at the table. He could feel all of them looking at him. Eli, who was always sickly and who would marry soon and bring another woman into the family. Thirteen-year-old Aaron, who had saved his money and bought a set of "English" clothes he kept hidden in the attic just to try on from time to time, as if the clothes would somehow make clear to him a way of life he couldn't begin to understand. And David. Adam should have been closer to David—there were only ten months between them—but there was nothing similar in their appearance or their dispositions. David was dark-haired and short and stocky, taking after their mother's side of the family, and he was deeply serious about everything, like Jacob. He took his glasses off and wiped the lenses with his handkerchief in an effort at preoccupation. David had worn glasses as long as Adam could remember, but they did nothing to hide the accusation he could see in his eyes now.

He glanced at the women in his family, at his still-unmarried sisters Anna and Mary, at David's pregnant wife, Sarah, and at his mother, all of them dressed in their Plain clothes and their prayer caps, and all of them wearing the same fearful, worried expression as they hurried to get the food on the table ahead of Jacob's arrival. Daniel was the only one in the room who dared to give him a smile.

Adam had no idea how much of the argument they'd heard—clearly, enough to leave them strained and silent. He looked again at his mother, but she said nothing. She was a small woman, not beautiful by worldly standards, but beautiful to him. He was her first child, and he had always felt a special bond between them, just as he had always felt that she, more than anyone else, understood about Quinn.

Quinn had given him a book once—a shameful book, his father would have thought—about war and slavery and people so real they seemed to leap off the pages. *Gone with the Wind*, it was called. The woman Ellen in that book had always reminded him of his mother—quiet, hardworking, keeping everything running smoothly in Jacob Sauder's house without him having the slightest notion of how it came about or that she was entirely responsible for it.

"Mom," he said as he went to stand by his usual place. "You aren't feeding us 'pigeons' *again*?"

Lena Sauder smiled at his teasing and patted his shoulder. It was his favorite dish, turnovers made of raw potato, boiled egg, onions and parsley, and then steamed. He would have gladly eaten them three times a day, and she knew it.

"I give yours to the pigs, you don't want it," she said, setting the last of the steaming bowls around the table. No one sat until Jacob Sauder was in his seat at the head of the table. At his lead, they all bowed their heads. The prayer was silent and unusually long—the reason for which escaped no one, except perhaps Daniel. Adam glanced up once to frown at the boy's fidgeting.

"Adam," Jacob Sauder said as soon as he had lifted his head. He accepted the bowl of lima beans his wife offered him. "You will plant the corn with David tomorrow. Do you hear me, Adam?" He avoided Adam's eyes.

"I have another job, Pop."

"Do you hear me, Adam?" Jacob Sauder repeated.

"I hear you, Pop." He slid his chair back and slowly stood. "I have another job. I intend to finish it. I . . . I want to take Daniel with me, since you seem to think it's a good idea to send him after me at the Tyler house. If you don't trust me, surely you trust Daniel." His mother caught his sleeve as he passed her chair on the way out, but he gently removed her fingers and left the room.

"Adam?" David said behind him.

"What?" He had been standing on the porch out of the rain, listening to the sound of the evening meal as it continued inside and trying not to stare at the lights of the Tyler house.

"I want to say that I don't think you mean to do the things you do."

"And what things are those, David? I haven't read a book in years."

"You're not still—" David began, then stopped, and Adam moved to sit on the swing. The boards were damp from the rain, but he sat down anyway, letting the swing slowly move back and forth.

"Still what? What is it exactly you want to know?" He stared into his brother's eyes, refusing to behave as if he'd done anything wrong when he hadn't.

Not yet.

His father's old accusation suddenly presented itself in his mind, but he pushed it aside.

"I want to know what you are going to do about Quinn. We all do. If you go against Pop, they'll shun you this time, Adam. Will you put the girls through that, and Mom and Daniel?"

Adam gave a tired sigh. "And what will they shun me for? For doing carpentry work in her kitchen?"

"You always make jokes!"

"So our father tells me."

"Go ahead, Adam. Keep on with the jokes. I am your brother. I remember what it was like in this house before. I have a wife with a baby coming. I have a right to know what it is you plan."

Adam looked away, scanning the quiet spring night, fighting hard not to lose his temper. "I plan, David, to finish the work Holland Wakefield hired me to do," he said, looking back at his brother's troubled face. "I plan to take Daniel with me to set your minds at rest—or do you think I'd fornicate with Quinn on the kitchen floor with Daniel there?"

"You have a dirty mouth!"

"Not my mouth so much as your mind."

"There is no talking to you! Our father is right to think what he does of you."

"And what is that? What does he tell you he thinks of me?" It galled Adam to think that they had discussed his shortcomings, but he baited his brother anyway.

"You have no discipline. No self-control!"

No discipline. No self-control. He wanted to laugh. By his own choice he lived celibate, alone. He stood up from the swing and walked toward the back door. "Then how is it you think I've stayed *here* for the last eleven years?" he said.

He let the door slam behind him, and he didn't stop once he was inside the house. He could hear the clocks ticking in the kitchen and in the sitting room, and the hiss of the gas lantern in the room where his mother worked on her quilts long after the others in the household had gone to bed. He met no one on the enclosed, winding staircase to the second floor, and he continued through the dark hallway to his room at the front of the house.

The room was large and sparsely furnished, with only an oak bed and dresser and one chair; he had no difficulty maneuvering in the darkness. He took off his clothes, hanging them blindly on a row of pegs on the wall. But he didn't go to bed. There were no curtains at the windows, and he intended to pull the dark green shade before he lit the lamp. Instead, he sat down in the straight chair his grand-

father had made for him when, as a young man, he'd first
moved into this room. He was so tired, and he sat alone in
the dark, staring across the fields at the lights in the Tyler
farmhouse.

Chapter Three

Quinn was down on her hands and knees. She had believed Adam when he said he wouldn't be back this morning, and she hadn't expected him. But she looked up to find him standing in the front hallway, his carpentry tools in the box he'd carried with him yesterday and the same young boy at his side.

"What are you doing?" he asked, surprising her further. She hadn't expected him to talk to her, either. He was frowning enough to indicate that he certainly didn't want to, but his eyes moved over her, finally stopping at the empty white china teacup she had in her right hand.

"I might ask you the same thing," she said, crawling a bit to the left of a stack of boxes. "I thought you weren't coming back." She was wearing gray sweatpants, a grey Mickey Mouse T-shirt, and running shoes, suitable attire for what she was doing, regardless of his obvious disapproval. "Don't you ever knock?" she added irritably. She sud-

denly felt that he was appraising more than her peculiar
worldly clothes, and, for some reason, she wasn't comfortable with the possibility that Adam, in spite of himself, still
found her attractive as a woman—even with Mickey Mouse
on her chest.

"I did knock—at the back door. No one came."

"Yes, well, I was busy." She kept crawling, then abruptly
stopped and sat back on her heels. "Hello, Daniel Sauder," she said to the boy with him.

"Hello, Quinn Tyler," the boy said shyly, glancing up at
Adam for what Quinn felt was permission to have done so.

"Quinn, what are you doing?" Adam said. He didn't like
towering over her, and he didn't like trying not to notice how
her breasts moved under the shirt with the mouse on it.

"Looking for a spider," she said, crawling around some
more boxes. "It's here someplace. Want to help me, Daniel? The kitchen's that way," she added to Adam. "You are
here to work on the kitchen, aren't you?"

"I gave Holland my word."

She looked up at him. And an Amishman's word was
everything; he'd keep it, even if it meant coming here.
"Right," she said, going back to her search. Daniel knelt
down beside her.

"There it is!" he cried as the spider suddenly crawled
across the floor toward the toe of Adam's shoe. She headed
it off, dropping the cup gently over it halfway there.

"Now what?" Daniel whispered, again coming to kneel
beside her.

"Good question," Quinn whispered back, and he smiled.
He reached out to gently touch the cup, then look into her
eyes.

"Do you want to kill the spider, Quinn?" he asked solemnly.

"No, Daniel. I'm going to relocate him—outside. I don't
like spiders much, but you can't go around squashing

something just because you think it's ugly, can you?'' She gave a wink and a short nod toward Adam. ''I mean, where would your big, frowning brother be if people went around doing things like that?''

''Squashed?'' Daniel said, giggling at her heavy-handed joke.

She grinned. It was the kind of thing she would have said eleven years ago if she'd found Adam as out of sorts as he was now.

But Adam clearly didn't share her amusement; he stalked into the kitchen without a backward glance. Her grin faded. She would do well to remember that whatever made Adam Sauder smile these days, it wouldn't be prompted by her.

''Whatever I am now, Jacob had no hand in.''

Oh, God.

''Now what?'' Daniel said again, and she smiled at him. She had to stop worrying about Adam.

''Well . . .'' She reached into a nearby box, searching until she found an envelope. ''I'm going to lift the cup just a little and slide this in. And when the spider crawls onto the envelope, I'll let the cup down again and we'll have him. What do you think?''

''Good!'' Daniel said.

''Then let's do it.''

But she wasn't as ready to take on a spider as she thought.

''Go on!'' Daniel prompted, clearly delighted with this adventure.

''Yes. Right,'' Quinn promised. The distinct possibility that anything as fuzzy and multi-legged as that particular spider might end up crawling over her fingers was a real consideration, and she continued to sit there by the cup until Daniel held out both hands, palms up, and raised his eyebrows.

''What?'' Quinn asked innocently.

''You're not doing,'' he advised her.

No, she certainly wasn't. She crooked her finger, motioning for him to come closer. "Did I ever tell you," she whispered, as if she didn't want the creature under the cup to hear, "that I'm afraid of spiders?"

"The spider's afraid, too, Quinn Tyler."

"Is he?" she asked, smiling a bit because he sounded so wise.

"Yes. Spiders always run away."

"Always?"

"Always."

"All right," Quinn said, rubbing her hands together. "I'm ready. Here we go. Oh, I can't do it!" she said the minute her fingers touched the cup. "Daniel, I'm a big sissy."

"You can do it, Quinn," he said encouragingly.

"Can I?"

"Yes, but you have to be brave."

"I have to be brave. Brave..." she repeated to talk herself into it. She carefully lifted the cup.

Everything went as planned, except that the spider made a break for it, causing both of them to scramble—Daniel, after him, and Quinn, away from him.

"The cup, Quinn! The cup!"

She fumbled the cup, nearly dropping it, all but throwing it into Daniel's hands. "Daniel— Oh! Catch it!"

He did—it *and* the spider, quietly taking the envelope from her and trapping the spider inside the cup without difficulty.

"My hero," Quinn said, and he smiled his bashful smile.

"Where can he live, Quinn?"

"Any place you think is all right, except the woodpile. I don't want to bring him right back in." She sat back on her heels, watching Daniel march outside with his important catch, thinking how much he reminded her of Adam at that age. She looked up to find Adam watching her from the kitchen, and their eyes held. He wasn't frowning anymore.

Don't let me see it, she told him silently. *If I'm hurting you, don't let me see it.*

He abruptly turned away and began hammering nails out of one of the boards he'd pulled down yesterday, each blow delivered with more force than was needed.

Quinn gave a soft sigh and got up from the floor, fighting a wave of dizziness that almost always plagued her these days when she made any extreme changes in position. She was still slightly anemic from the latest flare-up of her ulcer, but the dizziness quickly passed. She really was feeling much better physically, if she discounted the sleepless night she'd just had. And she *was* going to look after herself. She was going to eat regularly and take her medication and rest. She was also going to worry, but that couldn't be helped— three out of four wasn't bad.

She could hear Adam dragging boards around in the kitchen, and Daniel had come back in.

"Where to put the cup, Quinn?" he asked.

"I'll take it. Did you find a new home for the spider?"

"In the barn—a good place in the corner."

"Wonderful. I thank you for your help, Daniel Sauder."

"You are welcome, Quinn Tyler."

They both grinned, until Adam called Daniel sharply from the kitchen.

"We are here to work," he said from the doorway. He was very careful of where he looked. He had at least a week of carpentry work in this house if he was to do what Holland wanted. And in order to stand it, he had to stay away from Quinn. He'd been deliberately vulgar in answering David last night, because he had been annoyed, and, if he was truthful, more than a little guilty of wanting exactly what David and his father suspected. Quinn was still beautiful to him, body and mind. And he was more certain than ever that she was still Quinn. He tried not to smile. Quinn and her spider. Quinn—kind to creatures, cruel to men. She was supposed to have loved him, and he would never understand.

He set Daniel to hammering nails out of the stack of pine boards that had been pulled off the back wall. He would salvage as many of the originals as he could, perhaps piece some behind the cabinets, to make the kitchen look as it had before. He wanted to do that for her, and he didn't dwell on the reason, other than the fact that he sensed her need to restore this part of her past. He could hear her unpacking boxes in the front hall, and, in spite of his resolve, he looked in that direction. He could just see her through the doorway, down on her knees again.

Quinn felt his eyes on her and glanced up just in time to see him move away. Perhaps they needed to sit down and talk, after all. Anything was better than the covert stealth they were both using to hide their mutual curiosity. She went on with the unpacking, leaving the computer until last, and trying to tune out the two sets of hammering noises that echoed through the still-empty house. She sighed. What was she going to do in this big place but rattle around? She was too much of a loner to take in boarders. Poor Quinn Tyler, people would say, nothing but that big old house and her computer.

She slid the carefully packed boxes of computer equipment into the living room, setting up her work area on the oak library table as she'd planned and noting that, with Daniel, Adam seemed more himself—or at least more the person she remembered. After a time she could hear a running conversation between them in their "at home" German. Riddles, she thought, because she recognized some of the words and the form, and because they laughed from time to time. She got the computer unpacked and working with minimal difficulty, and someone knocked on the front door.

"Quinn Tyler, someone is knocking," Daniel called from the kitchen. She smiled. He was such a dear little thing.

Edison Clark stood on the front porch, cardboard box filled with client files in his hands. He was what one might tactfully describe as portly. And he was balding. To make up for it, he wore a thick, drooping mustache that rather reminded Quinn of a turn-of-the-century tenor in a barbershop quartet. He had been her father's fishing buddy long before she had given him cause to become the family lawyer, and he usually looked as if he were about to do just that—go fishing. He favored a pocket watch with a gold watch fob and Pennsylvania Dutch cooking and helping people, and he was probably the best friend she'd ever had.

"I've brought you your bread and butter," he said, grinning. His grin promptly fled at the sight of Adam working in the kitchen. "Is that a good idea?" he whispered, eyebrows raised.

"I don't know," she said truthfully, "and don't start on me."

"You look like hell," he said, starting on her anyway. "What's happened to you?"

"Nothing," she said, wishing he'd lower his voice. But he was used to courtroom theatrics, and no juror ever dozed through one of his speeches.

"Nothing? Quinn, I saw you only a week ago, and you looked great. Now you're pale and—"

"I . . . I didn't sleep well."

He glanced into the kitchen. "No, I don't suppose you did. How are things with him?"

She shook her head without answering.

"Can't say I'm surprised. He took it hard, Quinn. I told you that ten years ago. Your being here again is the last thing he ever expected to have to deal with."

"Edison, could we not talk about this?" she said pointedly.

He grinned under his mustache. "All right. A house doesn't have to fall on me—at least I don't think it does." He handed her the box. "Now, what I'm going to need on these are regular reports on who owes what, who's got what and how much. I'll keep giving you updates on some of the earnings and expenditures and stuff like that. Can you handle that?"

"Sure," she said, carrying the box into the living room. "I thought I'd stagger it. I'll send you printouts on some the first of the month and the rest on the fifteenth."

"That'll work fine. Quinn?"

"What!" she said testily, recognizing the tone of voice.

He grinned again. "You're not going to like this, either."

"No, I didn't think I would," she said dryly. "What is it?"

"Jake called me."

She didn't say anything.

"You know Jake," he elaborated. "Jake Burroughs. Man you used to be engaged to. I took the two of you out to dinner once. I was even invited to the wedding, and—"

"What did he want?" she interrupted because she couldn't see a way out of it. She and Jake had parted by mutual consent and on good terms, if there was such a thing in a broken engagement. She had no doubt that he still cared about her, that in a platonic, altruistic sort of way, she was now rather like his favorite charity. But he was a bit irrepressible at times, and he'd been loud and long in voicing his opinion about her coming back here.

"So you do remember him!" Edison teased.

"Edison . . ."

"Aw, I know I'm annoying you, Quinn, but you look so damn solemn."

"Are you going to tell me what Jake wanted or not?"

"He wanted reassurance. He's worried about you—and you didn't tell me how bad the ulcer thing was the last time, Quinn. He's afraid you're going to isolate yourself out here and not take care of yourself, and next time you won't make it to a hospital soon enough. I thought he was being overly cautious, until I saw you today."

"I'm all right!"

"Are you?" he asked, his eyes probing hers for the truth.

She bowed her head for a moment before she answered. "I will be," she said, looking up at him. "I just have some things to . . . get used to."

"Quinn, Quinn," he said, sighing. "I don't know what to tell you. Or Jake."

"You don't have to tell him anything."

"No, I don't—if you want him to come out here to see for himself."

She frowned. That was entirely possible. Jake Burroughs was one of the best stockbrokers on the East Coast, and he hadn't gotten there by not finding out what he wanted to know.

"You can tell Jake that I'm feeling better. Now, wait," she said when Edison raised his eyebrows. "I *am* feeling better. I simply don't have a lot of stamina yet. When I'm tired, I'm tired, and it shows. I'm tired today because of the move and because I didn't sleep very well, and that's the truth."

"All that doesn't concern me nearly as much as the *reason* for the move, which is likely the same reason you're not sleeping. You know how potentially harmful this arrangement is?" he asked, nodding toward the kitchen. "His people remember, Quinn. It was a source of great shame for them. He's still not one of them the way he should be, and he's still sitting right on the edge of being shunned all the time, even if he is a good man. The Amish are a gentle folk, but they won't put up with flagrant disregard for their beliefs."

"Edison, it was his choice to come work on the house. He was here when I got here—Holland had already hired him. And he didn't have to stay. It's going to be all right. Really."

"Well, you'll have a hard time convincing me of that—*and* old Jacob Sauder. I'd hate to be in that household when he finds out you're back here."

"I . . . think he already knows. I saw him on the road yesterday."

"And Adam's here working this morning? Damn! The old man must be mellowing." Edison checked his pocket watch. "Well, I've got to be in court at one. You take care of yourself out here."

"I will. I'm not suicidal, you know. If I were, I would have stayed at the brokerage firm in Philadelphia."

He smiled and patted her cheek. "I can find my own way out. I'll speak to Adam before I go."

"Edison . . ."

"Quinn, I've known him since he was born—longer than I've known you. I'm just going to say hello."

It was what he might say *after* that that troubled her. She gave a resigned sigh and looked at the box of files she was still holding. She put them down on the desk by the computer; she might as well get started. It would take her mind off Edison's chat with Adam. Except she was too intent on eavesdropping.

But even that was hopeless. Edison had lapsed into the dialect German he'd taken pains to learn when he first came to practice in this area. Probably all the Amish here let him handle their legal work—transfers of parcels of land to older sons and the like. At least Adam was talking to *him*, Quinn thought, opening a file and trying to concentrate. But she could only think of the past, of Edison coming to her in

Philadelphia shortly after the baby was born, when she was trying so desperately to get on with her life.

"You're a strong person, Quinn. I admire you," he'd said, and she had smiled, in spite of her fear that the other shoe was about to drop. "It's my job to give you legal advice. It's not my job to meddle in your personal life."

"And?" she had asked quietly.

"And I wouldn't presume to tell you what to do, but I think I ought to make sure you're apprised of the situation." He waited for her reaction, and, when she didn't say anything, he went on. "I've seen Adam, Quinn."

"What do you mean you've seen him?" she said sharply. She knew that Adam had looked for her, that he'd hired one of the Mennonite boys who had a car to drive him to Philadelphia—Edison had already told her that. If anything could have made her lose her resolve, it would have been knowing that Adam was still here, aimlessly searching for her on the streets of Philadelphia.

"Quinn, this is killing him."

"It's killing me, too, Edison."

"Everything is done now, Quinn. It can't be undone. It would be a kindness to let me tell him—"

"No! I thought you weren't going to tell me what to do!"

"I'm telling you what *I'd* like to do."

"He'll hate me more than he already does, Edison."

"No. No, I don't think that's true, honey. But if it is, at least he'll know what's happened, and he can get on with his life. That's the reason for all this, isn't it? You didn't want to take his good life away from him? It's the *not* knowing that's so hard for him, Quinn."

"Edison, I—"

"Quinn, Quinn," he had said gently, patting her shoulder. "You've given your baby a wonderful chance. You were in an impossible situation, and you did the best you could with it."

"Did I?"

"Yes. You did. You did a good and loving thing for your child."

"Edison, I wanted him so badly...."

"I know, honey. I know."

"And Adam—"

"I know that, too." He smiled. "I remember when you were a little girl—how you cried when you found out the Amish weren't accepting membership applications."

She gave him a tremulous smile in return. "I thought it was something like the Auto Club, I guess. All I needed was the membership fee and someone to sponsor me."

"I'll tell him gently, Quinn."

But there had been no "gentle" way to tell him, and if he was the better for having been told, she couldn't discern it by looking at him now. She had known that, while he might understand intellectually that she was alone and afraid and in debt, he would never understand in his heart. Children were the most important thing in the world to the Amish, and she'd given his away.

The back door slammed finally, and Adam and Daniel were hammering again, much to her relief. She worked steadily at the computer until nearly noon, entering page after page of financial data she found refreshingly tame without some hotshot broker breathing down her neck every second to get the latest tally on his commissions. She paused for a moment, thinking she'd heard someone knock. She finally decided she hadn't, only to hear the timid knocking again.

"Now what?" she murmured on her way to answer it. There wasn't enough authority in the knock for it to be Holland. Or, God forbid, Jake.

Two young Amish girls stood on the front porch, one of them carrying a basket. They were both wearing eyeglasses, and they covertly inspected the red-framed ones

Quinn took off and let dangle on a cord around her neck. She knew that Amish girls were forbidden adornment, and she knew that, like all females, they made do with whatever they could—in this case, glasses. There was a good chance that neither one of them really needed spectacles, but wore them in the belief that it enhanced their physical appearance. Her translucent red frames were clearly worth noting.

"Yes?" Quinn said, trying not to smile.

"For Adam and Daniel," the older of the two said, holding up the basket of food for the *Mittagessen*, the noon meal.

"Out in the kitchen," Quinn said, standing back to let them come in. They both hesitated, and their somewhat startled expressions made her wonder what these girls had been told about her. The truth, she imagined, watching the girls dart glances around as much of her "English" house as they could see from the porch. "That way," she said, still holding the door open. They reluctantly came into the front hall, and Quinn pointed out the direction again on her way back into the living room to the computer. She tried to place which of Adam's sisters these two were, but nothing came to her except that the names would be German or biblical. How had she forgotten the names of Adam's sisters?

She glanced up at the conversation that suddenly came from the kitchen. German again—*loud* German. If Adam expected a meal hand delivered today, he certainly didn't sound like it. Quinn needed to eat, too, and she waited until the commotion died down and Adam and the others went out onto the back steps.

Why was he so annoyed? she wondered. His day had likely started before sunup; surely he was hungry, and his mother's cooking was famous in the area.

Chaperons, she thought suddenly as she opened the refrigerator door. Jacob Sauder knew she was back, and

Daniel and the other two were here to keep Adam safe. Quinn could see Adam through the kitchen window. He was still angry, and the girls sat and fidgeted on the porch steps while he spoke to them in a low, harsh voice, the basket all but abandoned. Edison had been right. This wasn't a good idea.

She took out some cheese and cold cuts and made herself a sandwich, shaking her head because old Jacob had little to worry about. Adam either snapped at her or ignored her. He didn't need two sisters and a brother to chaperon that.

She carried the sandwich and a glass of milk back into the living room. The morning had grown increasingly gray, and, though it hadn't yet begun to rain, the room seemed damp and cold now. On impulse, she decided to light the fire she had laid in the fireplace last night. Carrying firewood had been the only constructive thing she could think of to do after Adam left.

She was more lonesome than she wanted to admit. Would a fire in the fireplace help loneliness? She felt like the woman in one of Edna St. Vincent Millays' poems, the one who kept a kettle boiling for company. *Poor Quinn Tyler, with her empty house and her computer,* and *her fires.*

She smiled to herself. "Can't hurt," she whispered, lighting the kindling.

She sat down close to the hearth to eat her lunch, realizing after a few moments that someone had come into the room. It was the older of Adam's sisters. The girl stood awkwardly just inside the doorway, and Quinn waited as she had with Daniel, realizing that this girl must see her as some kind of hussy, an English *Windfliegel*, at best.

"My father asks if you will need a hired girl," the girl said finally, and Quinn nearly laughed. When Jacob Sauder wanted someone chaperoned, he didn't do it by halves, even if it meant exposing another child to the "English."

"No, I don't think so," Quinn said. Then she changed her mind almost immediately. She knew how suspicious Jacob Sauder could be, and she could use some help with the unpacking. Perhaps she could hire a maid-chaperon to get the house settled and make life a little easier for Adam at the same time. "No, wait," she said as the girl turned to go. "What I need is someone to help me get these things unpacked and put away. What's your name?"

"Anna Sauder."

"And the other girl?"

"Mary Sauder."

"Well, I want to hire both of you. To clean up and to put all the things in these boxes away. Could you do that?"

The girl nodded.

"Both of you?"

"I will ask."

"Good. How much do you charge?"

She took a piece of paper out of her pocket and handed it to Quinn. It was a painstakingly written notice of Anna Sauder's hourly wage.

"This will be fine," Quinn said, handing it back to her. "I'll pay this to each of you. You find out if that is agreeable to your father. Tell him that I want both of you to come when Adam comes and leave when he leaves, and I'd like you to start as soon as possible." She realized suddenly that she was sounding very much like the head of the brokerage firm accounting department and probably scaring this girl half to death. "And one other thing, Anna."

"What?" Anna said timidly.

"I like your glasses."

The girl gave a shy smile, reaching up to touch them before she backed out of the room. Quinn could hear her calling her sister, then caught a glimpse of both of them running across the plowed field toward the Sauder farm.

She sighed and sat down by the fire again, idly rummaging through a box marked Glass and Brass while she finished her lunch. True, there were brass candlesticks inside, and a number of glass vases and bric-a-brac. But there was also wood—primitive art, she supposed it would be called. She lifted the wooden figure of a cow standing knee-deep in flowers, painstakingly cut out and hand painted in bright colors. Adam had made it and given it to her on her ninth birthday. She had loved it—still loved it—and she had kept it in plain view on various mantels or open shelves ever since he'd given it to her. She unwrapped it carefully now, her fingers running lightly over the wood.

"Quinn," Adam said from the doorway, the fine edge of annoyance still in his voice.

Lord, she thought. She was so tired of this, his anger, her guilt.

"What?" she said sharply, letting his scowl put her on the defensive in a way that could only make matters worse.

"What have you said to Anna and Mary?"

"Anna asked if I needed a hired girl," she said, putting the wooden barnyard figure down. "I said I did. I'm hiring both of them." She picked up her glass of milk and drank some of it to have something to do. It was hard for her to get used to his being so... unhappy, when she'd expected him to have a wife and children of his own now, expected him to be settled and content with his life. She remembered one of her father's appraisals of Adam Sauder when she and Adam were still children: *"God made him merry."* It had been an apt description—once.

"Why would you hire my sisters?"

"Because I think Jacob wants us to be chaperoned, and I'm obliging him," she said truthfully.

"We don't need chaperons."

"I know that, but I don't think he does. I can use some help unpacking, and I think having your sisters here will make things ... easier."

"I don't need you to make things easier for me."

She looked up at him. She had always felt that his eyes were able to look directly into her soul, and she felt that now. He was still so handsome to her, handsome and strong—but not strong enough to have endured the trouble she would have brought him, she reminded herself. "I didn't do it for you. I did it for me. Quite frankly, I don't need the aggravation. I've had enough encounters with irate Amish fathers to last me a lifetime."

Now. Now *you can accuse me of making fun of you.*

She looked away. "Where's Daniel?" she asked, because it suddenly occurred to her that Jacob's well-laid plan had already gone awry.

"In the barn. Checking on the spider."

"Oh." The glass of milk was empty, and she tried to find something else to do, someplace else to look. There was no other place, and she raised her eyes to his.

I can do this, she thought a bit desperately. I can look at him and talk to him, and the past doesn't matter.

They both looked away.

"You've been sick," he said abruptly. She could feel him making comparisons, Quinn now with the Quinn he once knew.

"Edison was a little overexcited."

"I knew before I heard what Edison said to you, Quinn. With what were you sick?"

She glanced up at him but found his gaze too disconcerting. "Too much urban living, I think," she said, reaching into the box again.

"I don't know what that means."

"It means I have an ulcer, a stomach ulcer. They tell me mine comes from working too hard and caring too much."

"That doesn't make people sick."

"It does when you don't like what you're doing and you keep on doing it just because you're good at it and the pay's good. It's not the same as the hard work you do farming. You've always liked it so much it isn't work to you."

"You don't know what it's like to stay in a hot field from sunup to sundown. It feels like work, Quinn." To her surprise, he almost smiled.

"I haven't forgotten. I used to tag along after you in that hot field as long as I could get away with it. I haven't forgotten what Dad used to say about you, either. 'For Adam Sauder, to plow is to pray.'"

He did smile then, and he sat down on the raised hearth, his forearms resting on his knees, his work-roughened hands in plain view. She had always thought he had beautiful hands, and she tried not to remember the feel of them on her face, on her breasts.

"You didn't like Philadelphia so much, then?" he asked. He had caught her looking at his hands, and he folded his arms as if to keep them out of sight.

"Oh, I liked Philadelphia. I liked having people tell me what a good job I was doing, how important to the firm I was. But I'm a farm girl at heart, I guess. Always have been. I never got used to living and working with people who scramble to make money twenty-four hours a day. I missed—" She broke off. She wasn't going to tell him how painful her exile had been. "You know what I had forgotten? Birds. I didn't hear anything but sparrows where I lived. I keep catching myself listening now—robins, cardinals, mockingbirds. I even like the blue jays and the crows."

Her eyes collided with his, eyes that were pale blue and sad and holding hers again whether she wanted it or not. He was sitting too close to her, much too close.

"Tell me," he said quietly. She couldn't have looked away if her life had depended on it. "Where is your husband?" The fire crackled and burned, and she was growing too warm, but she couldn't move.

"Where is your wife?" she countered, realizing that they both could have given the same answer: *I don't have one—because of you*.

He looked away, his gaze falling on the wooden figure. "What is this?" he asked, picking it up.

"You know what that is. You gave it to me."

"I gave it to you," he repeated.

"Adam, you know you did. For my birthday, when I was nine."

"And you kept it?"

"Yes," she answered, bewildered by the incredulity in his voice.

He abruptly stood up, and she rose with him. "Why?" he asked, his hand clenching the figure tightly. "Why did you keep this?"

"Because . . ." She faltered.

"Tell me, Quinn. I want to know. It's ugly. You said this morning you don't keep things around you that are ugly—not spiders, and not this."

"It isn't ugly." She reached for it, but he wouldn't let her have it.

"Why do you keep it?" he asked again.

She took a small breath and looked up at him. "Because you gave it to me," she said evenly.

"Mein Gott!" he said with such pain that she took a step toward him.

But he didn't want her comfort. He moved sharply away from her. "Because *I* gave it to you? How can you say that to me?"

"Adam—"

"What do you want from me now, Quinn, when I have nothing left? Do you think I can't feel it—your *wanting*?"

"Adam, please—"

He grabbed her by her wrist with his free hand. "Tell me what you want!"

"Nothing!"

He abruptly let go of her, and again she tried to take the wooden figure from him. He was too quick for her. He tossed it into the fire.

"Adam, don't!"

He grabbed her when she would have retrieved it from the flames, making her look at him.

"I gave you a baby, too, Quinn. Where is he? You keep the wood and you give away the child? What kind of woman does that!" He turned her around toward the fire, holding her tightly against him when she struggled to get free, his arms locked over her breasts, his face pressed against hers as they watched the wooden figure burn. "There is nothing between us now. Not even wood. Do you understand?"

She didn't think her legs would hold her, and she sagged against him, feeling his breath warm and quick against her face. His touch, even in anger, was nearly more than she could bear. She didn't want him to see her cry—she *couldn't* let him see her cry.

"Answer me!"

"I understand!" she cried, trying to free herself again. "I understand! I've *always* understood!"

"What does that mean?"

"It means that I did what I had to do. It means that you won't make me feel guilty for it now. Let me go and get out. Get out!"

He didn't let go. He could feel her trembling. He didn't want to hurt her. He just wanted to—

"Quinn!" he whispered harshly against her ear, holding her until she stopped struggling. He wanted her to know that he understood, too. He wanted her to know that he knew she would have come to him—*if* he had been man enough to take care of her. "Quinn, forgive me!"

Forgive him? She turned her head to see Adam's face. Daniel was standing in the doorway.

Chapter Four

Daniel," Quinn whispered, and Adam let her go, stepping sharply away from her. Daniel stood just inside the room, his mouth pursed and trembling, his eyes huge and afraid.

"Daniel, come," Adam said. He reached out to turn Daniel around and point him toward the kitchen, and he thought for a moment that the boy was going to shrink away from him. My God, what had he done? He'd forgotten all about him. Daniel had no part in this misery with Quinn.

"It's all right," he said. "Let's go. We have work to do."

"Do you fight with Quinn?" Daniel asked, looking up at him.

"No," Adam said, hurrying him along into the wide front hall.

"She wants to cry, Adam," he insisted. He looked back over his shoulder into the living room. "The cow is burned. She wants—"

"It is not our business!" Adam said, maneuvering both of them among the boxes in the hall.

Oh, Quinn!

Daniel dropped his head, and Adam knelt down beside him so they would be at eye level. He took a deep breath, trying to calm himself, trying to regain some control, trying to think of what to say.

"Daniel?"

The boy kept his head bowed.

"Daniel, look at me."

He waited, and finally Daniel raised his eyes to his.

"You are my brother. I will tell you the truth. Quinn ... Quinn has been my friend since we were both little like you. My friend, Daniel. Do you understand?"

"Like Aaron Lapp?" he asked, his eyes probing Adam's. "Smiling Aaron," he qualified in case Adam might not know which among all the Aaron Lapps in the area, young and old, he might mean.

"Yes. Like Smiling Aaron," he agreed. Aaron Lapp was a likable young man who lived on a farm nearer to town. He, too, was the oldest son in a family with too many mouths to feed solely by farming. He had become an apprentice in a local cabinet shop to help make ends meet, and he frequently came to the Sauders to ask Adam's advice on carpentry.

"Even if she is English?"

"Yes." He watched as Daniel thought this over.

"Is she your friend now?"

"I ... I don't know, Daniel."

"Is that why you want to hurt Quinn now?" he asked solemnly.

Adam grabbed him by the shoulders. "Daniel, no! I don't want to hurt Quinn. I would never hurt Quinn." *I love her!* he almost said. "It's just that sometimes people get angry, and they say things, do things they don't mean. Quinn and I were angry. That's all."

"About what? About the cow?"

"No. About . . . something that happened a long time ago."

"When you were little like me?"

Adam smiled. "Well, not quite that long ago. But it still makes us angry to talk about it, you see."

"You and Quinn—don't talk about it anymore, Adam," Daniel said, flinging himself into Adam's arms. "Please!"

Adam held Daniel tightly, feeling the ache in his throat, the stinging behind his eyelids. He was a grown man, and it had been a long time since he, too, had wanted to cry. He held Daniel away from him so that he could see his face. "It's nothing for you to worry about."

"I feel worried," Daniel confessed.

"Don't feel worried, little brother. I am your big brother, and I say so."

"What will Pop say?"

What indeed? Adam thought. Once again, Daniel's eyes probed his for the truth. He hadn't thought that Daniel understood much about the friction between their father and him, but he obviously knew it existed. "I don't know. He will decide when he asks you what you've seen here in Quinn's house."

"He will ask," Daniel said, clearly resigned to the ordeal.

"Yes, and you can tell him. He is our father, and we honor him. We tell him the truth."

Daniel nodded, then gave a big sigh of relief. "I bent a nail," he said, suddenly remembering now why he'd sought Adam out in the first place.

"Did you? Can't you get it out?"

"No, it's too hard. Will I get big like you, Adam, or will I be a runt?"

Adam laughed in spite of his inner turmoil. "A runt," he said, knowing his depreciation of Daniel's size would precipitate one of their bouts of teasing and wrestling and tickling. "Enough!" he cried after a moment. "Runt or not, you'll soon be too strong for me. Show me this bent nail of yours."

Quinn stood by the hearth, watching the last remnants of the wooden figure Adam had made for her as it burned. She turned her head sharply at the sound of laughter in the kitchen. She wanted Adam out of this house. She'd told him so, yet he was laughing in the kitchen. She whirled around, striding across the hallway with every intention of throwing him out. She didn't care if the carpentry work was never finished. She would *not* put up with his being here.

She stopped at the kitchen doorway. Adam and Daniel were kneeling on the floor, their heads together as Adam showed him how to straighten a bent nail.

"No, no. Turn the hammer the other way," he was saying. He was so patient with Daniel and his hit-and-miss hammer. He would have made a good and caring father. "Now, push down. Hard! There, you see? It's not so hard. You did it."

"Adam," Quinn said, and he hesitated before he acknowledged her, his face closed and tight. "What did you mean?" she asked when he finally looked up. She had fully intended to tell him to leave, but, looking into his eyes, that suddenly seemed not to matter.

"About what?" he asked, his eyes shifting away from hers. He stood up slowly, as if to give himself time to prepare for coping with her questions. She glanced at Daniel. The boy was wearing his worried look again, but that didn't matter to her, either.

"You know about what. About my... forgiving you. What did you mean?"

"This isn't the time, Quinn." He turned and said something in German to Daniel, who immediately began to gather up the hammers and put them into the carpenter's helper.

"It is the time, Adam. I want to know what you meant."

"Daniel and I are going now," he said, taking the toolbox from Daniel's hands and knocking his brother's hat crooked in the process.

"Adam..."

"No, Quinn! I've told you. There is nothing between us now. We don't talk about this ever again. The time for talking is long past. Daniel, let's go."

He straightened Daniel's hat for him and went out the back door so that he wouldn't have to come any closer to her. He couldn't bear it anymore, her nearness, not when he'd just had his arms around her, felt her warm and trembling against him. Not when he could feel her questions now, her *wanting* something he couldn't give. He heard her call him as he stepped off the back porch, but he kept walking.

He could feel Daniel's eyes on him from time to time as they cut across the field to Sauder land. The sun was shining now, and he thought that if he stopped and turned around, he would see Quinn, standing on the porch steps, eyes shaded, watching him go.

But the sun went behind the clouds, and he didn't turn around. It was going to rain again, and his father and brothers would be coming in from the fields. Daniel said nothing, walking forlornly along beside him. He should say something to make the boy feel better, but there was nothing he could say. He had other things on his mind—his father, for one. The old man would ask Daniel everything, and he would have to explain whatever Daniel told him. But he couldn't explain, and that was something Jacob Sauder had never understood. Whatever existed between Quinn Tyler and Adam Sauder had always been there, and it was unexplainable.

He sent Daniel to search for the newest batch of kittens and headed straight for the house, stepping on the randomly shaped pieces of slate that led to the back door. The slate was shiny and wet, and he tried not to remember another time, a time when he was little and holding Quinn by the hand as they jumped from one flagstone to another in the rain. He wanted to talk to his mother before the old man came up from the field, so he set the carpenter's helper on the back porch by the door instead of taking it directly to the barn. His grandfather would have to forgive him this one delay in taking care of his tools.

"Adam," Jacob Sauder said from the kitchen. "The rain comes too hard for planting today. It washes the seeds away. Does it come too hard for carpentry at the house of the English woman, as well?"

Adam braced himself before going inside. A pot of cabbage simmered on the stove, filling the house with its aroma. He didn't see his mother about.

"Are you making trouble for us, Adam?" Jacob asked quietly.

Adam ignored the question, going to the water bucket on a small table by the back door. He took the dipper off a peg on the wall and plunged it into the bucket, drinking deeply, savoring the familiar metallic taste of the cool water.

"You have no answer for me, I see," Jacob said.

He faced his father squarely. "No, Pop. I don't." He hung the dipper back on the peg. "If I go there, you are unhappy. If I come back, you are the same."

The old man looked away, staring out the kitchen windows across the yard to the barn. "Where is Daniel?"

"In the barn looking for his kittens."

"I can feel the trouble coming to this house. Perhaps he will tell me why it is you make such a fuss to go to the English woman's house to work and why you come home too soon.''

Adam fought down an angry reply. He would not be threatened by anything Daniel might say, and he didn't want to argue. He wanted to talk to his mother. He went into the front of the house, but she wasn't there.

"Mom?" he called at the foot of the stairs.

He heard her answer him from somewhere on the second floor.

"Mom?" he called again when he reached the second-story landing. She was in the big room at the front of the house, a room used for storing out-of-season clothes and making quilts and putting up unexpected guests. He found her and Mary going through a stack of shirts and undergarments on the floor, winter things that would be carefully mended before they were put away.

"It's not time to eat," his mother said, smiling.

"I'm not hungry," he replied.

"Then you are not my Adam," she said matter-of-factly, making him return her smile when he felt nothing like smiling. He stood awkwardly, not knowing what to say now that he was here, particularly with Mary listening.

"Mary," his mother said after a moment, "take these things down to the kitchen."

"But we are not done."

"Take them on. I'll be bringing the rest. Or I'll make Adam carry them."

"Adam doesn't carry underdrawers, Mom," Mary said, picking up the pile and taking them out.

"You used to," his mother said to him. "When you were little. Do you remember that? How you would carry the things in from the clothesline to help me?"

"I remember." He looked around the room, remembering, too, the times he'd played up here with his brothers and sisters when the work was done, hide-and-seek, blindman's bluff.

"You had better tell me what it is," his mother said quietly. "I can't bear to look at so sad a face."

He sat down on one of the trunks that lined the walls, and he was silent. He had wanted to speak to her, but now that he was here, now that she had given him the opening, he was suddenly tongue-tied. It was as if he were a boy again with a problem or a pain, and he wanted his mother to fix it.

"Do you fight with your father again?" she asked.

"No—no, not a fight. I worry him, and—" he looked into his mother's eyes "—I can't help him with this. This time I have to help myself."

"Yes" was all she said. She went back to folding winter clothes.

"Quinn is . . ." He faltered.

"Quinn is back," his mother said for him. "After so long a time. And you can't stay away from her. You think I don't understand you, Adam, but I do. You are my son. My first baby. And Quinn has always been in your heart. I have seen how much you try to make yourself believe something else— that she is English, that she has no business being there, always so close to you. But she *is* there. From the time you are little."

"I don't want to hurt the family. I don't want to hurt you. I don't want to make you ashamed of me."

"Suffering comes from God to make us strong, Adam. I have seen *you* suffer. All this time, and it is not better for you. Maybe there is less hurt for me to see you better than you are now, even if you—" She stood up suddenly and began gathering the remaining pile of clothes, but then she put them down again. She walked to a cedar chest that sat under the front windows, opened it and took out a quilt wrapped in tissue paper. "This is the quilt the women made for Quinn."

"For Quinn?"

"When her mother died. Her father gave us the dresses her mother wore to the school, and we used them for the quilt pieces—to honor her, to make a remembrance for Quinn. She left before it was finished. I have kept it here for her."

The quilt was red and blue and black, with an intricate center star pattern that was typically Plain. He reached out to touch it, knowing the hours of work the women would have put into it. He could smell its cedar scent from the chest, and in his mind he could see Quinn's face, the reverence it would hold at receiving such a gift.

But she hadn't received it. She'd run away with his son inside her, and she'd come back alone.

"She will have the quilt now," his mother said.

"She won't take it," Adam said. "There's too much trouble between us."

"She will take it from *me*. Your trouble has nothing to do with this," his mother answered. She wrapped it back into the tissue paper. "Carry the clothing downstairs and give it to Mary, please, Adam."

He grabbed the pile of clothes and followed his mother downstairs. "Mom, don't—"

"I will give Quinn the quilt," his mother said firmly. "It is hers."

"Mom..." he began again. But this was a household matter—the dispensing of quilts. It was her domain, and even Jacob himself would not interfere. "Are you going now with it?"

"Yes. The rain has stopped," she said as they entered the kitchen. "Mary, you watch the cabbage pot until I get back."

His sister was there, but Jacob was nowhere in sight. No doubt he'd already gone after Daniel.

"Quinn is . . . upset now," Adam offered as a stumbling block in lieu of the rainy weather.

His mother looked up at him. "Your doing?"

He did not want his mother talking to Quinn. "Not all mine," he said a bit testily.

She made no reply to that, and there was nothing he could do but watch her go. He picked up the carpenter's helper he'd left by the door and headed for the barn. Jacob and Daniel were making their way toward the house.

"Where is Mom going?" Mary called after him, but he wasn't about to get into that with his sister, not with Jacob so close at hand.

"Adam!" Jacob called, and Adam steeled himself for yet another confrontation. Daniel bounded up the walk and on into the house, out of the way.

"What is this thing that happened at the English woman's house?" Jacob demanded.

"Quinn!" Adam shouted, the anger he'd had earlier for Quinn spilling over at his father. "Her name is Quinn!"

"I know what she is called. What I want to know is what happened there."

"Daniel told you," he said, moving to get by his father.

"Daniel! Daniel says there is a burning of the cow!" Jacob said, not letting him pass. "What foolishness is that to tell the boy to say? Now you make your little brother lie for you?"

"I haven't told him to say anything. Daniel tells the truth. You know that." He walked toward the barn, willing himself to say no more. He was angry, but he didn't want to argue with anyone else today. He just wanted to be left alone. He had no idea what Quinn would say to his mother. Nothing? Everything? He looked toward the Tyler farm, seeing his mother disappear just over the rise at the edge of the fields.

* * *

Quinn wandered aimlessly through the empty house. She had long since given up working at the computer. She needed to get out for a while, away from this place with so many memories, but she had nowhere else she wanted to go. She moved some boxes about, regretting her impulsive hiring of Adam's sisters. What on earth was the matter with her? She needed to keep Adam and everything that reminded her of him out of her life, not make it impossible to think of nothing *but* him.

Yet trying not to think about him had never worked, not in all those years away, where she never saw him or anything remotely Amish.

Someone knocked at the front door, and she closed her eyes. She didn't want to deal with anyone or anything else today. She moved quietly into the front hallway, immediately recognizing the woman who waited on the front porch.

"Mrs. Sauder," she said, opening the door wide for her. She couldn't have been more surprised if old Jacob himself had been standing at the door.

"Lena," Adam's mother corrected, reminding Quinn of what she already knew, that the Amish did not hold with such formalities. Titles were but an indicator of false pride. Even their children called adults by their first names.

"Lena," Quinn repeated, trying to mask her surprise. "Come in, come in. What have you got there?" she asked, though she really wanted to know about Adam. Was he still angry? Was he fighting with old Jacob. She stood back to let Lena Sauder come inside. She wished that the house were in better order. She never would have had it up to Lena Sauder's standard of housekeeping, but things could have been slightly less chaotic than this.

Heaven help me, she thought. All this time, and I still want Adam's mother to think I'm good enough to be Amish.

"I have brought you the quilt, Quinn. The remembrance quilt for your mother. I have been keeping it for you, for when you came home again."

She said it so matter-of-factly, Quinn thought. Not *if*, but *when*. She looked down at the tissue-wrapped quilt, and Lena Sauder placed it into her arms. Quinn carried it into the living room and sat down on the sofa, putting the bundle carefully in her lap so she could unwrap it. She recognized the quilt pieces immediately, the blues of the dresses her mother had worn to the Amish school.

Mama, she thought, the pain of her mother's dying more real than it had been in years. She looked up into Lena Sauder's eyes.

"I—it's—" She broke off, dropping her head because the tears were so close. She stared at the quilt, rubbing her hands lovingly over it, admiring the fine stitching, the hours of painstaking work, while she bit her lip and tried not to cry. She hadn't known, hadn't even considered that Lena and the women would have done this on her behalf. She hadn't thought that Lena would keep it for her, bring it to her now—especially now. "It's so beautiful," she said, her voice husky and low. "Thank you. I'll cherish it always." She tried to meet Lena's eyes again but couldn't.

Lena's hand came to rest on her shoulder. The hand was gentle and warm, and the fact that it belonged to Adam's mother was nearly more than Quinn could bear. Lena Sauder had always been kind to her, but she didn't deserve her kindness. A tear spilled out of her eye and rolled down her cheek, and Lena sat down beside her, her arm sliding easily around her shoulders. Quinn savored her comfort. She had once thought of Lena Sauder as her second mother.

"Just yesterday, I was thinking about you," Lena said. "Remembering. When I stand at the kitchen window, I can see the fence on the ridge. Do you know the one?"

Quinn nodded, not trusting herself to speak.

"One winter I am looking out that same window, at the same fence. Adam was just a boy—ten years old, or eleven maybe. He had to put in the new fence posts—carry them up the slope and fit them into the holes and put the rocks and the earth around them. It is so cold that day—fine snow coming—and I look out the window now and again because I am a mother and I want to see he is working all right. But one time when I look, I don't see my one boy—I see two boys, one bundled in a red wool cap and red mittens. Two boys, working and working to get done ahead of the dark and the snow. But, no. It isn't a boy at all who is working so hard to help my Adam. It is Quinn Tyler—my little English."

"You gave us fried apple pies and hot cinnamon milk when we were done," Quinn said, resting easily in Lena Sauder's embrace.

"To make your noses run so you don't catch the grippe."

Quinn laughed softly, and Lena gave her a hard squeeze.

"Quinn, I have something I want to say to you. About Adam."

Quinn took a deep breath and forced herself to sit up. "What?" She managed to look into Lena's eyes.

"I know what a hard thing you did for him so he is not lost from us. You went away and—"

"He hates me, Lena," Quinn interrupted, her face crumpling as she finally voiced the fear she'd carried so long. She hadn't been able to say it to anyone. She hadn't had anyone who would have understood, no one who knew how much she'd cared for Adam Sauder.

Lena patted her gently, putting her arms around her again to soothe her as if she were a child.

"No, Quinn. Adam is hurt and he's angry. But he doesn't hate."

"He wants his son. He knows that I loved him, but he can't forgive me for that."

She felt Lena stiffen. "His son?" The comforting arms dropped from around her.

Oh, dear God! Quinn thought. Adam hadn't told her. It never occurred to her that he hadn't told his mother and Jacob. She stood up, putting the quilt aside and wiping at her eyes.

"Quinn!" Lena said sharply, and Quinn turned around to face her.

"You will tell me this thing! You had a baby with my Adam?"

"Yes," she said evenly.

"And Adam knows this?"

"Yes."

"And where is the baby now?"

"Lena, I don't want to talk about this."

"Nor would I, Quinn Tyler. What have you done to him, my poor son!"

"Lena . . ."

"I will go now."

"Lena, *please*!"

"And I will not see you, Quinn Tyler, until I can find the forgiveness in my own heart."

Quinn followed Lena to the front door, knowing there was nothing she could say or do. Then she went back into the living room and stood by the front window to watch Lena Sauder until she was gone.

Why didn't he tell her?

The question repeated and repeated itself in her mind. Did none of them know, then? In her mind, miles away in Philadelphia, she had faced the ordeal of Jacob and Lena finding out. It had been real; she had thought they knew. She had thought they *all* knew. She wouldn't have come back here if she'd suspected for one minute that she would be the one to tell them. Dear God.

Old Jacob.

Her father was dead. If she had to face Jacob again, she would have no one to stand by her now.

You can do it, Quinn, she told herself.

She wasn't a child anymore. She could deal with Jacob Sauder if she had to.

There is nothing anyone can do, she reminded herself. It's done. It can't be undone. How many times had she said that since she'd last lived here? A hundred? A thousand?

Adam. She wanted to see him, talk to him.

She sat for a long time in the dark, holding the quilt made from her mother's dresses.

Chapter Five

Quinn awoke shortly before dawn. The house was cold, and she toyed with the idea of building another fire. Instead she opted for a sweat suit and a walk over the remaining Tyler land, standing for a time on the back porch and watching the morning mist rise from the low ground and hollows as the sun came up. She closed her eyes and listened. She had missed this, too, the damp freshness of the morning quiet broken only by bird song. No, not only bird song. There was more. She could feel the breeze rustling the new leaves and the tall grass, and somewhere, not far off, she could hear the rattle and clank of chain and tack in the still morning air, and the peaceful monotony of a cajoling human voice. Someone—a Sauder—was plowing. It was a good morning for it. The ground would be soft and wet from the rain. In her mind she could smell it, the newly turned earth, could imagine it cool and soft between her bare toes.

She stepped off the porch and walked around the yard, looking at the house and the lay of what little land she had left as if she'd never seen it before. She had enough acreage to plant *some*thing, and it was hard to tolerate a fallow field. She'd speak to Edison about it. He could find someone to plow it for her. She could manage a small garden herself— tomatoes, squash, cucumbers. Lord, she'd missed home-grown vegetables. The thought of such delicacies made her stomach rumble, reminding her that she hadn't eaten.

She walked back to the house, uncomfortably aware of her state of mind. She was waiting. Hoping. Praying Adam would come to the house today. She had no idea how Lena would handle the news of Quinn Tyler's having had a Sauder child. She would speak to old Jacob surely, and then...

Her mind refused to surmise about that. Jacob was not a violent man, but he was devout, and evidently Adam hadn't told him the worst of his sin. She wanted desperately to know what was happening at the Sauder place, but she had no way to find out. She certainly couldn't go there. She sighed heavily, stopping for a moment to grieve once again for the old apple tree. She reached out with the toe of her running shoe to poke the dead stump.

"You can't bring it to life again," Adam said from the porch, making her jump. The lilac bushes had concealed him; she had no idea how long he'd been waiting. His hair was damp under his hat, freshly combed. If she got close enough, she knew how he would smell—skin that was soap-and-water clean, clothes that had dried out in the sun. Apparently he intended to stay and work. A basket and his carpenter's box sat beside him on the porch.

"No, I can't bring it to life again," she said, knowing it wasn't necessarily the apple tree that she spoke of. She stood with her arms folded over her breasts and didn't get any closer.

"I thought you were still sleeping."

"No," she said again, taking a few steps in his direction. He didn't seem angry. Lena must not have said anything. If she had, he wouldn't be speaking to her so civilly. If she had, he wouldn't be here at all.

He reached out to pull a leaf off one of the lilac bushes. "You're going to have to do something about these bushes, Quinn. They've got the black spot."

She said nothing to that, and he let the leaf fall.

"Well, do you tell me I can go inside to work, or do you leave me standing here on the porch?"

She frowned. The remark should have been sarcastic. It wasn't. He wasn't teasing her exactly, but almost. Almost.

"Yes, of course," she said, climbing the porch steps too quickly. She'd forgotten that they were so rickety, and she was off balance when she reached the top. Adam stretched to steady her, his hand firm and warm on her elbow. She looked into his eyes, her mouth pursed to say that she didn't need any help, but she didn't get the words out. She stood there, her eyes locked with his. Hers, she was certain, were wary and filled with questions; his... For once, they were unfathomable. She had no idea what he was thinking, feeling. She knew only his closeness, his hand still firmly clasping her arm.

"There's Quinn Tyler!" Daniel called suddenly from behind them, and Adam let go of her arm. "We knocked and knocked on the front door. Were you sleeping?"

Quinn smiled. The "we" included Anna and Mary, one dressed in a plain green dress, the other in a deep-blue one, and both wearing their white prayer caps with the strings dangling and their typical aprons. Somehow, when she'd really expected no one today, the whole clan had arrived. "No. Not sleeping. Just walking around."

Her smile broadened. She could tell by the girls' expressions that they considered the activity typically English and entirely trifling. "Let's get to work," she said, leading the way into the house and only vaguely concerned about whether or not they'd noticed Adam's touching her.

She left Adam and Daniel in the kitchen and took Mary and Anna to the stacks of boxes in the hallway, starting them on the linens first. The cartons were heavy, and she and the girls were struggling to get the necessary ones up the stairs when Adam intruded with his greater strength and carried the boxes to the second floor as if they weighed nothing.

"Anything else?" he asked, clearly annoyed at having to interrupt his carpentry.

"No, nothing, thank you," Quinn said coolly.

Anna looked perplexed. "What?" Quinn asked her.

"The boxes were heavy, Quinn Tyler. Didn't you want Adam to help us?"

"Of course, I wanted him to help us," Quinn said loudly enough for him to hear her. "I just didn't want him to be so arrogant about it. There are only two ways to be strong, girls—mentally and physically. And each of us has only one of those. It's not *our* fault God put all our strength between our ears."

To her surprise, she heard Adam laugh, really laugh, when he reached the kitchen. She set the girls to cleaning out the linen closet, then lining the shelves with flowered paper.

"Will you tell us where you want the towels and sheets to go, Quinn?" Anna asked, clearly worried at the responsibility of the task.

"Put the sheets and pillowcases on the higher shelves. The rest you can do however you think is best."

She went back downstairs to Adam and Daniel's vigorous hammering in the kitchen. She had to find something for her breakfast. She was determined not to ask Adam anything about Lena. If he didn't know she'd told Lena about their child, she wasn't about to bring it up. He'd know soon enough, and, if she were truthful with herself, this sudden and uneasy truce of his was not unpleasant.

She rummaged around until she found a can of cream of chicken soup. She heated it on the hot plate and made toast in the toaster—not standard breakfast fare, but more than soothing. She ate with relish—it was quite good, actually—and she stayed out of Adam's way, casting glances in his direction from time to time from her perch on a bar stool in the corner.

He ignored her, his mind on pulling boards off the wall and his conversation only for Daniel.

When she had finished eating, she washed the pot and the one bowl she'd used, then went into the living room to work on Edison's financial records. She found that in spite of Lena Sauder's visit and her subsequent sleepless night, in spite of Adam's being in the house, she could concentrate—for a time. But with the fifth folder of financial data, her mind began to wander.

The house was alive this morning, not deadly quiet the way it was when only she was there. Anna and Mary laughed together upstairs—the Amish strived to teach their children to be happy in their work. And Adam and Daniel told their riddles.

How she'd always longed to be part of a big family like this, a part of *his* family. And yet, she couldn't deny that she'd tried to make him "worldly." She'd fostered Adam's desire for learning. She'd brought him books, told him about the movies she'd seen, let him listen to her "English" music. Once, they'd danced together in the moonlight on a creek bank. She even remembered the song, "I Love How You Love Me," by the Paris Sisters. It had been considered an oldie, even then. They hadn't yet become lovers, but she and Adam slipped away to talk, to listen to the music that was forbidden to him, to simply be together. He was always so filled with questions about the things she saw and heard in her world, and the song had come on the small transistor radio she'd brought along. Adam, non-dancing Adam, had held out his hands. They'd stepped into each other's arms, the way he knew English couples did, and awkwardly they had moved together to the music. She had never forgotten. The feel of his body against hers, his heady masculine smell, his breath soft and warm against her ear as they danced so innocently.

"Quinn," Adam said behind her, and she jumped.

"What's wrong with you?" he asked, his voice taking on the sharp edge she dreaded.

"Nothing's wrong."

"Then why do you jump out of your skin every time I speak to you?"

"Adam, I didn't know you were there. You startled me, that's all."

He stared at her, and she could feel him deciding whether or not he believed her. "Are you afraid of me?" His eyes probed hers.

"No, I'm not afraid of you."

"You're just . . . nervous, then?"

"I guess so," she acknowledged. "City living and all that. What did you want?"

"I need you to help me."

"Me?" she said, unable to keep from sounding incredulous. Somehow that was the last thing she'd considered, that Adam Sauder would ask for *her* help.

"Yes, you. You are too much of a big shot to help?"

"No, I'm not too much of a big shot." She got up from the computer and followed him into the kitchen. "What is it?"

"There's a piece of molding that's fallen down into the wall. The hole is too small for me to get my hand in, and Daniel's arm is too short to reach it. I think you can do it.

Reach up in there," he said, showing her the hole. "The piece is diagonal between the studs, I think."

She looked at the hole, then at him. "Adam, you know there could be spiders in there."

"Yes, I know that," he assured her. "Daniel, here, knows it, too. Don't you, Daniel?"

"Yes," Daniel said.

Quinn needed more incentive than she was getting. "How do you know the molding is in there?"

"Because I dropped it in there. See that hole higher up? For some reason, somebody put it in that hole. Just the tip was showing. I knocked it the rest of the way in trying to pull it out."

"Couldn't we just leave it?"

"Yes, we could do that, but I think it's part of the fancy original ceiling molding—one of the pieces your father made. I thought you'd want to keep it. I don't want to have to pull off any more boards to get it if you can reach it."

She looked at the hole again. She did want to keep the molding. She just didn't want to stick her hand in there.

"And you want me to put my hand in that hole with the spiders," she said.

"That's what we want," Adam said. "Don't we, Daniel?"

"Yes," Daniel said again. They were both trying not to grin. It was becoming obvious to her that her aversion to spiders had been discussed at length before she'd ever been summoned.

"You two are just too cute for words," she said.

"We are," Adam agreed.

"I'll be right back."

She went into the hallway to rummage through the boxes, coming back with one red-and-blue-striped knee sock. She put the sock on over her hand, pulling it all the way to her shoulder. She stuck her well-covered hand and arm into the hole and located the molding easily enough. Dislodging it was something else again, but after a few minutes of blind maneuvering, she was finally able to get it free.

"Good job," Adam said when she brought it out.

"Thank you. Do you see this here?" she asked, pointing to the sock. "Spiderwebs. All over my arm."

"You were very brave," Adam said to pacify her.

"Just don't let this happen again," she admonished them.

"No, we won't. Will we, Daniel?"

Daniel grinned, and Quinn left on the heels of their laughter, laughing herself once she was out of the kitchen. But her smile quickly faded. It was so easy—too easy—to put aside all the hurt and the pain and the sorrow. She was behaving as if nothing had happened between her and Adam Sauder, and she couldn't afford to do that.

She went back into the living room, determined to work at the computer. She needed to get the financial data entered, and she needed not to resurrect any more old feelings.

"Quinn?" one of Adam's sisters called from upstairs. Quinn wasn't familiar enough with their voices to tell which.

"Yes?" she called up the stairs.

"Come see, Quinn."

She climbed the stairs, feeling the strain of the past two days in the last few steps. She was tired—too tired in light of her promise to Jake and Edison to take care of herself. She hesitated for a moment on the landing to catch her breath.

"It's done, Quinn," called Anna, who seemed to do all the talking. Mary, the younger of the two, was dutifully subordinate, staying quietly in the background.

"It looks fine," Quinn said truthfully as she inspected the stacks of carefully placed linens. She couldn't have done better herself.

She turned them loose in the bathroom next with various spray cans they seemed delighted to try. She went back downstairs, deciding to set up the refrigerator, even if she had to leave it in the hall outside the kitchen door for a while.

The cord wouldn't reach the wall plug. She tried moving the refrigerator, but it was an older model without wheels, and she could barely budge it. She caught a glimpse of Adam out of the corner of her eye, and this time she didn't jump.

He put his hammer down. "Where do you want it?"

"Closer to the wall socket so I can plug it in."

"Come, Daniel, you, too," he said, not, Quinn suspected, because he needed Daniel's help, but because he wanted Daniel to feel that he did.

Such a good father, she thought yet another time and promptly pushed the thought aside.

Together the three of them moved the refrigerator close enough for the plug to reach.

"Anything else you want the mentally weak to do?" he asked, and again she was struck by his lack of vindictiveness. She looked up into his eyes.

What are you doing? she demanded silently.

His eyes slid away from hers, and he reached across her to retrieve his hammer from the top of a box where he'd laid it. He was too close again, too close and too obliging.

"I'm going into town," she said abruptly. "I have to get some groceries."

"I'll come with you."

"You'll come?"

"I need nails. Unless you're afraid to have me ride into town with you."

"I'm not afraid of you!" she snapped, but she was. She'd never been so afraid in her life.

"Then there is no problem, is there?"

Yes, there's a problem, and you know it! she wanted to say. It took everything she had to stop herself.

"I have to find my purse."

She walked away from him, ostensibly looking for her purse and her keys but in actuality seeing nothing. What was the matter with him? He couldn't be seen riding around town with her!

"It's in the kitchen," Adam said. "On the counter by the hot plate."

She went to get it, and he called upstairs in German to his sisters, and then to Daniel, who was watching her search through her purse for the car keys. He wasn't taking Daniel with them. She could tell immediately from the boy's crest-fallen look.

But she said nothing. She could be alone with Adam Sauder. She wouldn't be afraid of him. She would show him that she could be alone with him. He followed her out to the car, getting in and trying to keep his knees from pressing against the dash. He was much too tall to be comfortable.

"There's a lever under the seat in front. Push it to the side if you want to move the seat back."

"No," he answered, staring straight ahead, as if such a flagrant concession to personal discomfort was a road that would lead straight to his destruction.

Fine, she thought. He could suit himself.

She drove into town quickly, meeting no Amish horse and buggies to slow her down. She attempted no conversation with Adam, nor he with her. They simply rode in silence, each acutely aware of the other's presence.

"Turn in there," he said shortly after she'd pulled onto Highway 340. "At the flea market."

"Adam, you don't want to go in there," she protested.

"Why not?"

"Because..." *You're with me,* she almost said. But she bit down on it, deterred by the challenge she saw in his eyes.

She pressed her hand against the burning ache in her stomach. "You won't find nails *here*, will you?"

"I will if Abe Zook is here today. He sells them cheaper than in town. Park the car over there. It won't take long to see."

She parked where he indicated.

"Aren't you coming?" he asked as he got out of the car. "Come on, Quinn. You may see something you want for your house." He opened the door on her side and stood waiting. "Are you afraid of the flea market, too?" he asked. Although he didn't speak the words, his voice challenged her, *There is nothing between us Quinn. Why can't you act like it?* "What else are you afraid of? How did you live in so big a place as Philadelphia when everything scares you?"

"Everything doesn't scare me," she said as she got out. If he didn't care, there was no reason she should, she told herself, knowing it wasn't true. *She* had nothing to lose in being seen with him. She trailed after him, trying to stay far enough behind so that no one would think they were together. He waited until she caught up. Together, they walked down an aisle of vendors, Amish women and girls with their hand-lettered, often misspelled signs. HONY FOR SALE. APPLESAUS FOR SALE. She bumped into an Amishman coming in the opposite direction. He was barefoot and dirty, his feet tough and nearly black from going without shoes. He had two small boys with him, equally dirty, and the combined stench that rose from their three unwashed bodies nearly took her breath away.

She stepped away from him as if she'd been burned, only to find Adam watching.

"Philadelphia has made you too good for us," he commented.

"It hasn't made me too good," she snapped. "For some reason that man and his children weren't following your cleanliness-is-next-to-Godliness rule. He was dirty and stank!''

He walked on ahead of her, and this time he didn't wait for her to catch up. She followed at a safe distance, pretending to be interested in the nearest booth—jars of bean chow-chow and pickled cauliflower and celery. She watched out of the corner of her eye as Adam conducted his business with another Amishman who kept showing him boxes of nails. Adam came back empty-handed.

"Now what's the matter?" Quinn said.

"Too short," he answered succinctly, walking past her toward the parked car.

"What is an Amishman doing with all that hardware anyway?" she asked from behind him.

"A store was going out of business. He didn't want the store, but he did want the inventory. He bought it to sell here. Low overhead, you see. And good prices to get the people to come and to come back. He's making extra money for his family without having to send his children out among the English to work."

"Clever man," Quinn said as she caught up with him.

"Yes," Adam agreed, finally looking at her. "A clever man."

Quinn's car was boxed in by two others when they reached it, no major problem for a woman used to city living. Quinn pulled forward and backed up, maneuvering inch by inch until she could get the car out.

"Good job," Adam said when she cut the steering sharply for the last time. She glanced at him. He meant it, and she smiled, getting them onto the road again and heading toward town.

"Let me out here," he said when they were still several blocks from the second place he wanted to try for nails.

"I can take you the rest of the way," she insisted. It was crazy for him to walk with her right through half of Amish

Lancaster County, and then not let her take him to where they'd likely see no one.

"No. The tourist buses are in town. I can walk there easier than you can drive. I'll wait for you here on the corner."

She let him out, watching for a moment as he strode down the street. He was a beautiful man, strong and gentle and kind, and, once again, this time simply by being seen with him, she'd likely ruined him.

A car horn blew sharply behind her, and she drove on. Down the main street, lines of tour buses with logos from all over the eastern United States were creeping into town, backing up traffic at the stoplights and intersections. The entire downtown smelled of diesel exhaust fumes. She was finally able to get out of the press and into a grocery store parking lot, but it, too, was crowded. She didn't linger over her shopping. She'd be glad to get out of this and back home.

"Is it always this busy?" she asked the girl at the checkout counter.

"It is during the tourist season," she said without looking up. "Five million tourists last year—and they all came in here at least once. There's something about traveling on a tour bus that makes people think the next place they're going to stop to eat will be out of everything."

"Miss! Excuse me!" a large woman wearing a straw hat and white heart-shaped sunglasses interrupted. "Quick! Where's the candy aisle!"

The chekcout girl pointed. "See what I mean?" she said to Quinn.

Traffic was still congested as Quinn drove back through town, and Adam was waiting on the corner where he'd gotten out. She could see him plainly; she just couldn't get to him. Two tour buses had stopped on the street, and he was now standing stoically in the center of a rush of disembarked passengers with cameras. They either didn't know that the Amish did not like having their pictures taken or felt that their tight itinerary excused them from courteous behavior.

She rolled down the car window. "Adam!" she called, but he couldn't hear her over the bus engines. "Adam!" she yelled again, without success. She leaned on the car horn, causing him and most of the tourists to look in her direction. "Hurry!" she called, because she had stopped dead in the street with yet another tour bus all but in her trunk.

Adam disengaged his arm from the grasp of a young redhead in a halter top and skimpy shorts who was trying to get him to stand beside her for a picture. Quinn flung the car door open for him.

"Drive!" he said before he was all the way inside.

"Did you get your nails?" Quinn inquired when they'd gone less than a block. He was more rattled than she'd thought, seeing him from a distance, and she couldn't keep from teasing him.

"Yes, I got the nails." He showed her the crumpled paper bag in his hand, then sighed heavily. "I thought I was going to have to run for it." He glanced back over his shoulder as if he thought the girl in the shorts might be hanging on to the back of the car. "And it's not funny."

"I'm not laughing," she assured him.

He looked at her, and she kept her face carefully neutral. "See?"

He shook his finger at her. "The *outside* is not laughing," he said suspiciously. He sighed heavily. "There may be something to this never wearing shoes and never taking a bath," he observed. He glanced at her, and they both laughed.

They came out of one snarl of traffic and right into another. "When did it get like this?" she asked. "It wasn't so crowded the other day."

"The last few years or so. When the weather gets warm, here they come in their buses and their vans. Open season on the Plain People. Every year it gets worse."

"For you. Not for the ones who make a living off the tourist trade."

A small red car pulled out in front of her, and she slammed on the brakes. "This is worse than Philadelphia. I'm sorry," she said, realizing she'd nearly thrown him into the windshield.

"So am I," he answered. Their eyes met and held, and suddenly they weren't talking about the influx of tourists anymore.

Quinn looked away, trying to keep her eyes on the road, her mind on her driving. The car suddenly felt too hot and stuffy for her, and she rolled down the window, bracing herself for whatever his look suggested he was about to do. But he remained silent, staring straight ahead again in the start-and-stop journey out of town. The heat and the noise of idling engines, car horns and irritated voices surrounded them, making conversation impractical, had either of them wanted to talk. Quinn certainly didn't, and she was thankful that, for the moment, Adam seemed lost in his own thoughts. She only wanted to get back home, except that Adam would be there, too. Lord, how she needed some peace in her life! She had merely exchanged one grief for another, her loneliness in Philadelphia for a renewed guilt about Adam Sauder here.

But her relief at Adam's silence was short-lived. He waited until they were back at the Tyler house, until she'd pulled the car into the yard and was ready to get out, until Daniel was jumping down the back porch steps to meet them.

Then he reached out and put his hand on her arm. "Quinn," he said quietly. "What did our baby look like?"

Chapter Six

Adam knew she wouldn't answer. Daniel was bounding up to the car, and she wouldn't have the time, but he still asked. The question was there between them; it had been since the first day, and he couldn't *not* ask it. Her eyes blinked with the pain he'd given her, just as he knew they would, but he'd still asked. She shook his hand off her arm and flung open the car door, remembering only when she'd gone a few steps that she had groceries to bring in. He tried to help her with the bags, but she wouldn't let him. Clearly, his question had reminded her of the time she'd had to make do without his help.

"We *will* talk about this, Quinn," he said out of Daniel's hearing, but she gave no indication that she heard him.

"Is it eating time, Adam?" Daniel wanted to know. "Is it?"

"Not yet," Adam said in German, watching all the while as Quinn hurried into the house. It struck him again that she wasn't well. She was too thin, even in her strange, baggy, men's-looking clothes. Perhaps she didn't wear dresses anymore.

He followed her into the house. She was on her knees, putting things into the refrigerator, when he came in. Mary and Anna watched both of them from the kitchen doorway, Mary fiddling with her glasses in her nervousness about keeping him apart from Quinn the way their father wanted.

"What did you say, Adam?" Daniel called as he ran up behind him.

"I said, not yet!"

"Not yet? This is a hungry time, Adam!" Daniel pulled on his brother's arm to get him to go in the direction of the food basket they'd brought and left sitting in a window in the kitchen. Adam suddenly smiled, because he could see the telltale smudges of strawberry jam on the corners of Daniel's mouth.

"What is this on your mouth then? I will be lucky if there is anything in Mom's basket left."

He let Daniel urge him toward the basket, then took it and him out of the house and onto the back porch to eat, leaving Anna and Mary to marvel over Quinn's refrigerator now that he was far enough away for them to relax their vigilance. He sat down on the steps in the warm sun, taking his hat off and putting it aside, trying not to smile as Daniel mimicked him exactly. He noted again that the lilac bushes needed to be sprayed, and he reached to pull at the wobbly top step. He would fix it before he left here. The step was dangerous, and he didn't want Quinn to fall.

He sighed heavily and glanced at Daniel. He was tired suddenly, and the boy was waiting as patiently as he could manage for his portion from the basket.

"Anna! Mary!" Adam called abruptly. They had lingered long enough with Quinn and her English refrigerator.

They came quickly, crowding around the basket and waiting while he bowed his head over the cheese, frizzed beef, bread, fried apple pies and biscuits and jam his mother had packed for them. He raised his head, aware that his sisters were more interested in him than in his offering thanks for their dinner. They were supposed to watch him, and he'd gone off into town with Quinn alone. Now they were looking for some sign of whatever it was they were supposed to monitor in him. He carefully lifted the four jars of lemon tea out of the basket and passed them around. There was an extra jar in the basket, cabbage juice his mother had sent to Quinn for her stomach troubles. He'd forgotten to give it to her. He could hear Quinn in the kitchen now, and he got up with it, leaving his chaperons uncertain and worried again as he took the jar inside.

Quinn looked around sharply as he came in the back door, her eyes wary. She had a pot of something in her hand, and she stirred it vigorously before she put it on the hot plate.

He set the jar on the counter. "Mom sent you this to help your stomach. It's cabbage juice. Drink some every day, she says. Three times a day. She will send you more when it's gone—" He broke off because she was looking at the jar so strangely.

"When did Lena give you this?"

"When? This morning. Why?"

"I just . . . wondered," she said.

"It isn't spoiled, Quinn."

"No, I didn't mean that," she said quickly, picking it up as if he'd just given her some rare and precious gift. "I was just . . . surprised." He thought for a moment that she was going to cry.

"Tell Lena that I—I thank her very much." She put the jar down again. "You won't forget to tell her?"

"I won't forget. Quinn?"

She turned away from him to stir the pot on the hot plate. "What?"

"I'm waiting for you to answer me."

She didn't pretend that she didn't know what he meant. "This isn't the time, Adam."

"It will have to do. Daniel and my sisters will be here as long as I am. I would have said what was on my mind in the car, but I didn't—"

She turned to look at him. "Didn't what?"

He stared at her, for once feeling detached, separated from her by his need to know about their baby. He struggled to stay that way. Yet all the while, some part of his mind insisted that he see how beautiful she still was. More beautiful than he remembered. She'd been a girl when he last saw her, and now, for all her thinness and her strangely cropped hair, she was a lovely woman. "I didn't want to give you any more pain. But I need to know this. I *need* to know. Do you understand?"

"I understand," she said quietly.

I always understand, she had said before, and that is what he saw when he looked into her sad eyes now. Did she?

He waited. She glanced toward Daniel and the girls outside on the porch. Daniel had the giggles, the kind that little boys invariably get over nothing and the kind that unfailingly annoys their older sisters.

"He...was very small," Quinn said, looking back at him. "Only five pounds. He came a few weeks early, but he was healthy. His hair—he had a lot of hair. It was dark like mine. The nurse in the nursery told me that he liked to be bundled up in a blanket, liked to be wrapped up tight and touching the side of the bassinet. He was too young for us to know what color his eyes would—"

"Didn't you know how important a child would be to me!" he interrupted, surprised at his sudden rise of anger. "How could you not know that? Children are everything to us. There is no purpose in our lives—not for a man or a woman—without children.''

"I knew, Adam. Probably better than anyone who isn't one of you. Your way of life was mine as long as I could get away with it."

"And you still gave my child away!"

"Yes. I did what I thought was best."

"What *you* thought. You had no time, no need to ask the baby's father."

"My baby's father was lost to me."

"Your baby's father was in *hell*!" he hissed at her. He made a sweeping motion with his arm, sending the jar of cabbage juice onto the floor. It spun and rolled, but it didn't break, and the giggling stopped abruptly on the back porch. Quinn stooped to pick up the jar. He stared down at the top of her head, wanting to reach out, to touch her shiny dark hair, to put his arms around her. He turned on his heel and went back outside.

He stayed on the porch as long as he could, until Quinn had gone back to her computer, but he gave no explanations to Anna and Mary and Daniel. What they had overheard and what they would tell Jacob, he had no idea. He didn't care.

Quinn stayed well out of his way. He didn't blame her for that, but he still listened to her activity, hoping she would come into the kitchen again. He sent Daniel out to the porch with a stack of boards that needed the nails hammered out, but he could do nothing about Anna and Mary. Quinn put them to work unpacking boxes of books in the hallway while she worked on the things Edison had brought her. He couldn't get to her without Anna and Mary knowing, and he couldn't tell anything about her state of mind; he could only hear her clicking on the keys of the computer.

He worked on, pulling off boards, patching up the damage to the walls with the clean, reusable boards Daniel brought him from his project on the porch. The work was not difficult, but he intended to do it well. He would restore as much of the original wood as he could—for her—because he knew she wanted it, needed something around her from her past, or at least the part of her past when she was happy. He didn't think she was happy now, he knew his questions weren't helping her to overcome it.

He raised his head. Anna and Mary were singing a hymn, not a hymn in the English sense, but an Amish one that was usually sung at weddings. It was called *Guter Geselle*, "Good Friend." Quinn sang along with them; she had learned it when she was a little girl. Her voice was pure and disciplined, her execution of the erratic, chanting notes faultless. He could see her suddenly, standing in his backyard, earnestly singing that same song for him in the German she didn't understand.

My good friend, he thought in spite of himself.

Quinn, don't!

She had been that to him always, his good friend, and he closed his eyes against the pain of remembering. Everything happened for a reason. He'd been taught that all his life. But what was the reason behind this? What good did it do in God's overall plan for both of them to suffer so?

Quinn suddenly stopped singing, and he could hear her talking to Anna and Mary in the hallway, then going up the stairs.

He went to the kitchen doorway. "What did she say?" he asked in German.

Mary glanced at Anna before she answered. "She said she had to rest sometimes, and she'll be upstairs if we need to ask anything."

"She said I can run the vacuum cleaner," Anna put in, clearly pleased with the opportunity to use such a powerful forbidden convenience.

"If she has to rest, you don't run the vacuum cleaner until she comes down again," Adam said.

"But she said—"

"*I* said," he snapped. He cast a glance up the stairs, then retreated to the kitchen. For a brief moment he heard Quinn walking around overhead. He gave a short sigh and went back to work.

"You're hammering," Anna ventured through the doorway after a time. "She can't rest with you hammering."

"I'm getting paid to hammer," Adam said.

"I get paid to vacuum," she countered.

"You get paid to put away the things in the boxes and to clean the house. You have other things you can do until Quinn comes down again. I don't."

Anna pursed her lips to say more but didn't. She turned around and went back into the hallway. He could hear her voicing her complaints to Mary, who, not chosen for vacuuming, apparently was not impressed.

A man from the telephone company came shortly after Quinn had gone upstairs, and Adam intervened when Anna would have gone to tell her. He went himself, leaving the three of them standing in the front hall. He suspected from the lights he'd seen on Quinn's first night back that she'd taken her old bedroom, the room with windows he could see from his own room at home. The comfort and the anguish it had given him when their love was new, knowing that he could look out across the moonlit fields and see the place where she lay, as sleepless with longing as he was. And the comfort and the anguish it had given him when he'd crossed those same fields in the dark and hidden in the yard below, knowing that when he shined a forbidden flashlight on her window screen, she would come to him.

He walked quietly along the upstairs hall; she was in her old bedroom, as he'd thought. He reached up to knock lightly on the half-open door but didn't. He could see her plainly on the old-fashioned bed, curled up and sleeping under the quilt his mother had just given her, her shoes dropped carelessly on their sides on the floor. He could call her, knock as he'd intended, and she would wake, but he didn't do either. He stood watching her quiet breathing, realizing how much he'd once wanted this, to be in the same house with her, living, belonging together in all things, to legitimately have this privilege he was taking now, that of watching her in unguarded sleep.

She stirred, and he did knock, after all. She came awake immediately, and he worried for a moment that she might have been aware of how long he'd been standing there.

"There is a man from the telephone company who wants to know where to put the telephone," he said, and she sat up.

"I'll be right there."

"I can tell him where if you need to rest longer."

She worked hurriedly to get her feet into her shoes. "No. No, I'll do it."

Left with nothing else to offer her, he turned to go. But he stopped just outside the doorway.

"Quinn?" he said quietly because he knew that Anna and Mary would be trying to listen. "Our...the baby. Don't you ever want to see him?"

She had her shoes on now, and she stood up. Her eyes met his calmly. "Every day of my life, Adam."

"*Have* you seen him? Since he was born?"

"No."

"Why not?"

"I can't."

"Can't or won't?"

"Adam, I—I don't know where he is." It wasn't entirely the truth, but it would have to do for now. She tried to get by him, but he caught her arm.

"You could find out."

"I don't want to find out."

"How could you do this thing, Quinn?"

Again she looked him unwaveringly in the eyes. "It's the price I had to pay."

His fingers tightened on her arm. "For what you did with me, you mean?" He couldn't call their loving a sin, even now. She had been so much a part of him that, in the years since he'd been with her, no lawful wife could take her place.

She didn't answer him, reaching to pull his fingers off her arm, her touch nervous and cold to him. She walked on toward the head of the stairs.

"Quinn," he called, and she looked back, her face pale and grave, her eyes still deadly calm. Whatever her reasons for doing what she'd done, he realized that she had come to terms with it. Far from being comforted by her acceptance, he felt more abandoned and alone than ever, and totally of no consequence. Why was it that *he* hadn't mattered in any of this? He suddenly didn't want her to be calm and accepting. He wanted her to be as anguished as he was. Then he could understand. Then he would know that he and his blind devotion had meant *something* to her.

Didn't she see what had happened to him? He wasn't Amish anymore. He had tried so hard, but he *wasn't Amish anymore!* He still lived by the rules, by the *Ordnung*, simply because he'd had no alternative. But their goals in life weren't his. Jacob had told him over and over. *"You must stay one of us."* He had stayed, but he had brought them only his indifference, his apathy in the guise of obedience. He had loved this woman, and he'd refused to pretend that it wasn't so, regardless of the pain and embarrassment it had caused his family. And yet, standing here now, he deliberately meant to hurt her. "I think you would have done better to let God give his own punishments. He would not have been so hard on us as you have been."

He regretted the remark instantly. "Quinn, I—"

"No," she said, holding her hands up as if to physically keep him away from her if she had to.

"Quinn, wait—"

But she didn't wait. She left him standing in the upstairs hallway. Alone. Always alone. He followed her to the head of the stairs, watching as she descended into the hallway. He hadn't wanted to make her run away from him. He had wanted things to stay easy between them, like this morning when he'd gotten her to retrieve the lost molding. He wasn't like her; he hadn't *always* understood. He hadn't understood at all, and that was all he wanted—to understand. Perhaps if he did, he could get on with his life.

He went down the stairs. He could hear Quinn and the telephone man talking in the kitchen, and a new emotion surfaced. Jealousy.

"I didn't think you'd remember me," the telephone man said.

"For heaven's sake, why not? We had classes together all through high school."

"Yeah, well, you've been gone a long time, Quinn. Welcome back, by the way."

"Thank you, Bobby. It's good to be home."

"So the great Thomas Wolfe wasn't right after all?"

Quinn laughed. "Not that I can tell," she said.

Adam stood in the hallway trying to follow the conversation. Thomas Wolfe. Thomas Wolfe. The name was familiar, but he couldn't remember why. He was so—*ignorant*, for all the work Quinn had done years ago to enlighten him, bringing him the books about her world, explaining things to him, teaching him. He still hated it, the not knowing what other people, "English" people, took for granted. It surprised him how much he hated it. No. It surprised him how much his ignorance mattered to him now that Quinn was back.

He forced himself to walk into the kitchen, and he immediately began hammering, careful not to look at Quinn, or Daniel and the girls, or this telephone man. He was glad to note—covertly—that if Quinn was impressed with the telephone man's expertise in worldly devices, in the installation of the modern convenience, it didn't show.

"Daniel," he said finally, "we don't get paid for you to stare at this telephone."

He set Daniel to working again, not missing the fact that Bobby grinned and winked at Quinn, as if what Adam had said was immensely funny and they had just shared a private joke at Adam's expense. He turned his back on the pair of them, working hard, intently, as he always did when he needed to shut the world out. But it wasn't really the world that he needed to escape. It was the people in it. The English with their telephones and their Kodak cameras and their amusement at people who chose to live Plain.

"Daniel!" he said sharply, because the boy was intent on watching the telephone man again.

"I think we'd better get out of the way," Quinn said, taking the girls away with her into another part of the house.

In a moment Adam could hear the vacuum cleaner start with enough roar and force to make Anna happy. He kept working. Hard. If he had no interruptions, he'd be finished in this house this afternoon. The patching of the walls would be done, and he'd have no reason to return until the new cabinets were made. Perhaps he would tell Holland Wakefield to send another man.

It was what he wanted, he decided. To be free of his obligation to Holland Wakefield so that he wouldn't have to see Quinn again. He worked harder, pushing Daniel to get the boards he needed ready faster. By late afternoon there was nothing left to do but replace that found piece of molding Quinn's father had made. As he hammered it into place, he was suddenly aware of Quinn watching him. He hesitated a moment before he climbed down from the ladder, bracing himself for whatever he would see in her eyes.

He turned around. No anger, he thought in surprise. She was carefully inspecting the work he'd done, her face almost wistful.

"It looks fine, Adam," she said, moving around the room. "With a coat of paint, it'll look the way it used to." She finally gazed at him. "Do you know when I can expect the new cabinets?"

"Holland has already started one of the carpenters on them. They should be ready in a week or so."

She nodded and glanced around the room again. "It'll be nice to get the stove in."

"Quinn—" he began, unable to continue with inane conversation.

"Don't," she whispered, her eyes pleading. "Let's just be done with this, can't we?"

He wasn't certain precisely what she meant, and she moved to the counter to pick up her purse, glancing up once as the girls came into the kitchen.

"You've done a very good job for me," she said to them. "Both of you. If you need references for another job, you can give my name, all right? If your father asks, you can tell him that I'm well pleased."

She counted out the money to both of them, and Adam could feel how careful she was being not to look at him. He moved closer.

"Take Daniel and wait for me outside," he said to Anna in German, but she refused to do it, stubbornly standing her ground. He had escaped their surveillance once today, and she wasn't going to let it happen again. Jacob Sauder's was clearly the higher law. He pressed his lips together and began gathering up his tools.

"Anymore, if you have another spider, Quinn, I'll help you," Daniel told her.

She smiled. "Thank you, Daniel. You're just the person I'll call. Adam?"

He looked around at her, trying to keep his face neutral, his emotions detached, yet fully aware of the response her voice saying his name evoked in him.

"Tell your mother that I thank her for the cabbage juice."

"I've said that I will, Quinn," he responded more sharply than he had intended.

"Yes. So you did. I just…didn't want you to forget." She took a deep breath and looked at each of them. "Thank you all. I'd better get busy with Edison's files. You know the way out."

She turned and moved toward the front hall. Adam was standing between her and the doorway, and he didn't move. She came very close to him as she passed. He could smell her scent—soap and the sweet woman smell that was hers alone. He could almost but not quite feel the brush of her strange English clothes as she went by.

I want to touch you, he thought, and she glanced up into his eyes. For a moment he was afraid that he'd said it out loud.

"Should I pay you?" she asked. "Or will Holland do it? He didn't tell me."

"Holland pays me. Not you."

"Oh. Well." She gave a small shrug, her lips pursed as if she was about to say something else. Whatever it was, she didn't say it, escaping into the hallway. He could hear her going up the stairs instead of to her computer, and he finished gathering up his tools, checking the room one more time before he left to make sure everything was in order. There was no mess. No sawdust. No forgotten bent nails. He had no reason to say here. The job was finished.

Finished.

He picked up the carpenter's helper and led the way outside. There *was* still the wobbly step. He'd forgotten it until now, and he set the toolbox down. He inspected the step closely. It wasn't rotted, only loose. He carefully selected the nail he wanted and drove it through the top board and into the frame. Then another. And another. He tested the step to see if it was secure, letting Daniel bounce on it as a double check. Then he gathered up his tools and the carpenter's helper again and started out across the backyard, breathing in the fresh spring air, feeling the late sun still warm on his face. He looked around him. This was good land here, land that wanted to be cultivated and planted.

"Did you get the basket?" he suddenly asked his sisters.

"Yes, we got it," Anna said. "*You* have your mind too much elsewhere to remember things like baskets."

He walked on, oblivious to the insinuation in Anna's remark, savoring the late afternoon, the satisfying tiredness of a job well done. He glanced back once at the house. Quinn was standing in the upstairs window.

Chapter Seven

Quinn heard him before she saw him. He was whistling, and more to the point, he was whistling *alone*. There was no Daniel with him, no Anna or Mary. Illogically she'd been waiting all day for him to come back to the house. But, as the day wore on, she had finally given up. She had come to believe that she wouldn't see him again except at a distance, at some chance meeting in town or along the highway. She had even decided that that was for the best. He would never understand what she had done, and he would never forgive. And she had known that. She had come back here for no other reason than to get on with her life—with or without the burden of her guilt about Adam Sauder. She'd had the chance to talk with him, and they'd gotten nowhere. His feelings, and hers, were still unresolved, but there was nothing more she could do.

But now, here he was, strolling jauntily toward the house, and carrying a sapling tree with the roots wrapped tightly in a cloth sack. She moved to the kitchen window to watch him proceed along the narrow road that cut between her fallow field and his carefully planted one. Walking out onto the back porch as he came into the yard, she stood on the top step he'd repaired for her.

"Where is your shovel, Quinn?" he asked without prelude, his eyes flicking over her in a way that told her he appreciated the fact that she was a woman.

"I don't have a shovel."

He looked back in the direction from which he'd come, then set the tree down at his feet. "I'll have to go get one then."

"No, wait," she called after him. She went back into the house to get her car keys. "I've got an entrenching tool in the trunk. Maybe that will do."

"Entrenching tool?"

"It's like a shovel. I keep it in the trunk to shovel snow. It folds up. Soldiers carry them in their backpacks to dig foxholes and things like that—I got it at the army surplus store—I—" She broke off and tried not to smile. Adam was wearing that ask-a-simple-question look she'd seen thousands of times before whenever she'd bombarded him with "English" information he didn't particularly want. "Where are you going with that tree anyway?"

"I'm not going anywhere," he said, following her. "I'm here."

"Did I order a tree?"

"No. But you get a tree, even so."

"Oh," she said, unlocking the trunk. "Even so." She got the tool out. Adam took it out of her hands before she could unfold it.

"I can do it," he said. And he did so without difficulty. "Where do you want the tree?"

"Do I get to know what kind it is?"

"Apple."

"Apple," she repeated, looking into his solemn blue-gray eyes. She used to look into his eyes and see *her* there. Now she saw only the sorrow she'd given him.

"Four-in-one apple. I think you need a new one."

The look lengthened until finally they both glanced away.

"Yes," she said brightly—too brightly. "Mine seems to be gone. Well, if it's really mine, I'd like it planted close to where the other one stood. I know they grow well there."

He nodded and walked in that direction.

"This is a good place here," he said, pointing out a spot in the general vicinity of the old tree.

"Did you graft this one?" Quinn asked as he began to dig. The ground was soft from the rain, and he had no difficulty, even with so small a shovel. She watched his blue shirt pull tightly across his back, his muscles bunching as he strained to move the dirt.

"Yes," he said, not looking at her. "Grandfather Beiler taught me," he added unnecessarily, as if he'd forgotten— no, as if he refused to acknowledge that she had had any part in his past.

"I remember," she said. Just as he remembered how much she had loved that tree. "Adam, you don't have to do this."

"Yes, I do. Grandfather Beiler grafted the other one. Your father bought it from him. We guarantee our trees." A simple and innocent explanation for so tender a gesture.

She smiled. "This is some guarantee. The old one was chain-sawed."

"Even so," he said again, still shoveling dirt.

"I'll get a bucket of water," she offered.

"Good. Do you have a folding bucket, too?"

"Very funny," she said, heading toward the house.

"I thought so," she thought he said. She looked back over her shoulder. He was still shoveling, and he was smiling.

She came back carrying a white enamel bucket full of water, walking carefully so as not to slosh the water on her shoes. She set the bucket down, waiting until he had the hole dug deep enough to suit him. He loosened the sack but didn't remove it, setting the tree gently into the hole so as not to disturb the dirt on the roots.

"Now," he said to Quinn, indicating that she should pour the water. She poured carefully around the tree so as not to collapse the sides of the hole, until Adam said "Enough."

She knelt down and began to help fill in the hole, using both hands to scoop the damp earth.

"You'll get dirty," Adam said, careful to keep his eyes away from hers.

"I don't care about that. I want to—"

He caught her wrist. "I'll do it."

She felt his touch as if it were an electrical current that passed between them.

"You don't want to be digging in the dirt." He still had her wrist, and he still tried to avoid her eyes. He finally took the chance, giving her a quick glance. Her eyes were waiting.

"Don't I?" she asked.

He smiled, but he didn't look away. "Always you ask too many questions."

She pressed her lips together, fighting down the need to ask him the thing she really wanted to know. *Why didn't you tell your family about the baby?* And why hadn't Lena and Jacob said anything to him yet about his earlier omission? Surely he wouldn't be back here if they had. Her eyes searched his for the answers, and he abruptly let go of her wrist. He didn't like that, she thought. He could feel her "wanting" again, and he didn't like it at all.

She stood up, moving back a few steps to give him room to work. She looked around her. The shadows were growing long, the air cool with the coming dusk. She heard the dinner bell ringing at the Sauder house, calling the family to their evening meal.

"I can finish that," she said. "Lena won't want you to come to supper late."

"I'm not going to supper," he said, standing up to gently tread on the soft mound of earth around the tree. "Keep this watered, Quinn. Especially when the weather turns hot and—"

"Why aren't you going to supper?" she interrupted.

He turned his head to look at her. This close to him she could see plainly the weathered lines in his face that weren't there when she'd left here so many years ago. "Because I'm here to talk to you."

She didn't ask about what. She said nothing, feeling her anxiety rise. So. It wasn't finished after all. And sooner or later he would ask *his* question.

Where is our baby, Quinn? Where is our baby?

"You're scared of me again," he observed, bending down to pick up the shovel. He folded it and reached to take her car keys out of her hand. "Round is for the trunk," he said, holding up the correct key, and she nodded.

"I'm not...afraid of you, Adam," she said. She followed him to the car to show him that she wasn't. "It's just..."

"Just what?" he asked when she didn't go on. "You can say whatever you think you have to say, Quinn, but I feel it—this fear in you. It makes me wonder what it is that scares you. And it makes me feel sorry to know that I put it there." He unlocked the trunk, brushed off the shovel and laid it inside.

"You didn't—I mean, it isn't there. I'm *not* afraid," she said as he slammed the trunk lid down.

"Then are you worried that you'll feel embarrassed if people see us together? Are you worried about them seeing me with you and knowing that I'm the one you ran around with? I make you ashamed, as if I was like the man at the flea market who didn't take a bath? If I do, I can go. I don't ever want to make you sorry to know me.''

"Adam, no. I'm not ashamed to be seen with you."

"Then what are you, Quinn?"

She didn't answer him. She didn't know herself what she was.

"I *am* worried," she admitted finally.

"About what?"

"About you."

"Why?"

"Because . . . *because*, Adam! You know why! You can't work on my house and bring me trees. You can't let them think you've started up with me again."

"They will think what they think no matter what I do."

There was such resignation in his voice that she bowed her head rather than see it in his eyes, as well.

"Are you still my friend?" he asked quietly, and her eyes flew to his face. It was the last question in the world she expected.

"Are you?" he asked again when she didn't answer, his eyes searching hers.

"I am."

He smiled. "I am your friend, too."

"Adam, I don't want to do anything that will hurt you—" she began, but he wouldn't let her finish, holding up his hand to cut her off.

"Then don't," he said blithely. "You worry too much, Quinn. I'm not a boy now. I'm a man. And even when I was a boy, I was much stronger than you thought. I wasn't weak."

"I never thought you were."

"Didn't you?" he said evenly.

"No. I didn't."

"I would have taken care of you—and the baby—if you had given me a chance."

"I know that."

"You know that, and still it was you who would pick and choose for me. You still do it. Yesterday at the flea market you did it. I know what I want and what I don't want. I know what I can live with and what I can't. My sins are *mine*, Quinn, and you don't try to save me from them or from the consequences. Not anymore. Do you understand? Not ever."

With that, he walked off in the direction of the Sauder farm.

"Adam," she called after him. "Let me pay you for the tree." She wasn't sure he heard her, but then he waved his hand in refusal.

"It's nothing, Quinn," he said without looking around. She stood staring at his retreating back.

"Yes, it is," she whispered. "And you know it."

She went to bed early, and for all her agitation, she slept well. She woke up with the sunlight streaming in the bedroom window and with a feeling of dread, knowing that what she dreaded was *not* seeing Adam again. She showered and dressed quickly, then went about her work, trying not to listen for his step on the porch, his merry whistling across the yard. But she couldn't keep from it. She was waiting for him, just as she always had. As the sun set, she gave up again, only to have him knock at the back door. She should have been ashamed of how happy she was to see him.

"No tree?" she asked, and he smiled. How is it, she thought, looking at him now, that he's always so new to me? How is it that I look for every smile as if I'd never seen him smile before? She had never tired of seeing him or being with him. How could it still be like that after all that had happened? She had no answers, only questions, questions that he must surely see in her eyes.

But he wasn't the one who looked away, the one who'd grown so furtive. Today he was relentless about looking into her eyes. "Come outside," he said. "It's nice this evening. You're not busy with Edison's things, are you?"

"Yes—no—I'm almost finished—" She was rattling, and she knew it, because she wanted to be with him, and she shouldn't, and she was going to do it anyway.

"Then come out here. I would like to sit on your swing. Do you have lemonade made, Quinn?"

"Do I—?" she said incredulously. When she'd let herself imagine his coming to the house again, she hadn't imagined this particular inquiry. "Yes, I have lemonade made. I bought lemons yesterday."

He smiled again—not much, just a little bit of the old, teasing kind she recognized. "I saw them. That is why I asked. I thought if you were still the same, you wouldn't let them sit long."

"And if I didn't have lemonade and you were still the same, I suppose you'd ask me to make it," she said, coming out onto the porch just as he wanted.

"Yes," he said agreeably. He moved to sit on the swing, which faced the fallow field, taking his summer hat—straw with a black band—off and setting it aside. "You make better lemonade than Mom."

"That'll be the day," Quinn said.

"No, it's true. Mom wants to save sugar. You don't."

She looked at him doubtfully, not sure if she could accept that as a compliment or not. Somehow, it made her sound flagrantly thriftless. He raised both eyebrows in polite but mischievous solicitation. She couldn't keep from smiling in return.

"I'll be back in a minute."

She went inside and got two glasses down from the one usable cabinet in the kitchen, taking them to the refrigerator in the front hall to fill them with lemonade. How long had it been since she'd done this, shared lemonade and a porch swing with Adam Sauder?

She could hear the swing squeaking now and again as Adam idly let it move back and forth.

"The apple tree looks good," he said as she came back outside, his eyes lingering over her in a way that left her feeling flustered and unsure and intensely aware of herself. The look, as if everything about her pleased him, made her feel desirable and no less than beautiful and afraid that he'd suddenly see her flaws and realize that it wasn't true at all— all at the same time. "Lemonade doesn't bother your stomach?"

"No."

"Are you drinking the cabbage juice?"

She reached to hand him one of the glasses of lemonade, standing well away from him. She felt certain that he knew exactly the discomfiture he was causing. He knew, and he was going to do it anyway.

"Three times a day before meals. It's pretty good," she said.

"I have more instructions for you. You are to eat molasses mixed with peanut butter. It's supposed to build up your blood. If you do that, Mom promises you will be well soon."

"It's done me a lot of good just being here," Quinn said, hoping it was true, hoping she hadn't simply swapped one misery for another.

He smiled again, then drank deeply from the glass, tilting his head back so that she could see the strong, muscular lines of his chin and neck. He really had been thirsty, and she took advantage of the opportunity to gaze at him. Until yesterday, she would have thought that she knew everything about his face, every line, every scar, but she didn't. He was changed, older, and yet he was still the same, enough so to make her remember all the things she shouldn't be remembering. Such a well-loved face, one she had held between her hands and shyly kissed, passionately kissed. He looked tired to her, tired of body and of soul, and she had the sudden urge to put her arms around him and tell him that everything would be all right.

"Do you want some more lemonade?" she asked instead.

"No," he said, turning the now almost-empty glass around and around in his hands, regarding it thoughtfully. He reached and moved his straw hat off the seat and dropped it onto the porch. "The lemonade—it's good, the way I thought." He held up the glass. "Sweet. And really cold." His eyes suddenly found hers, holding them with no hint of uneasiness. "Sometimes things aren't as good as what you remember. You will sit down?"

She hesitated. If she didn't sit with him, they would surely get into that same discussion about whether or not she was afraid of him. And she wasn't afraid! Not of him, at any rate, she'd decided. If she was afraid of anything, it was of herself, of some bad judgment on her part that would make things worse for him.

"They will think what they think no matter what I do," he'd said.

"The question is so hard?" he asked quietly.

"No, it's not hard." She had no difficulty with the question at all. It was the answer that was the problem: Yes, *yes,* she wanted to sit by him.

She sat down. She was still holding her own glass of lemonade, and she sipped from it awkwardly. There was no sense in trying to make herself believe this was only a casual visit between old childhood friends, and that she did not recognize him as anything else, that he was not a beautiful man to her. He *was* a beautiful man, not just his body, but his spirit, as well. Gentle. Kind and loving. And he had been her lover. Her first lover. She had known with him what she had never known with anyone else. And she'd refused to marry Jake because of it.

Their bodies were not touching, but for her, his proximity was nearly as potent as actual contact. She suddenly could find no place to look. If she glanced anywhere in his direction, she was aware only of his acute masculinity, of a body made strong by hard, physical work, a body once beloved by her beyond the point of reason. And if she let her eyes meet his, he would see...everything. She stared out toward the fallow field.

"Tell me about Philadelphia," he said after a while.

"There's not much to tell. Everybody's in a hurry there. It's crowded. Nobody sends a neighbor cabbage juice."

"But you stayed a long time anyway." There was no challenge in his voice. It was a statement of fact, and she took it as such, one that required no comment from her. She hoped.

"It's a pretty dress you have on today," Adam offered. He still seemed to be completely at ease, as if he did this sort of thing every day. It suddenly occurred to her that perhaps he did. He was handsome, eligible; it was his duty to court someone, to sit on the porch swing with her and drink her lemonade.

But he hadn't married. Not yet.

She pushed the thought aside. "Thank you," she said, knowing that such a response was not necessary. Adam and his people didn't subscribe to what the "English" thought were the social graces. He said her dress was pretty because, to him, it was.

"I thought you had given up dresses and were always going to wear the mouse with the big feet on your shirts."

He was teasing her, and she laughed softly, amazed that he felt kindly enough toward her to do that. "No. The mouse is just...comfortable." She glanced at him. He was staring at her, his eyes traveling over her face.

How sweet it would be . . . she thought.

But she didn't let the idea complete itself. Nothing she did with him would be sweet, not really; it would cause more trouble, and she cared about him too much to give him any more grief than she already had.

"Sometimes you wore the purple dress, the one Daniel likes, in Philadelphia. To parties, he said."

"Yes."

"There were many . . . parties?"

"No, not many. Business gatherings mostly. I was never one for the party circuit."

"When you did go, did *he* take you?"

She forced her eyes to meet his. She could feel the tension in him, feel how close they were to another confrontation, and almost in spite of herself, she was deliberately obtuse. "Who?"

"This man you didn't marry."

She looked away. "Sometimes."

"He liked parties."

"What he liked was to make money. Parties, for him, were a way to do it."

"He made a lot of money then?"

"Yes. He enjoyed that—the way you enjoy carpentry."

He was looking out across the yard now, and he suddenly turned to her. "Will he soon come here after you?"

"No. Why would you think he'd do that?"

He folded his arms across his chest and set the swing to moving again. "I don't think it. I was only wondering."

"Wondering about what?" she asked, digging her heels into the porch to keep the swing still.

"About him. About why a man smart enough to make a lot of money at parties is stupid enough to let you go away from him."

"I . . . think we'd better talk about something else," she said, forcing a smile. "Tell me about the family."

"There's not much to tell. David is married. He and his wife have a baby coming. Eli will marry the first Thursday in November. Nobody seems to want to marry Anna. And Mary and Aaron and Daniel are too young to get married. It's all we Amish think about," he added. "Getting married." He was deliberately trying to annoy her now, and he was entirely successful at it.

"Then tell me about you," she said, determined not to let her annoyance show.

"Was there somebody I *didn't* marry, you mean?"

She smiled again, but it wasn't sincere. "Was there?" she said lightly. She regretted the question the moment she'd asked it.

"Yes," he said without hesitation. "Her name was Sarah. She was very... gentle. We would have had a fine farm and fine children."

"You should have married her."

"Don't tell me what I should have done, Quinn. No one can judge that but Sarah and me."

She sat there, staring straight ahead. Then, although she knew better, she allowed her eyes to graze his. Such beautiful eyes, pale blue-gray and filled with quiet sorrow. She would always feel his sadness, because his sadness was also hers. She shifted her position on the swing, and their knees touched. She had no strength, no desire to move away from him, but she did. She looked down, finding nothing to look at but his hand resting on his thigh.

"Quinn," he said quietly, and she looked up at him. His eyes were sad still, but she saw something else there, something intense and burning, something that made her knees weak and her belly warm. "I don't mean to be...unkind to you."

"You haven't been. You haven't been anything that I don't deserve." She tried to look away and couldn't.

"Yes, I have. Quinn, you are so beautiful still." His eyes probed hers, looking for things she knew she didn't have. His voice had gone soft, loving, surrounding her, caressing her as surely as if he were actually touching her. It was the voice of the Adam she remembered.

She tried to get up off the swing, but he reached out to make her stay, his fingers strong and warm on the underside of her arm. He didn't seem to mind doing that, touching her, but it was nearly more than she could bear.

"I have things to do," she managed, her voice steady only because she willed it to be.

"No. I'm sorry, Quinn. I had no right to say that. It's true, but I won't make you uncomfortable. Don't go." He released her arm.

She gave a short sigh—and stayed where she was.

"Where are Daniel and your sisters?" she asked for something to say, something neutral that would get them on to safer ground, because she wanted to stay on the swing with him.

"At home."

"Aren't they supposed to come with you here?"

"Are you *still* worrying, Quinn?"

She sighed again. She wasn't doing well at all at establishing any kind of neutrality. "I guess so."

"Don't. Rest easy. Look around you. The sun is nearly gone. The evening is quiet and beautiful. You said it had done you good to come back here, but it won't last if you don't settle down and find peace."

She looked out over the yard. She could see the first star of the evening just above the horizon. "I wish I could do that. Find peace," she murmured wistfully. "Adam?"

"What?"

The swing rocked slowly back and forth, and she could feel him staring at her again, studying her in the shadows. She decided there was no point in trying to be neutral, no matter how painful the alternative. "Why didn't you tell Lena about the baby?"

He waited a long time before he answered, and for a moment she thought he wouldn't. "It was *my* sorrow, Quinn. And my joy. And it was your . . . shame. I didn't want to make it worse for you."

"It wouldn't have made things worse."

"Yes. It would. If you ever came back here—like now. To the family, you are worldly. What happened between you and me would have always been your fault."

"I didn't realize that you hadn't told Lena."

"I know that."

"Was she—is she very upset?" She wanted desperately to take Lena's gift of the cabbage juice as a sign of forgiveness, but she still had to ask, knowing that Lena would be kind to her regardless of her personal feelings. She met his eyes again, knowing, too, that he would tell her the truth but that she would see it in his eyes first.

"Yes, Quinn."

Her heart sank. "She must be very upset . . . now."

He made no reply to that, clearly understanding what she didn't say—that his mother would be upset because he was here with her. He suddenly drank the last of his lemonade and stood up.

"I can see you'll get no peace with me here," he said, setting the glass down on the porch railing. "Good night, Quinn. The lemonade was good."

She nearly called out to him when he stepped off the porch and crossed the backyard. She didn't want him to go. *Don't! Don't!* she kept telling herself. *It's better this way.*

"Will you come back again?" she finally called, but he didn't hear her, and he didn't look back. She watched him until he was swallowed up by the twilight, finally putting her hands to her face in exhaustion. Her weariness was more mental than physical, and she knew that what Adam had said was true. She'd get no peace with him here. But she felt no peace with him gone, either.

If only she could . . .

If only. The lament of all unhappy humans. If only what? If only she hadn't come back here. If only she hadn't let Adam stay to work on the kitchen. If only she hadn't once loved him in the first place. And now there was nothing to do but wait, and for what, she had no idea. For the time to come when she'd wake up one fine morning and Adam Sauder wouldn't matter to her anymore?

But the waiting became excruciating. She could never quite suppress the intense feeling of anticipation she had, and every day it got worse. She kept expecting Adam to turn up in the evenings when his chores were done. But he didn't. And there was nothing she could do about it. Nothing she *should* do about it, except be both relieved and disappointed. She passed the time by getting the house into shape and supervising various workmen—the one who hooked up the washing machine and dryer, the one who installed the new range top in the kitchen, the one who painted the kitchen the soft yellow she wanted. She had the refrigerator moved from the front hallway to the kitchen, and Holland Wakefield came, with bad news about the rest of her cabinets. The cabinetmaker's wife was having surgery, and he wouldn't be working on them for several weeks. Unperturbed by the delay, Quinn asked Holland to recommend someone with a tractor she could hire to plow her field.

"Now, Quinn, you're not thinking of taking up farming, too, are you?" Holland teased.

"Just enough to get me a tomato or two," Quinn said. "Come July, I want a ripe, red tomato that's just picked and still hot from the sun. And a big fresh buttermilk biscuit with the butter oozing out the sides."

"Sounds good to me," Holland said. "There's an old man on the other side of town who'll do it. He can't farm much anymore, but he sure can plow. His wife can't hardly get him off that tractor of his. I think he makes just enough side money to keep her from selling it out from under him. I'm going right by there. Want me to tell him to come see you?"

"If you don't mind, Holland. He won't charge me an arm and a leg, will he?"

"Oh, hell, no, Quinn. He knew your dad. He wouldn't charge you anything that wasn't fair."

Holland was as good as his word. The old man came to see her—tractor, bib overalls and all—and his plowing rates were definitely reasonable. She put him to work on the fallow field, listening to the sound of his plowing from time to time as she worked at the computer, remembering when her father was alive and readying that same field for planting.

When she heard the tractor stop, she got up from the library desk to look out the window, but the old man hadn't finished. He'd merely paused to have a word with someone—Adam Sauder. She had no idea what they were talking about; she could tell only that the conversation was friendly because they both laughed. The old man went back to plowing, and Adam came toward the house.

She stopped at the mirror she'd hung over the living room mantel, brushing her hair into place with her fingers, shamelessly pinching her cheeks to put some color in them before she met Adam at the door.

He was all smiles when she answered his knock. His shirtsleeves were rolled up, and he was more tanned than when he'd been there last. "It's good!" he said, looking back at the old man and the tractor.

"What's good?"

"You're getting the land plowed again. The ground is rich there. What will you plant?"

"Nothing," she said, coming out onto the porch. He looked so scandalized at that revelation that she nearly laughed.

"You have to plant *something*, Quinn. It's not too late yet for corn, tobacco seedlings—"

"Now what would I do with corn and tobacco?" she asked, teasing him shamelessly. He was a true farmer. It was incredible to him that she wouldn't do something with such good land. "I don't smoke, and I don't have any pigs or chickens."

"You will lease the land, then?"

She hadn't considered that. "You think anybody would want it?"

"It's late in the season, but yes, I think so."

"For what?"

"For what?" He shrugged. "I would have to look at it."

"Then look, and tell me. If I'm going to lease it, I'd like to say what it's good for."

"Come with me," he said, suddenly turning back to her when he was halfway down the steps. "You'll want to see up close, how the soil holds the rain and such. Come on," he insisted, but she stood there thinking how crazy their relationship had been since her return. They vacillated from the comfortable oneness they'd enjoyed all those years ago to outright animosity, and she was constantly off balance because she never knew which situation she'd find herself in.

The old man was just finishing the plowing, and she went back into the house to get him his money.

"You got some fine farmland there, missy," he yelled to her over the noise of the tractor. She nodded and handed him a check for the amount she owed him. She stepped back from the tractor, giving him a small wave as he rode out of the yard.

Adam was waiting for her at the edge of the field. "Come on," he called again. "This is good! You have to see!"

She smiled and walked in his direction.

"Are you sure this land can be leased?" she asked when she reached him. "It hasn't been prepared. It hasn't been limed and harrowed."

He sat down on the ground and began taking off his shoes. "It's still good to play with."

"To play with?"

"If he can spare the time, a man sometimes likes to see how good a farmer he is. Not with the land he needs to survive, but with something extra like this. Just to see. It's like...a little showing off. Just enough to make him feel good, to make the others talk about what a good man he is at growing things, but not enough to offend. You see?"

"I see. You want to make the troops go 'Ah.'"

He glanced at her, and she realized he didn't understand her analogy. She let it go.

"You come with me now," he said. "Take off your shoes."

"No, thank you," she demurred. "You walk the field barefoot. I'll wait here."

"You used to like walking in new plowing without your shoes. But I forget how English you are now—a big city woman who keeps her shoes *on*."

"I don't happen to like walking barefoot in the mud," she insisted.

"Don't you?" There was the barest hint of a smile at the corners of his mouth.

"No, I don't. I was always afraid of stepping on earthworms."

"Then why did you do it so many times?"

To be with you, she thought, but she didn't say it.

"Come walk with me, Quinn. Who will see you? Your friends from Philadelphia? If they come, I will tell them you can't know about land with your shoes on. The Amish are famous for farming, so your city friends would believe me."

"I'm sure they would," she said, gazing at the newly turned ground. She tried not to smile; she wanted to pretend she was young and happy, earthworms or not.

"Come on, then. Before it gets dark."

She looked up at the sun and laughed. It was barely past noon. She slipped off the red canvas espadrilles she was wearing and wiggled her toes, stepping boldly onto the raw ground. The earth between her toes was soft and damp and wonderful and without earthworms as yet; the sun was warm on the top of her head. She took a few experimental steps. "Ah, Scarlett O'Hara, eat your heart out."

Adam was grinning from ear to ear.

"What?" she asked.

He shook his head.

"What?" she insisted.

"Well, for once I know what you're talking about. You gave me that book to read. *Gone with the Wind*. Scarlett O'Hara loved the red soil of Georgia—but not more than Quinn Tyler loves *this*. Come on," he said, holding his hand out. She took it without hesitation, her small hand lost in his, his fingers rough and warm around hers. Barefoot, they walked the plowed ground together, the way they would have when they were children, lost in the joy of such a simple pleasure and lost in the joy of being with each other.

A noisy flock of crows flew overhead. "You remember *Gone with the Wind* after all this time?" she asked, looking to watch the birds disappear into the treetops on the far side of the field.

He glanced at her. "It's not hard. My head is not so full of books as yours."

"Well, you've got a lot more up there besides English books—all the things you know about living and working the land, for instance." She paused. "I...I probably shouldn't have done that—brought you those books to read."

"Why not?" he asked, stopping to look her directly in the eyes.

"It only made you unhappy." She held his gaze for a moment, then started walking again.

"Not unhappy, Quinn. For me, the books were bread to a man dying of hunger. I needed to know about things then, about places and history and the stories in books. I was wondering, who is the Thomas Wolfe you and the telephone man talked about?"

"A writer. He said you can't go home again, or something like that." She could feel him digesting this information as they walked. He had always had such a fine, quick mind, and, rightly or wrongly, it had always given her pleasure to tell him about whatever he'd wanted to know.

"That depends, I think," he said. He looked into her eyes again, and this time she held his gaze.

"On what?"

"On if you're looking for yesterday or tomorrow." Characteristically, he made his profound announcement and jumped to another subject. "This is good land," he said, clearly pleased with what the walk was telling him. "You can grow anything here. But for now, this late, corn will be best. The ground will have to be sterilized with steam for tobacco."

"It wouldn't be worth the trouble this late, would it?"

"It depends on how much the farmer wants it. Tobacco is money."

Quinn suddenly remembered herself. She was standing in the middle of a field, hand in hand with Adam Sauder. True, he seemed much more in control of his feelings than she, and their being together was not nearly so distracting for him, but if someone should see them here . . .

They were no longer innocent children, regardless of how much she wished it. She couldn't turn back time any more than she could be Amish.

He stood beside her, quiet and still, but he knew. She could feel the anger in him. "Now what is it?" he asked.

"You know what—"

"Yes. I know what. Nobody knows better than me!"

She tried to pull her hand free of his, but he wouldn't let go, his strong fingers clamping down hard on hers as he tried to keep her close to him.

"Don't. Don't run away from me, Quinn. Not if you—"

He suddenly let go and stepped back from her. "I am being a fool."

"Adam," she said, but he walked away from her. "Adam!"

She'd hurt his feelings, and she hadn't meant to do that. She was *not* ashamed of him or anything that had happened with him, but she couldn't seem to convince him of that. She hurried to catch up, grabbing him by the arm to make him stop. He shook her hand off with such vehemence that she recoiled as if he'd struck her.

"Adam, I didn't mean anything—"

"That's the trouble with you, Quinn. You don't *mean* anything."

"I don't deserve that!"

"And I don't deserve—" He broke off and turned away from her, looking out toward his own land. "Sometimes, when I'm here, it's like it used to be. And I keep forgetting that you don't want anything that has to do with us." He looked back at her. "Can't you see this is killing me?"

"Then why do you keep coming back?" she cried. "Why don't you stay away? For both our sakes?"

He gave a short laugh, shaking his head as if he couldn't believe her stupidity. He started walking again, then abruptly turned back to her. "You want to know why I come here? I'll tell you then. I'll give you the same answer I would have given you when I was twenty-one. Or sixteen. Or ten. I'll give you the answer that will make you laugh." He paused, seeming to gather up his courage to say it. "I love you, Quinn Tyler. And you know that." He stared at her, as if he expected some response, and when none came, he stalked away toward where he'd left his high top farmer's shoes sitting in the grass.

Stunned, she followed him. He was putting on his shoes, and she tried to make him look at her. "Adam, please."

"It's funny, isn't it?" he said, but he kept putting on his shoes and avoiding her eyes. "*I* laugh, all the time. My mother, my father—they laugh. Even now they stay up late in the night talking, it's so funny to them. Now you can laugh, too. You and your damned English friends."

"Adam!" she cried, flinging herself on him when he got up, her arms wrapped tightly around his shoulders. "Don't! Don't!" She pressed her face into the side of his neck, trying to take his pain away by sheer force of will. He was hurting so, and she couldn't bear it.

He stood as if he were made of stone, rigid and separate from her. She wanted him to put his arms around her. She was crying; she could feel the tears she never wanted him to see streaming from her eyes, taste them as they ran down over her lips. She wanted him to press her close to him, to hold her the way he used to. It was true. It was the same between them. Nothing had changed. She still belonged to him, and she was glad, so shamefully glad, that he hadn't married.

His hands reached up and clamped down hard on her shoulders. She thought that he would kiss her; she knew how badly he wanted to. He was trembling, and she leaned into him, her mouth close to his, her lips parting. But he held her roughly away from him.

"I want you, Quinn," he said, his breathing rapid and harsh. "Can you feel how much I want you? You don't understand at all, do you? There is more to us than *this*!" He let her go then, leaving her on the ground on her knees, leaving her with nothing but the growing realization that eleven years ago she had made the best decision she could for him—and it had been wrong.

Chapter Eight

The spring rains came in earnest. Quinn stood by the upstairs bedroom window, staring at the wet countryside, trying to remember a line of poetry. It was something about the sound of rain, coming as gently, as quietly, as a woman's voice. But this was a farmer's rain, steady and warm and soaking, the kind that made tender seedlings take root and grow. Her gaze shifted to the small garden plot she'd marked off close to the house, to the two rows of tomato plants drenched and drooping in the afternoon drizzle. She had planted each one the way her father had taught her, working the ground until the dirt was soft and fine and free of weeds, digging each hole and mixing the fertilizer into the soil with her bare hands before she set the plant. She held her hands out in front of her now. Her fingernails were ragged and broken, nothing like an accountant's hands— which was just as well. She was nothing like an accountant.

She looked out across the field toward the Sauder place, her eye catching some movement along the fencing nearest her property. She strained to see but could tell only that the walker in this wet weather was Amish.

She didn't hesitate, hurrying downstairs to get her yellow rain poncho off the peg by the kitchen door. She put it on, on her way out, knowing that, wearing it, she was nothing if not conspicuous. Her mind was already at work looking for some excuse—she was going the long way to the mailbox, she was out for a walk—anything to explain her presence on the edge of Sauder land if the person happened not to be Adam.

But she had no need for explanations. Whoever was on the other side of the fence saw her well in advance and bolted—Daniel, she suddenly realized.

"Daniel!" she called after him. She knew he heard her, but he didn't answer, stopping only once to turn and look at her before he disappeared into a grove of willows.

She stood staring in the direction he'd gone. Why had he run from her? Daniel had no reason to, or none she could imagine. If she expected anyone to run at the sight of her, it was Adam. He had said he still loved her, and now, clearly, he must be ashamed he'd said it. She hadn't seen him since. She'd kept a lonely vigil at the windows that faced the Sauder farm, and she'd seen no one near her property until today.

And Daniel had run away from her.

She needed groceries; she was feeling better physically, and she was going to heed Lena's advice about the peanut butter and molasses. She went back into the house to get her car keys and purse.

She didn't want to go into town, knowing that, rain or not, the tourist trade would likely be booming. Instead she headed for a little Amish community store a few miles away.

IT'S A WILD, WILD, WONDERFUL
FREE OFFER!

HERE'S WHAT YOU GET:

1. *Four New Silhouette Special Edition® Novels—FREE!* Everything comes up hearts and diamonds with four exciting romances— yours FREE from Silhouette Books. Each of these brand-new novels brings you the passion and tenderness of today's greatest love stories.

2. *A Useful, Practical Digital Clock/Calendar—FREE!* As a free gift simply to thank you for accepting four free books we'll send you a stylish digital quartz clock/calendar—a handsome addition to any decor! The changeable, month-at-a-glance calendar pops out, and may be replaced with a favorite photograph.

3. *An Exciting Mystery Bonus—FREE!* You'll go wild over this surprise gift. It will win you compliments and score as a splendid addition to your home.

4. *Money-Saving Home Delivery!* Join Silhouette Books and enjoy the convenience of previewing six new books every month, delivered to your home. Each book is yours for $2.49—26 cents less per book than the retail price, plus 69 cents for postage and handling per shipment. And you may cancel at any time, for any reason, and still keep your free books and gifts, just by dropping us a line. Great savings and total convenience are the name of the game at Silhouette Books!

5. *More Mystery Gifts Throughout the Year!* No joke! Because home subscribers are our most valued readers, when you subscribe to Silhouette Books, we'll be sending you additional free gifts from time to time—as a token of our appreciation!

GO WILD
WITH SILHOUETTE® TODAY—
JUST COMPLETE, DETACH AND
MAIL YOUR FREE-OFFER CARD!

GET YOUR GIFTS FROM SILHOUETTE®
ABSOLUTELY FREE!

Mail this card today!

Printed in the U.S.A.

PLACE
JOKER
STICKER
HERE

PLAY THIS CARD RIGHT!

YES! Please send me my four Silhouette Special Edition® novels FREE along with my free Digital Clock/Calendar and free mystery gift as explained on the opposite page.

335 CIL 813F

NAME _____
(PLEASE PRINT)

ADDRESS _____ APT. _____

CITY _____

PROV. _____ POSTAL CODE _____

Prices subject to change. Offer limited to one per household and not valid to current Special Edition subscribers.

SILHOUETTE BOOKS "NO RISK" GUARANTEE

- There's no obligation to buy—and the free books remain yours to keep.

- Unless you tell us otherwise, every month we'll send you six more books, months before they appear in stores.

- You may end your subscription anytime—just write and let us know, or return the shipment to us—at our cost.

IT'S NO JOKE!
MAIL THE POSTPAID CARD AND
GET FREE GIFTS AND $11.00 WORTH OF
SILHOUETTE® NOVELS — *FREE!*

If offer card is missing write to:
Silhouette Books, P.O. Box 609, Fort Erie, Ontario L2A 5X3

Business
Reply Mail

No Postage Stamp
Necessary if Mailed
in Canada

Postage will be paid by

SILHOUETTE BOOKS

P.O. Box 609
Fort Erie, Ontario
L2A 9Z9

She met a number of Amish buggies on the road, all of them moving slowly on the rain-slick pavement. She peeked at each driver as she passed, and she knew perfectly well that she wasn't looking merely for someone familiar. She was looking for Adam Sauder.

Something was wrong. It had to be. If Adam still loved her, he'd want to see her, if for nothing more than to make sure she was all right. She knew that; after all her chief concern was, was *he* all right? She was never going to forget the look on his face when he'd told her he still loved her, and she'd only stood there.

Oh, Adam.

The grocery store was rimmed only by Amish buggies, the horses standing forlornly in the rain. She parked as close as she could without crowding any of the vehicles, smiling a bit at one of the buggies that clearly belonged to a teenage boy, one who was in his wild time of "running around" before he joined the church and became a staid member of the Amish community. The buggy had more rearview mirrors than its driver could possibly use and a bunch of vivid blue-green peacock feathers dangling just inside the door. She was a bit startled to read the bumper sticker that had been carefully placed in the middle of the big triangular reflector on the back. Feel The Thrill Again and Again and Again, it proclaimed. Only when she was closer did she realize that it had to do with fishing. I Support Catch and Release, it further declared in smaller letters. She laughed and ran the rest of the distance from her car to the porch to get in out of the rain.

The porch, which boasted soft drink and ice machines, was crowded with families waiting for a break in the weather, the women patient, the children eating bags of corn and potato snacks, the men talking and laughing as men caught with a little time on their hands always did. Quinn could pick up a few words of the local German dialect—

rain, weather, horses—but then the conversation abruptly stopped. She was suddenly ringed in stares and silence. She went into the store, hearing the silence change to a quiet murmuring behind her. The man who ran the store regarded her with the same silence—not with hostility or malice precisely, but with an attitude Quinn would have described, for lack of a better word, as incredulous. The man's wife, who had been sweeping the aisles between the shelves when Quinn entered, stopped to stare, as well. Enduring their scrutiny, it occurred to Quinn that she must be experiencing something akin to what Adam felt that day on the street corner while he waited for her to pick him up. She tried to effect the same dignity he had displayed, selecting the items she wanted as quickly as she could without having to ask where anything was. The things she couldn't immediately find, she let go. She knew that "English" people came in here all the time, and whatever had precipitated the situation she now found herself in, it wasn't her non-Amishness.

The proprietor had a long gray beard, but his hair was still dark and thinning on top. He said nothing as he counted up what she owed, and Quinn met his eyes without reticence when she handed him the money. The front door opened, and a few of the men who had been standing on the porch came back inside. She took her change and the box the proprietor had put her groceries into and moved carefully among them to get outside, feeling their complete attention all the way to the door. Before she could get to her car, she had to wait for a young bearded Amishman to turn his horse and buggy around, his small children peeping at her out the side window as the buggy went by.

She didn't go home. She drove into town after all, straight to Edison Clark's office. His receptionist was new to her, a quietly efficient older woman, who advised Quinn that Edison would be in court until three. But Quinn didn't leave. She waited, sitting in a leather wing chair by the front window and turning the pages of magazines she never really saw. And all the while, she could feel the receptionist's quiet concern for one of Edison's potential clients, one who was so obviously in distress.

Shortly after three, the receptionist excused herself to go to the post office, discreetly locking Edison's inner-office door in the event Quinn turned out to be some sort of pilferer. Quinn continued to wait, relieved to be alone for the moment. She caught sight of Edison coming from across the street, and she suddenly had misgivings about what she wanted from him, misgivings that lasted until he came in.

"Well! This is a surprise," he boomed. "Didn't I bring you enough work to keep you busy? Where's Margaret?"

She smiled, or tried to. "If that's your receptionist, she's gone to the post office. Edison, I—" She broke off and pressed her lips together, certain she was going to make a fool of herself and cry. Not that she hadn't cried in front of Edison before. But she had no real reason for feeling the way she was feeling now, and she didn't want to try to explain it.

"What's wrong?" he asked, cutting short the pleasantries.

"I don't know. I want you to find out for me."

He looked at her thoughtfully. "Go on."

"It's—it's Adam."

"Quinn, Quinn," he said, shaking his head in concern.

"I want to know if he's all right, Edison."

"Is there any reason he shouldn't be?"

"No."

"Then is there any reason you think he isn't?"

She didn't answer immediately. She looked into Edison's eyes and decided how much she wanted to tell him. "He's . . . been coming to the house."

"To work on the kitchen," Edison supplied.

"Since the work on the kitchen," Quinn corrected, refusing to look away from her friend's intent stare.

"I see. And?"

"And nothing, really. He came by a few times. He brought me a new apple tree, I gave him lemonade, and I walked a plowed field with him. But if somebody saw us, they might have gotten the wrong idea about . . . things."

"Yes, they might. *If* they saw you. And *if* the 'they' you're worried about happened to be old Jacob or a bishop or somebody like that. Is that what happened?"

"I don't know."

"Then what did happen?"

"I haven't seen him for days, and—"

"You were expecting to, I take it."

"Yes—no."

"Now, an answer like that, Quinn, can't mean anything but trouble," he said, poking the air in her direction with his forefinger.

"Maybe so, but it's the only answer I've got."

Edison sat down on the edge of Margaret's desk, his arms folded over his chest. "And?" he said again.

"I went to the Amish grocery store to get some things. Everyone there was so . . . quiet. The place was crowded, and everyone just stopped talking when I came in. It wasn't because I was English, Edison. It was because I was *me*. I want you to find out if something's happened."

"I told you how close Adam's been to getting himself shunned."

"I know you did. I want to know if it's happened."

"Well, I guess I can find out for you. I've got to go out to see one of the bishops tomorrow about some deeds. I think he'll tell me if I ask."

"Good," Quinn said, giving a brief sigh.

"Quinn. Is there a reason for Adam to be shunned?"

Again she met Edison's eyes. "No," she said evenly. The desire, the passion that had risen between them had been more hers than his. Surely Adam couldn't be blamed for her behavior.

"Then it'll be all the harder for him."

"What do you mean?"

"The frame of mind Adam Sauder's been in, all it's going to take is somebody accusing him of something he hasn't done."

"I don't understand," Quinn said when he didn't go on.

"I don't think he's Amish anymore, Quinn. He hasn't been for years, really. He's stayed, and he's gone through the motions, but out of respect for old Jacob, I think, not because he still believes."

"No," Quinn protested. She had suspected that possibility herself, but it was completely unacceptable to her. "He has to believe, Edison. He *has* to."

"Honey, I know you sacrificed a lot for him to stay Amish, but you did it without asking him. I told you what I thought about it then, and I haven't changed my mind. Unless you're sitting on the bench, you've got no business trying to be the judge of what's best for somebody else—and even then it's iffy. I've learned that in thirty-some years of practicing the law if I haven't learned anything else. But I can see this thing's worrying you, and I'll do what I can to find out."

"You'll call me as soon as you know?"

"Yes, I'll call you. Or I'll come by. Whatever I find out, I'm not going to sit on it."

"Edison, thank you."

"Don't thank me yet, Quinn. I may be bringing you more information than you want to know."

She gave him a small smile and left the office, stepping once again into the rain. Perhaps the information Edison brought her would be painful, but whatever was happening in the Amish community, knowing was far better than imagining. She sighed as she walked to her car, realizing for the first time what her disappearance eleven years ago and the subsequent *not* knowing must have done to Adam.

He'd been in hell—his own words—and she'd put him there, when she'd wanted only to protect him. You can't judge what's best for somebody else, Edison had said. Certainly, it was a lesson neither she nor old Jacob had learned.

When she arrived home, Holland Wakefield was just backing his truck out of the driveway. Quinn rolled down her car window to talk to him.

"You going to be home the rest of the afternoon, Quinn?"

"Yes, I'll be here."

"Good. We got your kitchen cabinets ready. Some of my boys got rained out today, and I thought I'd have them come on out here and get as much done as they could. Ain't no use in having them sit around with time on their hands. That okay?"

"Fine, Holland." She was almost certain Adam wasn't one of the "boys," but she didn't ask.

"They'll be here in a little while then." He gave her a wave and backed the rest of the way out.

Quinn carried her groceries inside, taking the time to put them away and eat, appetite or not, before the workmen came. If the truth be told, she was glad to have someone in the house for the afternoon. She had too much she *didn't* want to think about, and she didn't want to be alone.

However, she soon realized that solitude would have been better. The sound of hammering in the kitchen only served to remind her of Adam, and one of Holland's men considered himself a country-western singer. His voice wasn't bad, really, but his choice of sad, hurting songs left Quinn ready to scream. She didn't want to hear about love that still burned no matter what happened or how much time passed.

When she couldn't sit staring at the computer screen any longer, she went upstairs to stand by the windows that faced the Sauder farm. In the distance she saw three Amish buggies coming down the secondary road. All three of them turned in at the Sauders'.

The telephone rang downstairs, and she ran to answer it. It was a timid-sounding young woman who wanted to sell a photograph package that would include Quinn and her entire family with a special rate for children under three.

"No, thank you," Quinn said, abruptly hanging up the receiver. She glanced briefly around the kitchen. The men were hard at work, including the singer. They would easily finish the work today, she thought. And if nothing else worthwhile came out of her return home, this part of the house would be in good shape again. She looked back at the telephone.

Call me, Edison! she thought. Logically, she didn't expect him to drop everything and go find out about Adam, but her persistent feeling that something was wrong had little to do with logic.

She suddenly realized that Edison wouldn't be calling her today. He had said he'd see the bishop tomorrow. She was agonizing for nothing. She might even be worrying for nothing. Everything *could* be all right with Adam—except for the fist of anxiety she had in the pit of her stomach. She simply couldn't get rid of it, no matter what she tried. And she tried everything—a long walk after the workmen left, evening television, a book she'd been meaning to read. Nothing she did broke through her worry. It was simply there, real and nearly tangible, she felt it so acutely.

She stayed up until nearly midnight, finally going to bed with a glass of warm milk and the grim determination not to anticipate the worst. She lay for a time in the darkness. Then, unaccountably, she got up from her bed to turn on a lamp, sleeping the rest of the night with it on in case Adam needed to see her lights from across the field, needed to know she was there.

Edison came by the house early, finding her sitting on the back steps watching the sunrise and drinking coffee, which she shouldn't have been drinking with the stress she'd been putting on her delicate stomach. The morning was clear and fresh and breezy, and, as usual, Edison looked like anything but a lawyer. He was wearing "brier pants" with long leather patches from thigh to ankle that hunters wore to protect their legs in the underbrush. The porch was still damp from yesterday's rain, but he sat down beside her anyway.

"You're going to get your rump wet," she said.

"So are you."

"I'm sitting on the *Intelligencer-Journal*."

"I'm wearing my L.L. Bean waterproof hunting britches," he countered.

She smiled, and he gave her a fatherly pat on the head. He was being kind, and she braced herself for whatever he would tell her.

"I thought I'd find you up. You got any more of that?" he asked, motioning toward her cup.

"Yes," she said. She made an attempt to get up, but he held up his hands.

"Sit still. I can get it. I'd rather talk out here anyway. I don't get much chance to see the sun come up."

In a moment Quinn could hear him rattling cups in the kitchen.

"Do you need any help?" she called.

"No, I've got it." He returned and sat down beside her. He nodded toward the vivid orange and red and gold in the eastern sky.

"You know, if there's a sin in the world, it's not taking the time to appreciate beauty like that."

"Yes," Quinn said. Now that he was finally here, she didn't press him. Aside from his kindness, the fact that he'd come out this early suggested that something was indeed happening with Adam. "I finished your financial reports. You can take them back with you."

He nodded, then sipped his coffee. "You think we've beaten around the bush long enough now?"

She managed a small smile. "Yes. I do. Have you seen the bishop, or is it too early?"

"Well, you've got to get up early if you want to see a bishop when he's an Amish farmer. You've got to catch him between the milking and his breakfast, so you get invited to breakfast, too. You know what I had to eat? Eggs. Cornmeal mush. Liverwurst. Ham. Oatmeal. Fried potatoes. Biscuits with apple butter. That's what I need the coffee for. I made a pig of myself, and now I need to wash it all down."

"I thought we weren't going to beat around the bush anymore," Quinn said before he could go on rhapsodizing about food. "What did the bishop say?"

"It's what you thought, Quinn." Edison looked out toward her small garden. "You planting tomatoes?"

"Edison!" she said in exasperation. "I'm scared enough of what you're going to tell me. Will you just get on with it?"

"All right, take it easy, honey. It's this. Adam was refused communion at their last Sunday worship. If he'd repented and made a public confession before the church, it would have been all over. You know the Amish believe in forgiveness, in accepting anyone who's strayed, back into the flock if they show they want it. But he walked out. He wouldn't do it."

"He's being shunned, then," Quinn said, surprised to find that she'd been holding her breath.

"Yes."

"What is he accused of?"

"Being . . . involved with you."

"How involved?"

"You know how involved, Quinn."

"He's not my lover, Edison." She abruptly stood up. "He can't confess to something he hasn't done. I'm going to have to see Jacob."

"I wouldn't do that, Quinn."

"I told you, Edison, Adam isn't guilty of anything!"

"Then it's up to him to say so, not you. Now, if you think you're going to set Jacob Sauder and a bunch of Amish bishops straight about anything, then you've either been away too long or you're not as savvy about living Amish as I thought. You *cannot* interfere, you understand me?"

"Edison—"

"Not if you care about Adam Sauder. This is his problem. Not yours. And you keep out of it."

"They're shunning him, Edison!"

"Quinn, he knew what he was doing in coming to this house. And he knows what to do to get unshunned—if he wants to do it. He can confess to having the *will* to sin. He can repent of that. As it is, the bishop tells me he won't say anything one way or the other. Not a word."

"He said no matter what he did, they'd believe whatever they wanted to believe."

"My feeling is, he didn't give them much choice."

"He'll lose everything. All his property will be sold," she said, unable to keep from enumerating what would happen to him.

"Yes."

"No one Amish will talk to him, sell him anything, eat with him. Jacob won't have to do anything for him he'd do for David and his other sons—no land, no inheritance. He'll live in the house, but he'll be dead to them. They'll all turn away from him. Even little Daniel can't have anything to do with him."

"Yes. That's the way it'll be."

"How will he stand it, Edison?"

Edison looked at her for a moment before he answered. "The truth is, honey, I think he's been through worse."

Had he?

"My sins are my sins."

The phrase echoed through her head. She suddenly realized that Adam had known even then that he would precipitate this.

Adam, Adam, what are you doing!

"Quinn, I mean what I say. If you care about Adam, you'll stay out of it. If you interfere, believe me, he won't thank you for it."

She believed him. Adam had said as much himself.

"You don't try to save me—not anymore. Not ever."

"Edison?"

He looked at her over the rim of his coffee cup.

"It was all for nothing, wasn't it?"

He sighed. "Quinn, I don't know. I'm pretty much of a fatalist myself. Things happen the way they happen, and we mortals just have to do the best we can."

The best we can. She thought about that after Edison had gone. She had no "best" anymore. She'd used it all up eleven years ago.

"Are you worrying again, Quinn?"

Yes, she was worrying. Adam had given her no alternative. In her mind's eye she saw the Sauder farm. Where would Adam be? In the fields? No, that wouldn't be likely. His father and brothers wouldn't be allowed to accept his help in running the farm. Perhaps he wasn't even there anymore. Perhaps he'd moved out rather than suffer the ostracism of shunning. In any case, he'd have to get a job somewhere, perhaps as a hired hand with one of the Mennonite farmers or with Holland Wakefield. That thought made her feel a little better. Adam was a good carpenter. Holland would be glad to have him on a permanent basis.

Adam!

She made herself work. Work was the cure for everything. She braved the trip into town, fighting the tour buses to get to the hardware store to buy a hand cultivator for her small garden and the spray she needed for the blight on the lilac bushes. She worked outside for the rest of the day, and, when it was dark, she showered and had her supper in the almost new kitchen. Then she began working on a new stack of financial reports Edison had left for her. Edison had lived in this area long enough to believe in the work cure, too.

The evening was warm. She had left the house open, and she could hear the peaceful night sounds of crickets and frogs and an occasional passing car. Once she heard a number of Amish buggies, but she didn't get up from the computer to see where they were going. She knew where they were going—the Sauder farm. She turned on the radio, finding a station that played the old fifties and sixties hits.

Shortly after nine, someone knocked on the front door. She stood up and walked into the hallway, knowing she was visible to whoever waited on the porch. She could see the silhouette of a man through the screen, and she hesitated.

"Quinn Tyler," the man said.

"Yes?" She took a few steps closer.

"It's David Sauder."

She walked rapidly to the door, unlatched the hook and held the screen open. "Come in," she said, standing back to give him room.

He stood stubbornly where he was. "No. I will not come into your house."

"Suit yourself," she said. She remembered him well, and he could stand anywhere he pleased. She only wanted to know what had brought him here. "What's wrong?"

He wasn't a tall man, and they stood nearly eye to eye. He had always seen her as a danger to Adam, and in that, perhaps he had been right. He stared back at her now, his eyes hidden behind the thick lenses of his glasses, his lips pressed into a hard line. Clearly, being here was distasteful to him.

"David, what's wrong?"

"I don't come of my own choosing," he said finally.

"Fine. I can see that. You don't like me, but you need something. Are you going to tell me, or do I have to guess?"

"It's not *me* who needs anything from you, Quinn Tyler. My mother has sent me. I come for her—"

"Why?" Quinn interrupted.

"She wants you to come to the house."

"You mean now?"

He turned away and stepped off the porch.

"David? Is something wrong with Lena?"

"Not with her," he said, walking rapidly away toward the Sauder farm. Quinn rushed out the door and followed him, trying not to stumble in the dark. David, like Adam, was in prime physical condition, and it was all she could do to keep up.

"With Adam? David, is something wrong with Adam?"

"Don't ask me these questions, Quinn Tyler. I came here because my mother asked. That is *all* I will do."

Chapter Nine

The stars were out, but there was no moon. She followed
David Sauder along the dirt road between the cornfields,
and she didn't try to keep up any longer. He was more accustomed to getting about in the dark than she was, and she
had a stitch in her side from hurrying. She was sure, too,
that David wouldn't let her come any closer to him than she
already was, and that, whatever had happened, he held her
entirely to blame.

She stepped into a hole in the dark, and she stumbled
briefly, but she didn't fall. David strode on ahead of her. She
had been right about the Amish buggies she'd heard earlier
being en route to the Sauder house. As she got closer, she
could make out a row of them parked at the edge of the
field. But she could see no one around, hear nothing but the
crickets and frogs and a quiet whirring sound she identified
as the windmill behind the barn. There were no lights in any
of the windows on this side of the house.

"Wait here," David said over his shoulder when they reached the main yard. She waited, standing under the trees at the edge of the slate path to the back door. The wind rattled the new leaves overhead, and she shivered, not with coldness so much as with anticipation. One of the dogs, a short-haired mongrel, approached her warily. She didn't think David would have left her to the mercy of some vicious canine protector of the Sauder property, but she was by no means certain.

"Well, come here," she said softly, extending her fist for the dog to sniff. "And stop worrying." The dog immediately began to fawn around her legs, and she reached to scratch it behind the ears. The dog had had a bath today; she could smell the strong scent of brown laundry soap in its fur. "Hasn't been a good day for you, either, has it?" she whispered, letting the animal lick her fingers. "What with baths and strangers in the dark."

The dog's enthusiasm grew, and she knelt down to keep it from jumping up on her. She looked up sharply at the sound of the screen door opening, and the dog bounded off toward the house, giving excited barks along the way.

Quinn expected Lena, but it wasn't Adam's mother who had come out of the house. It was Jacob who quieted the dog with one sharp command. Her heart fell. She remembered Adam telling her once that, when he was little, he had been certain that God himself looked like Jacob Sauder. Watching Jacob approach, she could identify with Adam's feelings completely, and she felt as she always had whenever she met him face-to-face—inappropriate and unacceptable. It suddenly occurred to her that perhaps he didn't know that Lena had asked David to bring her here. Perhaps he was coming now to send her away again.

She glanced at the windows behind him. She could see a woman—not Lena, because she was obviously in the latter stages of pregnancy—carrying a gas lantern into the kitchen.

The woman—David's wife, she guessed—set the lantern on the table and waited for the group of men who followed her to be seated. Church elders, Quinn thought. What was happening now? If Edison's information was correct, they'd already decided on Adam's excommunication. She had no idea what else they could be doing.

"So, Quinn Tyler," Jacob said, drawing her attention away from the activities in the house. "You have come."

"Yes," she said. She willed her voice and her knees to hold steady. She couldn't see his face in the darkness, but she could sense the tension in him. She braced herself for his anger, but she refused to let the threat of it make her meek. "But I don't know why—"

"You are here because *she* asks it," he interrupted.

Quinn understood immediately the "she" Jacob meant. Amish marriages were built on respect, not passion or love as the worldly knew it. There were no open displays of affection between a husband and wife, and she was not surprised that Lena was not referred to by name. But Jacob Sauder's simple statement, and his apparent permission for Quinn to come here, spoke volumes about his regard for the woman he'd married.

"Her heart is not strong, and she cannot find the rest she needs otherwise," he said. He looked back toward the house. "Now you are here, and I can do no more for her. The other elders will have to say if it is good to let you stay." He looked back at her in the darkness, and Quinn waited, her heart beginning to pound. "They are deciding now," he went on. "We will wait here until they tell us."

"I want to see Adam," she said, feeling the fear rise. She was afraid to ask where Adam was in all this, and she was afraid not to.

"Even so. We will wait here."

Even so! Quinn thought in exasperation. "Why did you send for me if I can't see him?"

"It was a hard thing, asking you to come here," he said sharply. "I think now I shouldn't have done it. You are headstrong like Adam. It will take time for them in there to know what is the best thing to do. In this, I ask that you respect our ways."

"I have always tried to do that," she said quietly. But she was angry. If he only knew how much she'd respected his ways. She didn't want to offend him, yet she had no doubt that her very existence was likely offensive to him, and nothing she did now would change that. She walked a few steps away from him, looking around at the neat, orderly house and yard. Everything was trimmed, raked, weeded. Typically Amish. No clutter in their homes, no clutter in their lives. The place hadn't changed—even in the darkness, she could tell that—and neither had Jacob Sauder. The dog fawned at her feet again, and she reached down absently to pat its head. She looked toward the kitchen windows. The elders still sat en masse at the table.

"It may be Adam will not want to see you," Jacob said after what seemed a long time.

Was he pleased at that possibility? She couldn't tell. "Jacob, please. Where is he? Tell me what's wrong."

"You are an outsider."

"Please! Don't send for me and then tell me I'm an outsider!"

"Adam has shut himself away. We cannot talk to him because of the shunning. Do you understand?"

"No, I don't understand!" Quinn said, becoming alarmed now. "What do you mean he's shut himself away?"

"He is out there in the barn. In his grandfather's workshop. He goes in yesterday, but he doesn't come out again. My wife is afraid of this long silence—Quinn, where are you going!"

"I'm going to find Adam. How do you know he's not hurt?"

"I have heard him working. Even now he is working."

The back door suddenly opened, and the elders descended into the yard.

"Wait here," Jacob commanded, going to where they gathered on the slate path. Quinn watched the black-clothed Amishmen come together, heard their soft murmuring of German as they conferred with Jacob. She stood with her arms folded, ready to scream with impatience at these doings. She wanted to see about Adam, and she wanted to see now, whether the elders sanctioned her visit or not. But she forced herself to wait. If Adam was working, doing some kind of carpentry, then he must be all right.

She took a deep breath, her eyes turning toward the western sky and the distant rumbling of thunder. It was going to rain again. She could already smell it on the wind. She strained to hear some sound from the barn, but she heard nothing, only the night sounds and the windmill and the muted voices of solemn Amishmen.

"I will show you where Adam is," Jacob said behind her, making her jump.

"I know where the workshop is," she replied, already heading toward the barn. "I've been there before."

"Wait!" Jacob called. "You will need a light."

He walked with her to the lower barn doors, reaching inside and feeling along the wall until he found the lantern hanging on a peg. He lit it carefully and adjusted the wick. "Take this," he said, but he didn't give it to her immediately. He held the lantern higher, as if he wanted to see her face.

"Let me go to him, Jacob," Quinn said impatiently, waiting for him to stand aside.

He handed her the lantern. "I have done you great wrong."

"Me? You haven't done anything to me."

"I have thought ill of you. I have thought you were a selfish English woman who didn't understand us for all the times you were a child here in this house—an evil woman who enticed my son into evil ways. My wife has told me how you had the...right to take Adam from us. You could have taken him with only a word. That word you did not say. I think that you didn't say it because you knew in your heart that, for him, living Plain was more than—" He suddenly broke off.

How careful he was not to mention the baby, Quinn thought. Perhaps that sin was too unspeakable. "Yes," she agreed. "I knew what living Plain meant to him." And she *had* known, just as she had known that she and Adam Sauder were separate halves of the same whole. She had known both those things, and she had made her choice. "None of that matters now."

"It matters to me. I am an old man. I don't want to face God with such ill feelings in my heart. I ask your forgiveness."

"Jacob, I don't—"

"Bitte!"

She stared at him in the darkness. *I gave away my baby,* she thought. *Don't you understand? I gave away my baby!* Everything else was of no consequence.

But she said nothing, particularly the words he needed to hear. She was suddenly too aware of her irrevocable loss, too aware that Adam was excommunicated after all and it had all been for nothing. She could forgive no one until she could forgive herself. She tried to move by him, but Jacob reached out and caught her hand, holding it tightly in his two rough ones. "You must tell me I have done you no harm in this."

"It doesn't matter!" she said, and he abruptly released her hand. "I—we both did the best we could, Jacob. I see no need for forgiveness for that."

"You have no reason to feel charity for me, that I understand. But you can find out what is in my son's mind, Quinn Tyler. Talk to him. Tell him he knows what he must do—for himself, for this family."

"He isn't going to listen to me, Jacob. He'll do whatever *he* thinks is right. That's why I left here the way I did eleven years ago—because I knew I couldn't keep him from—" She abruptly stopped. She didn't want to talk about that with Jacob.

The old man looked up at the night sky for a moment, then back at her. "Before, I have told you this, Quinn Tyler. We bring up our children in the way they should go so that they will never depart from it. Adam will be lost out there in the world. They, the ones who leave us, are always lost out there among the English."

"And has he been happy here?"

"We are not put on this earth to be happy."

"And we're not here to choose what is happiness for somebody else!"

She abruptly turned away, remembering that night on the porch so long ago.

"Do you love him enough?" Jacob had asked her then. If she let him, he'd ask her that again. Did she love Adam enough to do what *he* wanted? For all his talk of forgiveness, Jacob hadn't changed. Once again he wanted to make her his ally.

But Adam was beyond her influence now, because he knew his child was lost to him and because she had been away for so long. She couldn't press him about anything, whether he still cared for her or not.

"Are you still my friend?" he'd asked.

Yes, she was still that, regardless of what had happened between them. She didn't want to tell him anything on Jacob's behalf; she only wanted to know that he was all right. Jacob would have to take up his own case.

She held the lantern carefully as she stepped into the barn. It was dark and quiet, smelling of dust and horse, leather and aged wood. She moved silently past an open "courting" buggy and a row of horse collars hanging on pegs, hesitating to listen to the faint sounds coming from the carpentry workshop. Adam was indeed working. She could see the lantern light through the chinks in the wall up ahead. She walked on, looking around sharply at a noise behind her— Jacob and the elders, gathered now at the outside door to wait. They were not about to permit her to see Adam Sauder alone. Her toe caught on the uneven flooring, and she gave a soft cry as she tried to right herself. The noises in the workshop abruptly stopped.

She stood very still, listening, sensing that behind the door of his grandfather's carpentry shop, Adam was doing the same. She took a deep breath and moved on, setting the lantern down on the floor and going the rest of the way without it. She could see several years' worth of almanac farm-and-garden calendars on the walls as she approached, and the lantern cast her shadow long and thin onto their pages.

When she reached the workshop door, she rested the flat of her hand against the rough boards for a moment before she tried it. She had no idea what she would say and no right to say it if she had. She pushed on the door, but it was braced from the inside and didn't budge. She tried again, but it didn't open. Clearly, Adam had heard her, and he had barred the door against her. Because of the shunning, he would have no need to bar it against anyone else.

She leaned her forehead against the wood, trying to remember. Had he always wanted to be alone like this when he was troubled? Yes, she decided, but he'd wanted to be alone with *her*, to talk to *her* about whatever bothered him. She remembered when he'd had to quit school, and when Jacob had tried to make him see that he couldn't keep associating with the English girl. She had sat with him on a creek bank well away from both their houses and felt his pain as if it were her own.

"There is nothing in you that would harm me," he'd said then, and they'd both believed it. They had been so innocent.

"Adam?" she said. She could hear him moving around, but he didn't answer her. She waited, her head still resting against the rough wood. There was a small square opening cut in the lower corner of the door, and a calico cat poked its head out to peer at her. She made no move to touch it, but it suddenly withdrew as if she had.

"Adam?" she said again. She caught a glimpse of movement behind her. Jacob and the elders had moved closer. She turned her face away from them.

"I just want to know if you're all right," she said, feeling her desperation rise. "Do you hear me?"

The silence lengthened.

"Edison told me what happened. Adam, can't you—"

"Are you alone, Quinn?" he suddenly broke in.

She looked back over her shoulder at Jacob and the men, wondering why he wanted to know. "No. The elders from the church are here. And your father. Adam—"

"Go away from me," he interrupted. "Now."

He was close to the door; she could feel him there on the other side.

"Adam, listen! All those times I brought you books to read... Sometimes, when everything was so hard for you, when you missed going to school so much, you pretended you didn't want them. But I knew you did. I could tell when I looked at you. I could tell how badly you needed them—

it didn't matter what you said. How can I know what you want now if I can't look at you?" Her voice quavered, and she closed her eyes, trying to regain her composure. "Adam, let me see you," she whispered. "Let me—"

He heard her quite plainly, and that softly whispered plea on the other side of the door nearly tore him in two. It was all he could do to resist it. How had she come to be here? Quinn!

He couldn't let her in, no matter how much she pleaded, no matter how much he wanted to see her. He was so tired, and he had to be alone. If he let her in, they—his father and whoever else was out there—would always think that *she* had persuaded him to do what he knew he had to do. Worse, the day might come when he would think that himself. This was his final chance to make some sense of his life, and he was going to be very careful with it. The only way to do that was to stay separate from Quinn, entirely, so that Jacob and the others would know she was without blame, that he'd come to this himself, when he had no hope at all of a life with her.

"Adam? You know if you need anything, I'll help," Quinn said, keeping her voice low to avoid being overheard.

"I don't need anything, Quinn. I only want to be left alone. If I have any need, it's that."

The *Meidung*—the shunning. Eleven years ago, for the sake of the family, he had buckled under the threat of that punishment because he had thought Quinn lost to him and there was nothing else out among the English that mattered. Such a solemn and terrible ritual, like attending one's own funeral. He had grown up with the fear, of someone doing something that would bring the *Meidung* into the house. And how strange it seemed that it had finally happened. He had sat among the weeping women and the stern-faced men and listened to the account of his supposed sin,

and to the announcement that he was a threat to others and
had to be cast off from everything he knew and loved. And
yet, the alienation, the aloneness he'd felt since the shunning began was somehow no worse than it had always been.
True, no one spoke to him now, not even Daniel or his
mother, for whom, if he could, he would have spared this
trouble. He ate his meals alone after everyone else had
eaten, and he was no longer given the status he'd always
known as the oldest son. The days passed without the
constant "Ask Adam" from the rest of the family. It was
hard to suddenly behave as if he were not needed, when the
needs of this family had been what had kept him here after
Quinn had gone.

But he didn't delude himself. The real difference now was
that he was irrevocably at the crossroads in his life where he
must decide precisely what it was he wanted—to "repent"
and continue his marginal compliance as an Amishman or
to leave. He couldn't make the decision lightly, and he refused to be swayed by the terribleness of the *Meidung* or by
his longing for Quinn. In time, he knew that the strain of his
not belonging would become too much for all of them, and
he would be asked to leave the Sauder house rather than di-
vide family and community loyalties. He knew he had his
mother's sympathies, and Sarah's, and all of his brothers'
except for David.

Poor David. The shame was nearly more than he could
bear, and there was nothing Adam could do about it. David believed there was no excuse for Adam's behavior with
Quinn Tyler. Adam was a man now, not some infatuated
boy who'd let his pretty childhood friend seduce him.

"Adam, can I tell Lena anything? She's—"

He closed his eyes against the need to give in. "What you
can do is go away from me!"

He could hear the fear in her voice. And worry. And caring. He had no doubt that she still cared about him. He'd

felt that from the first day she'd come back. But did she love him? Or did she hold for him the same charity she held for encroaching spiders, something to be moved out of her sight, albeit kindly, but moved nevertheless?

That, he didn't know. He knew the passion was still there; it had leaped up wild and strong between them the day they'd walked barefoot over the plowed field. Even now, the memory of it left him restless and aching. He still loved her with all his heart, and his desire for her had nearly overwhelmed him. How angry it had made him to have *that* within his reach again. It would have given him such joy to make love with her, but he'd wanted so much more.

He had but one certainty, and that was that he would never be satisfied with illicit meetings in the dark again. This time he would have every part of Quinn Tyler, every hope, every dream, every weakness and fear. He would have every part of her—or he would have nothing.

"It never bothered you to leave me before," he said finally, knowing it would hurt her.

She stepped back from the door, then pounded it once hard with her fist. "All right! All right. If that's all you want, then it's the least I can do for you." She turned away, grabbing up the lantern as she went.

"He wants to be left alone," she said to Jacob. "That's all he'll say. I'm sorry."

She made her way through the group of men, remembering at the last moment to give back the lantern.

"You will need this to light your way, Quinn Tyler."

"No, thank you. I'll go home the long way by the paved road." She headed across the Sauders' backyard toward the macadamized road that bordered both farms. The mongrel joined her as she passed the vegetable garden and the grape arbors. Suddenly something moved in the vines behind her.

"Anymore don't hurry, Quinn Tyler!"

"Daniel! You scared me. You'd better go back inside."

But he didn't go back inside. He flung his arms around her waist instead. "I want to cry, Quinn Tyler," he said, his voice muffled against her. The wind was picking up. A flash of lightning illuminated the house and yard, and a crack of thunder rolled across the night sky.

She held him tightly. "Oh, Daniel, I know." She felt like crying herself. "Go inside now. It's going to storm."

"No. I can't talk to Adam. Quinn Tyler, is he going away from this house?"

"He didn't tell me. He only said he wants to be by himself for now."

Daniel leaned back to look at her, his features a blur in the dark. "Can you make him stay with us? Can you ask him? I can't talk to him." He let go of her and rubbed both eyes hard with his fists. "So bad I want to cry." He took his hands down, and the wind rattled the grape arbor behind them. Quinn reached out to touch his hair, but this time he fended her off. Clearly, like his brother, he needed answers more than he needed comfort. "I'm too big for crying. What will he do, Quinn Tyler? What will he do?"

"Daniel, I don't know that. I think he has to decide. And we just have to wait."

"Anymore I don't want to wait."

"Daniel!" David said sharply behind them. "Get into the house!"

"Can Adam stay at your house, Quinn Tyler?" Daniel asked desperately, pulling on her hands to keep her attention before David got any closer. "Can he? You wouldn't have the shunning there."

David came forward as if to cuff him on the ear. "Daniel! Get inside!"

The boy let go of her hands and disappeared around the corner of the house.

"He's afraid, David," Quinn couldn't keep from saying.

"We are *all* afraid, Quinn. All of us. Does it make you happy, this thing you've done?"

"No, I'm not happy! And I haven't *done* anything!"

"You came back here. Already you've led my brother into—"

"I love your brother!" she said vehemently.

He made a derisive sound. "And what good does it do him, this love of yours? You ruin him. You ruin this family. You see how Daniel is, how we all are. We have the *Meidung* in this house because of you!"

"David," a woman said worriedly, the woman Quinn had seen through the window. Neither Quinn nor David had heard her approach, and he looked sharply around at her. It was clear that he was not ready to forgo having his say, and he lapsed into the German dialect to speak to her, spewing angry words too rapid for Quinn to follow. There were only two words she understood—her own name and that of the woman. Sarah.

The gentle Sarah Adam had almost married? she wondered briefly as she stood there, temporarily forgotten. Whatever Sarah said displeased David even more. That was all Quinn could tell, and, whatever the words were about, she didn't care. She wasn't waiting any longer. She was going home.

"Wait, Quinn," Sarah called after her.

"It's going to rain. I have to go," Quinn said without looking back. She walked on toward the road, the playful dog pouncing at her heels.

"But Lena wants to see you!"

Quinn hesitated. Lena. She'd forgotten about Lena.

But she didn't want to cause any more trouble. David and Jacob were upset enough by her presence. "The elders will be coming back to the house. I shouldn't be there."

"Please, Quinn. She wants it," Sarah persisted. Clearly, she was a dutiful daughter-in-law. What her husband's mother wished, she would try to do.

Another flash of lightning lit up the yard, but Quinn wasn't able to see Sarah's face well enough to read her expression. She didn't exude the same animosity as her husband, but there was something there.

"All right," Quinn said finally. All the elders together couldn't be any more intimidating than Jacob alone. "Your name is Sarah?" she asked as she walked back toward the house. She didn't want to feed her jealousy at the possibility that this Sarah could be the one Adam had courted, but she needed to know if Adam had any allies at all. If this was the Sarah who had once planned to marry him, surely she must feel some kindness for him.

But Quinn was forgetting. Even if that were so, Sarah was David's wife now, and his feelings in the matter were likely to be hers.

"Yes. Sarah," the woman said. "Lena is waiting in the kitchen. She's not feeling well today. Last night she doesn't sleep much. Quinn," she added as they reached the back door, "I . . . never thought you wanted to hurt Adam."

They looked into each other's eyes, and, whether this was Adam's gentle Sarah or not, in that moment they seemed to understand each other perfectly. Quinn could feel the sting of tears behind her eyes, and she nodded, reaching blindly for the handle on the screen door. Sarah didn't come inside with her, but she had no difficulty finding her way; nothing had changed since the last time she had been in this house. She followed the hiss of the gas lantern into the large kitchen.

Lena was sitting at the table. Quinn stood in the doorway for a moment, not knowing quite what to do or say, remembering their last meeting.

"I will not see you, Quinn Tyler, until I can find the forgiveness in my own heart."

Had Lena found that forgiveness? Or at least some measure of understanding? In the eyes of the Amish, she had led Adam into sin. In the eyes of Adam's mother, she had also hurt him deeply, and it must have seemed a coldly deliberate act. Her sinning with Adam and then staying away from him all these years had been one thing; taking his son from him was quite another. Lena was Adam's mother, and no one deserved to be hurt the way he had been, not even in the name of love.

Tell me you understand, Quinn almost said, but she bit down on it, forcing herself to be still. Lena Sauder was a kind woman, a good woman. It was better not knowing whether she had her forgiveness, because if Lena couldn't forgive her, then what she had done was truly unforgivable.

"You have seen Adam?" Lena asked finally.

"Yes, but I can't tell you anything, Lena. He wouldn't talk to me."

The older woman sighed and pulled out the chair next to her for Quinn to sit in. It struck Quinn that Lena was not in the least surprised. Apparently she hadn't expected Quinn to accomplish anything, even though she had insisted that she come here.

"It isn't the talking so much as the knowing," Lena said as Quinn sat down.

Quinn propped her elbows on the table and rested her head in her hands for a moment. "I don't know what that means, Lena," she said tiredly. "I don't know what anything means anymore."

Surprisingly Lena reached out to her, and Quinn clasped her hand as if she were in danger of drowning.

"It means that Adam has put himself in a wilderness of his own making, and he can't see your lights across the way. But still, he needs to know that they are there."

Quinn looked away so that Lena couldn't see her face. Leaving her lights on all night had been a desperate, childish gesture, and she was embarrassed that Lena was so perceptive. She was sure now that, forgiven or not, it was for Adam that Lena had wanted her to come tonight, not for herself. But she didn't believe Lena's assessment of Adam's need of her.

"He didn't want me there. He locked the door."

"If he did, he locked the door *for* you, not against you."

Quinn shook her head, still not willing to accept it. "I don't—"

"I know my son, Quinn. I think he doesn't want you blamed, whatever he decides. He must think what to do now, what it is he really wants, and he wants no one to say Quinn Tyler talked to him tonight and made him go."

"Or stay?" Quinn asked softly.

Lena made no reply to that, looking at the windows as the first drops of rain splattered against the glass. "You must wait with us until the rain is over."

"No. No, Lena, I can't. I'll go home now."

"Quinn..."

She stood up. "No, I don't belong here. I have to go home."

She meant to squeeze Lena's hand one last time, but Lena stood up with her, hugging her tightly for a moment before releasing her to run out into the rainy darkness.

Chapter Ten

The telephone was ringing. She had left the house open in her haste to follow David, and she could hear it the minute she reached the front yard. But she made no attempt to answer it. She stood in the rain, looking at the tree Adam had planted and trying not to cry.

"It never bothered you to leave me before."

He didn't understand. Or if he did, he couldn't accept what she had done. She had to face that and stop punishing herself.

"This is killing me, too," she said aloud, the sound of her voice lost in the pouring rain. She had known full well how it might be when she came back here to live, and she'd had no surprises. Now she had but two choices, the same ones Adam faced: to go or to stay.

She took a deep breath and reached out to touch the leaves on the apple tree. It was thriving, and so should she. She just had to—

Had to what? That was the difficulty. She didn't know what to do to make the situation better. She didn't even know if it *could* be made better. Perhaps that was a solution in itself. Perhaps she should simply accept the fact that the part of her life that involved Adam Sauder couldn't be mended, that she was like someone with a serious physical injury, one that had left terrible scars that she would have to learn to live with.

She was drenched and shivering by the time she went inside. She went straight upstairs to a hot shower and dry clothes, thinking all the while of her mother. Taking a shower during a thunderstorm was breaking one of her mother's cardinal rules. But then, she'd broken more than one of them in her life. What would her mother say about Adam?

What should I do? she thought again and again as she stood under the hot water, and the answer was always the same. Nothing. Edison had told her that. There was nothing she could do for Adam Sauder. She tried not to think about him, about the aloneness he must be feeling that was so much worse than hers.

She couldn't wash the worry away, but the gods of lightning were kind this time, leaving her unstruck but with a longing for someone who would understand the turns her life had taken. She was exhausted but wide-awake, and she knew there was no sense in trying to sleep. Her throat ached, and her eyes burned with unshed tears for Adam. And for herself. And for their baby.

She wanted to believe Lena Sauder. She wanted to believe that Adam had asked her to go because he didn't want her blamed for whatever decision he was making now, not because he wanted nothing more to do with her. But, like it or not, she had to consider the latter possibility.

The rain had stopped. She put on jeans and a T-shirt, intending to risk working at the computer in spite of the now-distant rumblings of thunder, until she felt sleepy enough to go to bed. Impulsively she lit a fire in the fireplace to rid the room of dampness, and she concentrated on Edison's account figures, somewhat comforted by the precision of dealing with numbers. In this part of her life at least, there were no unaccountable variations. One and one were always two.

The fire burned into embers, and another thunderstorm came out of the west. She shut down the computer, and the telephone rang again. She went into the kitchen and reluctantly picked up the receiver. There was no one in the world she wanted to talk to.

"Quinn?" a man's voice said.

"Yes," she said into the receiver. She couldn't keep her voice from wavering.

"What's wrong?"

"Jake?" She closed her eyes and forced herself to sound calm. "Jake! How are you?"

"Don't dodge the question. What's wrong? I've been trying all evening to call you."

"Nothing's wrong. I—I was out for a while. I got caught in the rain." She wasn't making any sense, and she knew it. She tried to concentrate.

"What the hell were you doing out in the rain at this time of night?"

"Visiting."

A noise on the front porch caught her attention, and she stepped into the hallway so that she could see the front door, forgetting that she'd closed it. The old-fashioned door had a large oval window of beveled glass, and she hadn't had the time or the inclination to find a curtain for it yet. Since the hall light was on, she knew that anyone on the porch could see in better than she could see out.

"So," Jake said in her ear, "how are you doing?"

She walked down the hallway as far as the phone cord would reach, half expecting David Sauder to be out there again with the rest of what he'd wanted to say to her. But the porch looked empty. Just the wind, she thought. "Fine. I'm fine. What about you?"

"Oh, I'm better than ever. Now here's where you're supposed to be impressed—I made ten thousand bucks in commissions Thursday. What do you think of that?"

She cringed at a loud crack of thunder. Taking a shower in a thunderstorm was one thing; using the telephone was something else again. "That's nice. Jake, listen, there's a storm here, so I'll have to—"

The front door opened.

Adam came into the hallway. He stood for a moment, then walked toward her, leaving wet footsteps on the bare wood floor. He wasn't wearing a hat, and his clothes were drenched, his hair plastered down by the rain. He said nothing, but, oh, the pain in his eyes.

His name formed on her lips, but she, too, said nothing.

"Nice? *Nice,* Tyler?" Jake protested. "You're damned right ten thousand bucks is nice. The market's been a bitch—or haven't you been reading the papers?"

"No, I—Jake, I have to go. I'll call you tomorrow or—"

"No, wait, Quinn. I want to know how you're really doing. You sound like hell."

"Jake, I told you, everything's fine." Fine, she thought, staring into Adam Sauder's eyes.

"When are you coming to Philadelphia?"

Adam stood silently, waiting, dripping rain on the floor.

Dear God, she thought. *He's done it. He's broken with Jacob.*

"What?" she said to Jake because she'd all but forgotten him.

"I said, when are you coming to Philadelphia. I want to see you, Quinn."

"I can't come to Philadelphia. Jake, goodbye. I have to go."

"Quinn!" he called, but she wasn't listening anymore. She stood clutching the telephone receiver tightly against her chest.

"I don't think you told him the truth, Quinn," Adam said. "I don't think everything is fine." His eyes traveled over her face. She looked so forlorn to him. So little. And so sad. Her eyes were bright with unshed tears, although the mouse with the big feet smiled bravely on her chest.

Quinn. My beautiful Quinn.

"Why are you here?" she asked.

"I came of my own choice. I wasn't driven out or—"

"What happened with Jacob?" she interrupted. Something must have happened. He'd refused to see her only hours ago.

"I am no longer his son." He was so calm, so matter-of-fact. "He understands, Quinn."

"How could he understand? You're his first son. Adam, what are you doing here? I never wanted to take that away from you." *Too*, she'd almost said.

"He understands because I've told him. I can't live Amish anymore."

Quinn pressed her lips together, not trusting herself to speak. She was like Daniel, she thought crazily. She wanted desperately to cry, and there was nothing she could do to hold it back anymore. Her eyes filled with tears, which spilled over and ran silently down her cheeks. She hated for him to see her cry, and she turned away, going back into the kitchen to hang up the phone.

"This man who called you, he's not so stupid as I thought," Adam said from behind her. "He wants you to come back to him."

She stood in the middle of the kitchen, not knowing where to go next or what to do. Adam moved around her to see her face, but she bowed her head. She has always been like this, he thought. Always wanting to hide her tears from him. But there were tears he should have seen, the ones when she knew she was having his baby, the ones when she knew she was leaving him.

"Will you do what he asks, Quinn? Will you go to Philadelphia?"

She looked up at him. "No," she said, her voice barely a whisper.

His heart began a slow pounding in his chest. No. So easily she said it. As if it were never a possibility. Again he was determined to look into her eyes. They were the same in that respect. He couldn't know what she was feeling if he couldn't see her eyes. She looked so wounded, so cornered, like a rabbit in a trap, but still he had to know.

"Why won't you go to Philadelphia?" he said, and she looked away.

"Adam, you shouldn't be here," she said, attempting a composure she didn't feel.

"Where else should I be then? I promised myself I would never do this again, Quinn. I wouldn't come to you in the dark like when I was a boy. I'm a man now, but I'm here. Because I can't *not* be here. That's how it is with me. I . . . I want you to say how it is with you."

"There is still so much wrong between us," she began.

"Just tell me!" he said impatiently. "We can't settle anything if you won't tell me what you feel."

"I don't know what I feel."

"Then let me help you. Do you want me to go? This other man, this Jake, do we just leave you alone here? Is that what you want?"

"Adam, I can't—"

"Do you want me to go!"

"No!"

"Then what do you want?"

She took a few steps toward the back door. He went with her. "I want you to be happy," she said, turning around to face him.

"And this time will you ask *me* what it takes for my happiness? Or will you and my father decide and leave me out of it?"

"Adam, I—"

"Ask me what will make me happy, Quinn! Never mind—I'll tell you. It would make me happy to know at last what is in your heart. You're right that there is still much that's wrong between us. Maybe we're both too hurt, too battered to deal with the why of how we came to this. But we have to start somewhere. You have to tell me if there is anything between us now. I ask you again. What do you want?"

She tried to get away from him, but he caught her arm.

"Say it! Once and for all if you want me out of your life, then tell me. Tell me so I can believe it. You kill me with what I see in your eyes, the need you have. You *need*, Quinn, and I don't know what I have to give you."

"It's not just what *I* want!" she cried.

"No? Then who else is there? I have told you I love you. I have no pride when it comes to that. I didn't stop loving you while you were gone. But I tried, Quinn. I tried! So tell me, who else is in this? Jake?"

"No, not Jake. You're Amish, Adam," she said desperately.

"Yes. *I* am Amish. Me. Not you. I will decide what I want to do about it." He brought her around to face him. "Now, you look at me. You look at me, and you tell me. You have my word I will believe you. If you can give me nothing else, then give me the peace I need. Say it! Say, 'Adam, I don't want you. Adam, I don't love you.' Say it! 'I never wanted you or your son!'" His fingers dug into her arm, hurting her, but they didn't hurt nearly as much as what he wanted her to do.

"Please!" she cried, and he abruptly let go of her. She was trembling, and she couldn't stop. She tried to hold her body rigid so that she wouldn't sob out loud.

"It's not true," she whispered. "I wanted you—and our boy. I wanted you so much!"

"Quinn. Quinn..." he said, but she didn't understand the rest because he'd lapsed into German.

She looked up at him. She wanted to go to him so badly, but she only shook her head because she didn't understand.

"I said, don't cry," he translated. "Don't, Quinn. We've had enough tears, you and I."

"Oh, Adam." She reached out her hand to him, and, amazingly, he took it, his fingers interlacing with hers. He drew her to him, and she gave a soft moan as she sagged against him. She had had her reasons for separating them, good reasons, and they suddenly counted for nothing. He put his arms around her without hesitation, reaching up to rest his hand against her tear-stained cheek. He was wet from the rain, but his touch was warm, so warm. She held him tightly, her fists clutching the back of his shirt. He felt so good to her. She needed his strength, and she despaired at the possibility that he might withdraw it.

"Don't leave," she whispered urgently. "Please, don't leave."

"Why?" he asked quietly. One way or the other, he was going to make her say it.

"Because—I—Adam, I didn't know what to do! I didn't! I loved you so!"

Loved. Past tense.

He closed his eyes, holding her tightly. *And now?* he wanted to ask her. *What about now?*

But he didn't ask. He had lost his nerve, and she was too distraught. She seemed so fragile to him. So fragile, and yet she was so strong. He knew what she had done for him. She had tried to give the one thing he couldn't give her—his Amishness—and she'd sacrificed their child to do it.

"Quinn!" he whispered against her ear, all the love, all the pain he was feeling riding on the sound of her name.

She clung to him, her face pressed against his. His face was smooth, just shaven, she realized. She could smell the scent of soap on his skin. She suddenly understood his sending her away earlier, his being here now. He hadn't come to her the way he'd always done as a troubled boy, and he hadn't wanted to see her while he was unkempt and unfocused. It was even more than not having her blamed for his decision to leave the Amish. He had wanted to come to her as a man, a man who was in control of his life and who had made his choices deliberately, just as she had done.

"What was I to you?" he persisted, keeping the promise he'd made to himself. He had to know, even if the knowing ended it.

"Everything," she said without hesitation.

"Was I?"

"Yes! You still are."

Still?

He held her away from him, cupping her face in his hands. The softness of her cheeks was sweet against his rough and callused palms. He was afraid to hope, but he was driven by the years of not knowing. He asked anyway, his eyes searching hers for the truth. "And what am I now?"

Time stood still. There was nothing but the rain coming down and the sound of their breathing.

"My friend," she said quietly. "My lover. My... husband."

His heart soared. "Yes!" he affirmed, his mouth coming down hard on hers, the taste of her already in his mind. He was all those things. Always.

Always.

He intended to be gentle, to make the kiss sweet and lasting. But he was too hungry, too starved, too long without her. He tore his mouth away from hers, pressing another kiss against her jaw and then into the delicate fragrance of her neck. He was trembling. His hands shook with desire. His mouth found hers again, and she parted her lips, accepting the probing of his tongue as if she, too, were starved. He lifted her up off the floor, and her arms went around his neck. She weighed nothing, he thought as he carried her into the hallway.

"There is more to us than this" she remembered as he carried her up the stairs. There was more to their relationship than their physical attraction. And it was because there was more that *this* was so consuming. She had been in such pain for so long, alone for so long, and so had he. And it was *this* that they both needed to heal them.

He set her on the edge of the bed and let her turn on the small lamp by the bed. He kneeled down beside her, putting his head into her lap for a moment before he began to undress her. Her fingers entwined in his hair as he pressed a warm kiss against her belly, a kiss she could feel deep into the soft, secret, womanly part of her. She loved his touch, a touch that was both reverent and demanding. She loved his damp, sun-streaked hair, his pale eyes that shaded with his moods from blue to gray. She loved his taste, familiar and distinctive, and she wanted more.

"Adam . . ." she whispered.

He lifted his head to look into her eyes, the beautiful hazel eyes he'd always found so easy to become lost in. His passion was strong; he trusted himself to leave only the briefest of kisses on her mouth. And he wouldn't let her help remove her clothing or his. He wanted to do that himself, to peel away every vestige of her Englishness and his Amishness until they were only a man and a woman.

How beautiful! he thought. Her high, firm breasts that were neither large nor small but just fit the palms of his hands. Her hips and thighs and legs, with their silky, woman-soft curves. Her body was so smooth beneath his hands. Warm. Smooth. Soft. And willing. She leaned back on the bed, resting on her elbows while she watched him with half-closed eyes, accepted his worship with a soft sigh as he caressed every part of her. In that look, he could feel her wanting the touch of his hands, and the look alone was enough to make him catch his breath. He pulled down the quilt and the sheet on the bed, lifting her and placing her gently in the middle of it. He felt no shyness at having her see him remove his own clothing, no shyness that she should see how much he wanted her.

How beautiful! she thought as she watched his clothes drop away. He was neither awkward nor hurried. She loved his body. She had always loved it. He was trim and muscular from the hard, physical work he'd done all his life. She lay back against the pillows, languid with anticipation. Only the tremor of his hands, and his eyes grown needy and dark, and then his final nakedness gave away his rising desire. His bold desire. His unsatisfied desire.

He stood before her without shame, and she held out her arms to him. How many times had he imagined this? A bed with cool, crisp sheets, and Quinn, warm and pressing against him. And privacy. And time. All the time in the world to be with her. That it was really happening was incredible to him, that she was covering his shoulder and neck with warm, wet kisses, that her belly strained against his, and the twin hard peaks of her breasts flattened against his chest. The male part of him lay swollen and hard against her thigh, and when she reached down to touch him, her hand encircling, stroking, he heard himself grunt with un-abashed pleasure.

It was no longer enough to be the recipient. He wanted to touch, to kiss, to taste. He held her to him with both arms and legs as they tumbled together on the bed. The sweet woman smell of her, the sweet woman taste, drove him on. His hands slid into her dark, cropped-off hair. Strange, when he remembered her hair being long, braided some-times, and the braids coming undone. But he loved the sleek, crisp feel of her hair now. And it smelled so good. Like flowers, Daniel had said. She smelled like flowers. He stroked her body, cupped her breasts, probed the delicate, petallike folds of her womanness until she arched against his clever fingers. When he kissed her breasts, when his mouth gently suckled and his teeth gently bit, she writhed in plea-sure, sliding her fingers into his hair to keep him there. Such a joy it was to please her, to make her whimper at his min-istrations, to make her cry out his name.

"Adam!"

Who else had done this for her?

The thought rose unbidden, and he pushed it aside. That didn't matter to him. There was only the now and the need he had for her. Quinn, who had given him such joy and such misery and pain.

"My beautiful Quinn," he said, holding his body above hers, staring into her eyes. He could see everything she wanted to tell him there, the things he was afraid to hear, the things she was afraid to say. She reached to bring him down to her, but he abruptly scooped her up, kneeling in the mid-dle of the bed and holding her so that she had to lock her legs around his hips to keep from falling. He was a man, and he was strong and virile and delighted, and he wanted her to feel it. He held her as if she were no burden to him at all, and he kissed her, devoured her, her lips and shoulders and breasts. Every place he could reach, he covered with kisses, nipped with his teeth. He could feel that most female part of her, dewy and warm and straining against him. Then he tipped her backward, lowering her slowly, so slowly, back onto the bed. He was kneeling between her thighs, and his hands cupped her hips, sliding her closer to him.

Again her arms reached up; he smiled into her eyes as she embraced him. He kissed her lips, her nose, her eyes, then her lips again, letting his tongue explore the sweet taste of her mouth, savoring, remembering, experiencing it all anew, letting his hardness press urgently against the threshold of the place he was so desperate to be.

"Love me, Adam!" she whispered against his ear, and he felt the words, burning, all the way to the heart of his desire.

And then he was inside her, thrusting deep, his moan of pleasure lost in hers. She was so hot and tight and wet around him. So good. It felt so good. Nothing had ever felt so good. He tried to remember to be gentle—she was so small, and she'd been ill. He wanted to love her slowly, completely; he wanted to make her belong to him again, to make it last. He braced his weight with his hands, and the muscles in his arms trembled with the strain of holding back.

But he had been her first lover, and he knew. She had learned this most ancient of rituals between a man and woman with him. Virgins both, they had learned to pleasure each other together, and he had known her body as well as he knew his own. That hadn't changed. She didn't want his restraint. She wanted him, all of him, and she thrust her hips into his.

"Quinn, Quinn," he whispered, his body answering hers in a primitive rhythm he was powerless to stop. "It's so...good—you feel so good around me."

"You feel good," she murmured against his mouth. "I— love you—Adam."

From somewhere far away, he was aware of the thunder, of the rain beating against the roof, but he was lost now in a storm of his own. And Quinn was the center of it. He was drowning in the meaning of her words, in the exquisite joy of her body. Such pleasure. He had never known such pleasure, and the pleasure was not his alone. Her soft cries filled his heart to bursting. That he could do this for her, that she should want him so—like this—deep inside her—

And then the pleasure sharpened, and sharpened still more, and rushed through him to splinter into a fiery path of a thousand white-hot shards. He wanted to hold back; he thought he would die if he couldn't reach the end of it.

"I love you, Quinn!" he cried, feeling himself empty into her. "I love you," he murmured again and again. In English? In German? He didn't know.

She was listening to the rain, a quiet pattering sound now against the front windows and on the gutters. The lamp was still on, and she lay quietly at Adam's side, watching him sleep. He was lying on his back, the sheet only minimally covering his body, one knee bent, one hard, muscular thigh clearly exposed. When she was young, just on the threshold of being a woman, she'd dreamed of this, of having Adam in this house, in this bed. He would be her husband, and they'd sleep together, make babies together, grow old, be happy.

She loved him so!

Always.

Still.

Adam suddenly turned to her, taking her into his arms so that they were lying face-to-face. He pressed her close to him, and he gently kissed her eyes. "Is it all right?" he asked.

"Yes," she answered, resting her head against his, knowing that he was using one of his Amish idioms. He didn't mean "it." He meant her. Was she all right. Since their lovemaking. And before whatever in their lives was coming next. She felt that they were both dwelling on the now of their situation, not the past and not the future, and it was so good to be in limbo like this, she thought. And so... precarious.

"I want us to marry," he said quietly, dragging them both into reality. He put his fingertips against her lips to head off any protest she might make. "I want us to marry," he repeated. "I don't want to wait. I don't want to think it over. I want you. The wrong between us can't be fixed while we're apart. I want us together. Now."

She looked into his eyes and saw no trace of uncertainty, only his quiet strength and his love. He knew all her arguments, so she made none. She had but one question.

"Are you sure?"

"Do you love me?" he countered.

"Yes," she said firmly.

"Then I'm sure."

She hugged him tightly, burying her face in his neck as if she could hide them both from the difficulties to come.

"It's going to be harder for you," he whispered.

"No, it isn't."

"I... can't give you anything, Quinn. I have nothing but myself and what I can do with my own two hands."

She leaned back to look at him. "I don't want anything but you."

"You know I'll work for you, for us. Holland will hire me, I think. It shouldn't be too bad." He smiled, but his smile quickly faded.

"What?" she asked, her eyes searching his.

"We never did this before. All those times we were together, we never really talked about making a life together."

"No," she said sadly. "We didn't."

"Quinn, I never thought of marrying anyone but you. I should have said that. I should have made sure you knew. But your father was so ill then, and I young and stupid, and you suffered for it. Somehow I thought everything would just go on the way it was and—"

"Don't. Don't. No *if onlys*. All right? For my sake. Promise me that."

"Quinn—"

"I wouldn't have let you talk about it. I didn't want you to lose everything because of me. Now, please, for my sake..."

He seemed about to say more, but he didn't, smiling instead. "Tell me. Why were you looking at me so?"

"When?" she asked innocently, trying not to smile in return.

"When you thought I was asleep."

She kissed him softly on the chin. "Oh. Then."

"Yes, then. Why were you looking at me?"

"You're very beautiful?" she suggested, and this time he grinned.

"Me? Beautiful?"

"Very beautiful," she corrected.

"Ah. *Very* beautiful. And what else am I?" he asked, clearly at ease with her earlier inspection of his body and clearly fishing.

"What else? Well, you're—" she let her fingers trail over his chest and abdomen, watched his eyes flutter closed "—kind."

He opened his eyes again. "I see. Kind. And who am I kind to?"

She pressed the smallest of kisses on his chest. Then another. "To your family." And another. "To Jacob and Lena, and Daniel, and your sisters, and—"

"I'm not always kind to my sisters," he interrupted, letting out the breath he was holding.

"Yes, you are. You made them all marriage chests—Anna told me when we were unpacking dishes," she added when he was about to interrupt again. "She said no one had a brother as good as you."

"Anna said that?"

"She did."

"She must have had her hair twisted too tight—don't stop," he added because she'd found yet another place she wanted to kiss.

She obliged him. "She did not—have her hair—twisted too—tight."

"Then she was out in the sun too long—oh!"

"No, she was in the house with me. She said all her girlfriends in the—I've forgotten what you call them—the groups that meet at each other's houses on Sunday evenings..." She outlined his hard male nipples with her tongue.

"Supper gangs," he managed. "Quinn—"

She lifted her head. "Yes. In her supper gang. They all have crushes on you because you're so smart and handsome."

"I thought I was beautiful."

"Oh, well, that's only my opinion," she said, lowering her head again.

"I like your opinion," he said, lifting her chin so that his mouth could find hers. "I like everything." The kiss was soft and friendly, but it quickly escalated in degree and purpose. "I want you again, Quinn," he whispered, his mouth moving hungrily over hers. "I want you." His mouth left hers to suckle her breasts, and she closed her eyes at the hot, wet, exquisite pleasure it gave her. His hands, his urgent, knowing hands brought her leg up, stroked and teased and explored her most sensitive places until she moaned with the pure sensuality of it.

"I love to hear you," he whispered. "I love to hear you want me."

And then he was inside her, deep, so deep. His urgency compounded her own. She did want him. She wanted him very badly.

"Quinn . . . you are . . ."

But he didn't tell her what she was, and she didn't wonder. She had but one hope. That he would understand and that he would be kind to her, too.

Chapter Eleven

Adam woke with a start at the abrupt trilling of a mockingbird outside the window. He should have been disoriented, unsure about where he was, but he wasn't. He knew instantly, even before the soft body lying in his arms fully registered.

Quinn.

He closed his eyes again, savoring the memory of the night they'd just had. Unbelievable, he thought for the thousandth time. He was here. And Quinn Tyler loved him. She was so beautiful lying there, and he pressed a soft kiss against her temple before he eased out of bed.

"Adam?" she murmured sleepily.

"Go back to sleep," he whispered, gently stroking her hair. The morning was cool, and he pulled the sheet up around her shoulders.

He quietly dressed—in his plain Amish clothes. He wanted to get rid of them; they were only a reminder to him and to Quinn, but for now he had no choice. He was hungry, and he went downstairs to hunt through the kitchen for something to eat. He found cheese and bread and milk and a pear.

He walked out onto the porch, eating. The sun was just coming up, and the buildings of his father's farm—the silos, the barn, the house, the windmill—were silhouetted in a brilliant orange predawn glow. He could see the mists rising from the fields, and he knew that his father and brothers had already been at work for hours.

You can't go home again, he thought, remembering his walk in the plowed field with Quinn. In this instance, the writer Thomas Wolfe was right. He couldn't go back to the farm—but then, that hadn't been his home for a long time. His home, his true home, was wherever Quinn was. He walked the length of the porch, savoring the morning stillness, hesitating as he felt the give of rotted porch planking at the far end. He trod on it again, and suddenly nothing became more important to him than to fix it. He smiled. Happy or sad, he needed to work, needed the satisfaction of a job well done.

He walked out to the barn to look for something he could use to piece into the rotted places on the porch, but the barn had been stripped clean—there was nothing there except perhaps Quinn's transplanted spider. He walked back to the house. Voices carried in the early-morning air, and in the distance he could hear his father calling his brothers to some task. He stood listening, assessing his feelings about his estrangement at the same time. Nothing had changed. He was sad, yes, but he loved Quinn Tyler.

He went into the house, finding a hammer in the kitchen, and Quinn's car keys.

It had been a long time since he'd driven. That particular sin, that of having acquired a working knowledge of the automobile, no one could blame Quinn for. He'd learned when he'd been too old for school and too young for a salaried job, and he'd become a hired boy for one of the Mennonite farmers across the valley. He had liked driving, and it pleased him that he still remembered how. Quinn's small car was easier than the tractors and trucks he'd used before.

He remembered Quinn's instructions about the lever under the seat to slide it back, and he accomplished that without difficulty. He'd been so stupidly angry that day, angry enough to sit with his legs cramped all the way into town and back again. But he had been more angry at himself than at her, because he'd been squarely faced with the fact of how much he still wanted her. He thought of her now, sleeping, so soft and warm in the big bed upstairs. It he went to her, awakened her, what would she do?

He smiled again. When he came back, he'd find out.

He drove to Holland Wakefield's with minimal difficulty, worrying a bit that some law officer might want to see his driver's license along the way and he'd have to call Quinn to come get him out of jail. How *that* news would fly around the Amish community. *Adam Sauder, one day left—in jail he is the next.*

But no one stopped him, and he found Holland on the brink of leaving for a job in the next county. He tried not to grin as Holland recognized him, then realized that he had arrived in a car—alone.

"Well!" Holland said, clearly dying to ask but trying not to intrude into something that was none of his business. His eyes flicked over the car, and Adam could pinpoint the exact moment of Holland's second realization: this was Quinn Tyler's car. "Well," Holland said again.

Adam forced the grin to subside. "I've come asking for work, Holland. Do you have any carpentry for me?"

But Holland was still puzzling over the Adam-Sauder-in-Quinn-Tyler's-car situation, and Adam wasn't certain his friend had heard him. "Holland?"

"What? Oh! Yeah, Adam. I'm glad you asked. I got— Adam, are you legal in this car?"

"I didn't steal it, Holland."

"I know *that*. But have you got a license?"

"No."

"No? Well." Holland frowned. "Ought to be some way we can work this..."

"Work what?"

"I got a nephew that runs a bed-and-breakfast in Gettysburg. He's got some things he wants done—inside work mostly. If I take you down there, maybe he can put you up till the job's done. Take about ten days, maybe two weeks. You interested in something like that?"

"I need the money, Holland," Adam said simply.

"Well, then, let me see what I can do. I think the nephew'll be glad to get you. Otherwise, it'll be a long time till I can free up another carpenter to do it."

"I need something else, Holland. A favor."

"What is it?" Holland asked.

"An advance on my wage. I need to fix a rotted porch. I need some boards and nails."

"Go on out there in the shop," Holland said without hesitation. "Give me a list later of what you take. Anything else you want?"

"If you could lend me a saw and a square, just for today."

"The shop's full of them. Take what you need."

Holland was clearly puzzling again. "Okay, okay," he said with a sheepish grin. "I want to know what the hell you're doing in Quinn's car, but I ain't going to ask. I'll see you later—after I know what to tell you about going to Gettysburg."

Quinn was still sleeping when Adam returned, and he didn't wake her after all. He'd given her precious little rest during the night, and it was good for her to sleep now.

He rummaged in the trunk of the car, finding a tire tool he could use to pry up rotted boards. It worked almost as well as a crowbar, and the job progressed steadily. He glanced up once to see a car turning into the driveway, a sleek, new model of some kind that was low to the ground and silver in color. The man who got out wore sunglasses and clothes that were, to Adam, somewhat baggy looking—tan pants, a blue-and-white checked shirt, and a white pullover sweater. He thought it odd that each sleeve of the shirt and each sleeve of the sweater were rolled up together in one big roll just below the elbow, which must hinder bending the arms, but he'd seen enough tourists to know that there was no accounting for English modes of dress. They either wore too much, like this man, or nothing, like the girl in the shorts and halter who kept badgering him the day he'd gone into town with Quinn. He grinned to himself. Quinn to the rescue. He'd never been so glad to see anyone in his life.

But this man didn't look like a tourist. He looked like someone from the city. From Philadelphia perhaps.

He came up onto the porch, and Adam thought he was going to ignore him, but then he seemed to think better of it, stopping just short of knocking at the door. He lifted his sunglasses and shoved them to the top of his head. "I'm looking for Quinn Tyler," he said. "This is her place, right?" He eyed Adam warily, as if he couldn't quite decide what his function was here. Was he a hired man or what?

Adam pried up another board. It was too early for any kind of business call, for insurance salesman and the like. "Yes," he said succinctly. "But she's asleep," he added when the man was about to knock on the door.

The man frowned. "And how would you know that?" There was just enough annoyance in his voice to confirm Adam's suspicions.

"I know," Adam said obscurely, prying up yet another board. "Will you hand me that hammer there?"

He passed Adam the hammer. "Look, I'm here because—"

"You love Quinn," Adam finished for him, hammering the nails out of the board he'd just removed. He thought some of it was salvageable, a good three-foot length. He glanced up. The man was clearly taken aback.

"Who the hell are you?"

"Adam Sauder. You're Jake, right? Quinn didn't tell me your last name."

"Oh, she didn't," he said, the annoyance replaced now by the sharp edge of sarcasm.

"But then, I didn't ask," Adam said mildly.

"Look," the man said again, "I came to see Quinn."

"I understand."

"I don't give a damn if you understand or not, Sawyer!"

"Sauder," Adam corrected. "You came to see Quinn because you love her. Probably you still want to marry her. I want to marry her, too. But right now, she's asleep. She'll be awake soon, and you can talk to her then. In the meantime, Jake, do you know anything about porches?"

Quinn woke up shortly after nine, to the sound of hammering, and when she ventured to the head of the stairs, men's voices. She dressed quickly, arriving in the kitchen in time to see Jake Burroughs hammering and to hear his next typically Jake question.

"So how much does land run around here?"

"An acre?" Adam said. "For prime farmland, maybe ten thousand."

"Ten thousand!"

"Maybe more."

"Jeez. You have any idea how much Quinn could get for this place?"

"I wouldn't want to sell it," she interrupted. "Good morning, Jake. What brings you out here?"

He grinned his perfect, all-American, I-can-sell-them-anything grin. "I heard your porch needed fixing."

She laughed. "Among other things. How about some breakfast?" She spoke to Jake, but she was looking at Adam. He gave her a short nod, the best he could do in front of a stranger, and she smiled.

"Breakfast would be good, Quinn," Jake told her. "You know what I like," he added for Adam's benefit.

"Okay," she said, glancing at Adam again. Lord, he was handsome this morning. "Coming up, and it's potluck, Jake. There are no menu selections. Oh, I take it you two have met."

"You might say that," Jake said, going back to hammering.

She cooked what she had—eggs, bacon, toast and coffee, knowing that Adam was accustomed to a great deal more. His usual fare at home would be something like what Edison had described when he went to see the bishop.

But Adam seemed not to mind, eating heartily and keeping up a running conversation with Jake. Quinn said little basking in the quiet smile she saw in Adam's eyes whenever he looked at her. They might have been completely alone.

"I've got blisters on my hands," Jake grumbled at one point.

"Don't worry," Adam told him. "It's what happens when you work hard. You are a good apprentice carpenter, Jake. You should learn more—something for you to do when you get tired of making money."

"I'm not likely to do that, am I, Quinn?"

"I doubt it. So, did you come to tell me my stocks are wiped out or what?"

"No, I came to see why you hung up on me last night."

Quinn glanced at Adam, who abruptly stood up.

"I'll be outside, Quinn," he said, giving Jake a brief nod on the way out.

"Tactful to a fault, isn't he?" Jake said as the back door slammed.

Quinn looked at him across the table. He was an attractive man, dark haired, blue eyed. He was funny and irreverent, fashionable, rich and getting richer. But he wasn't Adam Sauder.

"So is he the one?" Jake asked bluntly.

"The one what?" Quinn said, meeting his eyes head-on.

"The one who went to bed with us every time—"

"Jake!" she interrupted.

"Yeah, I know. I'm being crude. I'm not as gracious as he is. You want to know what's funny? I *like* the son of a bitch. He's had me hauling and hammering boards half the morning, he's had the gall to tell me he wants to marry you, and I *still* like him!"

"I'm glad."

"You're glad," he repeated. "Does that mean you're going to marry him?"

"I . . . want to."

"You want to. He wants to. That sounds pretty definite, except for the look on your face."

"There are problems," she said obscurely.

"You mean his being Old Order Amish—yeah, he told me," he said when she frowned. "He said your mother taught at the Amish school he went to—something about the state being all bent out of shape about their teachers not having a teaching certificate, so his people hired her to meet state requirements."

"How in the world did you get around to that?"

"How the hell do I know? We exchanged life histories, I guess. Rivals like to check up on each other. I make a lot of money; he goes back a long way. Do you know there is nothing you can tell an Old Order Amishman about how you acquired your first Porsche that will impress him? So, how long have you known Quinn, I asked him. 'I've never *not* known Quinn,' he said. Funny you never mentioned him."

"There was no reason to mention him."

"I could probably differ with you on that. I think it's damned likely he's the reason we didn't get married."

"Jake, I don't want to talk about this."

"Well, I do, kid. I'll say this for you: you were honest with me all the way about what you were feeling before, during and after my grand marriage proposal. It's just that I think maybe I could have made you forget about him if you'd let me."

Quinn didn't want to hurt him any more than she already had, but he wasn't giving her much choice. "Jake, it's like Adam said. We go back a long way."

His eyes searched her face. "You know, last night I thought all kinds of things might have happened to you, besides a rainstorm. You didn't sound like yourself, Quinn. At the very least, I thought the ulcer had kicked up again or you'd had some kind of financial crisis. I thought you were too proud to tell me you needed looking after since we weren't...together anymore. So here I come to say I told you so and to save you, and you look better than you've ever looked."

She smiled. "I'm sorry. I feel fine. What can I say, except that I think it's the cabbage juice I've been drinking."

"You could say you're not going to marry him. You could say you'll forget all this rustic stuff you're into and come back to Philadelphia—"

"Jake..."

"Yeah, yeah, I get the picture. I saw the hot looks you two were giving each other over the buttered toast." He sighed. "Well, where does that leave us?"

She shrugged and smiled again. "Friends?" she suggested.

"No, hell, Quinn. I don't want to be your *friend*. I want to be...something sexual," he decided, trying to be flippant. But he couldn't maintain his teasing air. He reached to touch her cheek with his fingertips. "I don't suppose that's all there is between you and Sauder?" he said hopefully. "Something sexual? You know I could wait around if that's all it is."

She took his hand in hers and shook her head no.

He sighed again. "That's what I thought. Well, I'd better get out of here before Sauder has me giving the bride away."

He kissed her gently on the cheek, and Quinn walked outside with him. Adam was still working on the porch, and he didn't look up as they came out.

"I feel responsible for this, you know," Jake said as they stood on the porch steps. "I'm the hotshot consultant who wheeled and dealed your money into enough to buy this place."

"I would have come back anyway," Quinn said, knowing it to be true.

"Yes, you probably would have," Jake admitted. He looked up at the blue sky. "It's nice out here, you know?"

"I know."

"Well, Sauder," he said to Adam, "thanks for the blisters."

"You are welcome for that," Adam said, looking up from his work and giving a slight smile. "It's good to have a chance to learn things. For both of us."

Quinn walked Jake toward the car. "There's only one thing I wonder about," he said.

"What's that?"

He looked into her eyes. "Why you're still so damn unhappy. No, don't explain to me," he said when she would have protested his observation. He nodded toward Adam. "Explain it to him." Then he turned away and got into the car. Quinn stood watching him jerk the expensive sunglasses into place and back the silver Porsche out of the yard. She could hear the whine of the motor long after he'd disappeared from view.

"Is it like he said?" Adam asked from behind her. "Are you so unhappy?"

Quinn looked up at him. "I love you," she said simply.

"Which answers nothing," Adam said. "I can see, Quinn. I can see the same thing Jake Burroughs sees." He turned away and walked back to the porch, setting some nails into a length of the replacement flooring and hammering them into place. "You know what you get with me," he said, not looking at her.

She caught his arm when he was about to hammer another nail in, sliding around so that she was between him and the porch. "Tell me what I get," she challenged him, because she knew he was unsettled by Jake's visit, regardless of his superb handling of the situation, and because she knew that, except for her, he was alone.

"No parties and no purple satin dresses," he said, trying to get around her.

"That's what I *won't* get. Try again."

"Me!" he said angrily. "You get me! And that's all, Quinn. That's all!"

"Good enough!" she said. She was still in his way, and he moved her aside.

"Maybe you'll get tired of me," he said, hammering again.

"Maybe you'll get tired of living English," she countered, swapping worry for worry, if that's what he wanted to do.

"I have no property. No money. No silver car. Maybe you'll be ashamed of me."

"I can't cook and run a house like Lena. Maybe you'll have dirty underwear and starve."

He threw the hammer down. "You know what I think?" he shouted, jabbing the air with his forefinger.

"No! Tell me!" she shouted back.

But he didn't go on. He sighed, his face grave suddenly. "You haven't said you'll marry me, Quinn."

"You haven't really asked, Adam. You've only said what you wanted."

He thought about that for a moment, then nodded. "I keep making the same mistake, don't I? Thinking that I don't have to *say* what needs to be said. So I ask you. Will you marry me? In spite of everything, will you put your life with mine?"

His face was still grave, and she looked into his eyes, his beautiful eyes that made her forget all past and potential pain.

In spite of everything.

She didn't voice her reservations. Adam was waiting, and he was so dear to her. In her mind's eye, she saw him at the different stages of their lives. Adam, the boy. Adam, the man. It was true: the wrong between them couldn't be settled if they were apart. She was still afraid, but she pushed the fear aside.

"Yes," she said evenly. "I'll marry you."

He reached for her, and suddenly it seemed like a very long time since she'd been in his arms. He held her tightly, and she could feel the tension in him.

"I was afraid you'd go with Jake," he said after a moment.

"You heard what I told him last night. I told him I wasn't coming to Philadelphia."

He leaned back to look at her. "Telling the voice is different from telling the man." He reached up to smooth her hair back. "Your face is still sad."

"It's only because—" She stopped. Would they ever get away from it? Sadness. Distrust. The legacy of their youthful passion.

"Go on," he said, his eyes probing hers as they always did.

"I just didn't want you to lose—everything."

He pulled her to him. "Don't you understand by now?" he said fiercely. "*You* are everything. *You*. Even those years when I never saw you, we were together."

Yes, she thought. That was exactly how it was. If they'd never seen each other again, they'd still be together.

He nuzzled her cheek, then gave her a gentle kiss. Then another one at the corner of her mouth. And with a soft moan, his mouth covered hers. His touch was warm, and it scrambled her senses. She closed her eyes, giving herself up to the sensations his touch elicited, to the warmth of his lips and to the warmth of his body against hers, feeling him respond in return. His hands slid over her, one to find her breast, one to press her even closer.

"Quinn," he said, and she opened her eyes. He was smiling, his eyes filled with mischief. "I can't fix the porch now."

She smiled in return. "I'd be very disappointed if you could."

He laughed. "No, that's not what I mean. Well, yes, I mean that, too."

"Make up your mind, Sauder."

"Holland Wakefield's coming," he said to explain his dilemma.

She looked around as Holland's truck pulled into the drive.

"Hello, Holland," she called as he got out of the truck, wondering a bit that he seemed not in the least surprised that he'd just seen her with her arms around Adam Sauder.

"Quinn," he said, tipping his lumber company ball cap. "I see you got back in one piece," he said to Adam.

"Yes," Adam said, and Quinn thought he looked a bit sheepish. He rubbed the side of his nose with one finger, then grinned. "I was out driving," he advised her, trying unsuccessfully to keep the grin under control.

And pretty darn pleased about it, too, she thought. "Driving what?" she asked pointedly. She didn't miss the looks he and Holland exchanged.

The grin broadened. "Your car."

"*My* car?"

"It was the only car I had the keys to," he advised her further.

"Oh. Well, that makes sense. No use stealing one," she said dryly, wondering what else he'd done while she slept.

"How did you think I got the boards for the porch?" he asked reasonably.

"I don't know, but I can tell you I didn't think you drove off someplace in my car to get them," she assured him.

"Aw, he did a good job, Quinn. Didn't jump more than two or three ditches the whole time, and that was just because a constable was after him."

"All right!" Quinn laughed. "Don't tell me any more!"

"Well, son," Holland said, still grinning, "we're okay on the job. My nephew will put you up and feed you. But don't let him work you longer than eight hours unless you want to. I'll pick you up about five or so and take you on down there." He nodded toward the porch. "You might have time to finish the work you're doing there before you go."

"I don't think it'll take me five hours to finish it, Holland."

"No, that's not what I mean, son. I saw your old man in town this morning. He said if I saw you to tell you to come to the farm and get your clothes. I figure you'll want to go see him before you leave. Well, I got to get out of here. Quinn, honey, take care of yourself. And if I was you, I'd hide my car keys."

Quinn smiled a goodbye, but she didn't feel it. Adam went back to work on the porch, and she sat down on the steps close to him, watching him work but saying nothing.

"The job is in Gettysburg," Adam said after a time. "I need the money for our marriage."

She nodded, still watching him closely.

"It's good that it came up, this job," he went on. "It's at one of those tourist places, a bed-and-breakfast. Holland's nephew owns it. He needs some work done on the inside. It'll take about ten days, two weeks, maybe. Will it be too soon for you if we get married the Saturday afternoon two weeks from today?"

"No," she answered. She reached out to touch his arm so that he wouldn't start hammering again. "Tell me what you're feeling."

"About getting married?"

"No, about getting your clothes."

"I've left there, Quinn. It doesn't come as any surprise that Pop wants me to get my belongings."

"Don't patronize me, Adam."

He made an impatient gesture. "Quinn, I don't even know what that means!"

"It means that I want you to say to me, out loud, what you're feeling. Your sins may be your sins, if you insist, but your pain is mine. I don't want you to spare me."

He took a deep breath. "Quinn," he began, but he didn't go on. He came and sat down on the steps with her. "I feel you worrying, Quinn. And yes, I will miss my family. I told you Eli will marry the first Thursday in November. You remember Eli? He was about Daniel's age when you left. He was born too early, and he's always been sickly. But he's going to marry anyway. I admire Eli. I would have liked to be there for his wedding. I'll miss him, and Aaron and my sisters. And my mother. I'll even miss David and Pop. I'll especially miss Daniel. But my missing them takes nothing away from the love I feel for you."

She turned sharply away from him. "Dear God, Adam, I wasn't trying to make you say that. I wasn't trying to force you to give me reassurances."

"Quinn, Quinn, what am I going to do with you?" he said, taking her by the shoulders and making her look at him. "You can't make me say what I don't feel. Are we always going to go around and around like this?"

"I don't know," she said, resting her head on his shoulder.

"Don't make it harder than it is for us," he whispered against her ear.

"Adam—"

"I'm not the first Amishman to leave, Quinn. I won't be the last."

She took a deep breath. "All right," she said, straightening and looking into his eyes. "I'm going to do better. I promise."

He smiled and patted her cheek. "Now I have to ask you a favor."

"What is it?"

"I would like for us to be married in the meadow over there under the trees, where your property joins the farm. So I can invite the family."

"Adam, I don't think they'll come."

"Even so. If it's outside, they won't be breaking the *Ordnung* about entering other churches. And even if I'm being shunned, that doesn't extend to you. I want to ask them, and I want to make it possible for them to be there if they want to. If they don't come, that's their choice. I will understand."

She reached up to touch his face. "All right. I think it's the right thing to do."

He smiled. "Saturday two weeks?"

"Saturday two weeks," she affirmed. "What if the job isn't finished?"

"You don't worry," he said, giving her a bear hug. "It will be finished!" Laughing together, they tumbled back onto the porch. She reached up to touch his face, to run her hands into his hair, her lips parting as she saw the passion in his eyes.

"You make me forget everything," he said, his mouth brushing lightly over hers.

"Do you think this is a good place for this?" she whispered, and he grinned.

"I think if I don't get to work on the porch, I won't care if it's a good place or not." He kissed her soundly and let her up, pulling her to her feet so he could finish the job at hand.

Quinn went into the house, cleaned up the kitchen and worked for a while on Edison's accounting records.

"Adam, take off your clothes!" she called when she heard him come inside. She got up from the computer to find him.

David Sauder stood in the front hallway, his face as rigid as if it had been carved in stone. There was only the red blush on each cheek to tell her he'd heard what she said.

"I was going to wash his clothes for him," she said inanely, as if she could make him believe it, and hating herself for explaining yet unable to stop. "He's coming to see Jacob."

"You don't answer my knock on the door," David said stiffly. "So I came inside. I have brought his things here, where people say he is living now." His eyes flicked over the house. "I don't want to leave them outside and have him say we mistreat him."

"He wouldn't do—"

"You tell him, Quinn Tyler," he interrupted. "You tell him there is no need for him to come to our house. He is not to come on our land again." He pushed the box containing Adam's clothes at her.

"David," she said as he walked toward the door, but he turned on her with such anger that she took a step backward.

"You!" he said, pointing a finger in her direction. "I have nothing to do with a whore like you!"

"What did you say?" Adam said quietly from the kitchen doorway. He took a step closer, and David tried to get by him. "What did you say to her!" Adam demanded, grabbing him by the shirtfront and slamming him against the wall.

The answer was in German, and Adam lashed out at his brother with his fist. But David anticipated the effect his remark would have, and the blow only grazed his head.

"Stop it!" Quinn cried, following them into the kitchen as they dragged each other around. She was still holding the box, and she dropped it as they crashed into the kitchen table. "Stop it!"

Neither of them heard her, and she tried to get between them.

"Adam! Adam, please!" She was holding on to his arm with all her strength, and it gave David the chance he needed. He hit Adam hard, splitting the skin above his eye, and Adam lunged at him, causing them both to fall. He had David down, his fist raised.

"Adam!" Quinn screamed at him. "Don't! My God, don't!"

He looked at her then, and after a moment he let his hand fall, his chest heaving from the exertion, his face bloody. He still had David by the throat, and he seemed dazed, as if he had no idea how all this came to be. He moved away from his brother, sitting in the middle of the floor, his head bowed.

Quinn grabbed a towel and knelt beside him, trying to hold it over the cut.

"Please," she said to David, "just go."

"Adam, I didn't—" he started to say, but he suddenly stopped, going out the back door and letting it bang shut behind him.

"Don't fuss over me, Quinn," Adam said, getting up from the floor.

"Adam, wait. You're bleeding."

He didn't answer her; he went out the back door.

"Adam, where are you going? Adam—"

"I'll be back later," he said without stopping. "I have to settle this once and for all."

Chapter Twelve

Adam saw his father as soon as he entered the yard. The old man was working intently on a buggy wheel in the shade of trees, dragging it off the axle and setting it aside. He was wearing his straw hat and his usual black vest, the sleeves of his shirt rolled up above the elbows. His hands and the front of his trouser legs were greasy from the wheel.

Barefoot and humming to herself, Anna was pushing a hand cultivator through the rows of pepper plants in the vegetable garden nearby, shooing the flies away from her face as she walked. He heard the cultivator fall when she caught sight of him, and his father looked around sharply. Anna was already running for the house, as if Adam were some unclean thing she had to escape.

"Anna!" his father bellowed. "You work the garden! You do not worry the others with this!"

Anna hesitated, torn between having to obey Jacob and wanting to get inside. She turned back to the garden, picked up the cultivator again and pushed it raggedly down the row, casting furtive looks at Adam as she went.

Jacob waited until Adam came closer, his eyes immediately going to Adam's face and his torn shirt. "You come here like this? You let your mother see you like this?" he began, but there was the *Meidung*. He pressed his lips together to silence himself, but evidently there was too much he needed to say. "Come away in here!" he hissed at him. "Do not let your mother see you all bloody. Fighting yet! Who are you fighting with?"

"It doesn't matter," Adam said, following his father into the dark coolness of the barn. "It's not as bad as it looks."

"Did you stand in front of the mirror to decide that before you came? Why are you here, Adam? David took you your belongings. You know I can't talk to you."

"You don't have to talk, Pop. I want to do the talking. I don't want to argue with you. I only want you to listen."

"No!" his father said impatiently. "It's over, the time for talking and listening!"

"Pop," Adam said quietly, trying to hold on to his temper. The memory of Quinn's face at David's insult was still raw in him. He was only too aware that he had never *said* what he was feeling, what he wanted, either to his family or to Quinn. He was going to say it now. "You will hear this. If I have to sit on your chest, I'm going to say it. The only way you can keep me from saying it to you is to call David and the rest of them to throw me off the place. Do you want my mother to see that?"

His father made an impatient gesture with his hand and moved to sit down on a bale of hay near the doorway. He took off his hat and reached into his pocket, pulling out a blue bandanna and wiping his brow and then his hands. "I'm listening," he said finally, but in keeping with the *Meidung*, he said it to no one.

Adam came closer and sat down on another bale. He had both loved and hated this man who was his father, but he had always respected him. Jacob Sauder was strong in the *Unserem Weg*, the Amish way, and he meant for his sons to be strong with him. Now that Adam had Jacob's attention, he didn't know where to start. He had so much he wanted to say, and only this one chance to say it. The day was hot already, and a cool breeze wafted through the barn. The sparrows chirped and quarreled overhead, flitting from their perches along the eaves. He looked at Jacob closely, surprised somehow at how old he seemed today, and he leaned forward with the need to make him finally understand.

"I want to tell you the thing that has been so hard for me, Pop," he began. "Listen to me!" he cried when Jacob was about to get up again. "It's that you and David always behaved as if Quinn was some kind of—of crazy notion I had." He gestured with his hand. "Like wanting fresh strawberries in the dead of winter. That even if she had spent a great part of being a child *here*, she was a stranger to us and not real. You behaved as if you thought she was something I'd get over if I only tried hard enough. Or maybe I'd wake up one morning and what I felt about her would be gone. I did try, Pop, and you know that. It wasn't just for you and the family that I tried, but for myself, because after I knew about the baby, I didn't think anything was possible between us."

He paused, then went on. "But nothing helped. Not the lectures from you and the elders. Not going out to the Ohio relatives. Not trying to make myself think I wanted to marry Sarah. I still cared about Quinn. I always have. Even when we were children, it seemed my life was bound up with hers. I don't believe that will ever change, no matter where I go or what I do or where she is. It was wrong, what we did, having a child together when we couldn't marry. It's a sadness I'll carry all my life. But I don't want to carry the sad-

ness of not being with her, too. I lost my son. I don't want
to lose her.

"I know you think you failed. I know you think you're
not a good father because of me, because I can't do what
I'm *supposed* to do. It's not true. All the things you taught
me, I still have. All the things you made me, I still am. Even
if I'm away from here, I'll still love the land, and I'll still
believe that it's my calling to care for it, to replenish whatever I take. No matter what I do, I'll still try to be fair, I'll
try to behave honorably. And if I fail, it will be my failure,
my weakness, not yours. You need never be ashamed.

"'Be gentle unto all men,' you taught me. From the looks
of me, I need to try hardest of all with that. But, Pop, I believe it. I *believe* that's the way a man should live, with all
my heart, and I thank you for teaching it to me.

"I know you think that I should do my duty. So do I. It's
only on what that duty is that we differ. I believe my duty is
to Quinn. I *am* going to marry her, Pop."

His father moved restlessly on the bale of hay, then stood
up.

"Why can't I make you understand?" Adam cried,
grabbing at his father's arm to keep him from leaving. "I'm
only telling you what you see—what you've seen for the last
eleven years of my life!"

But Jacob held up his hands. "Sit down, Adam. The
place over your eye needs tending. Your face is not so un-
hurt as you think."

"I don't care about my face, Pop!"

"Sit down! Will you do nothing I ask of you?"

Adam bit down on an angry reply. *Were eleven years
nothing?* he wanted to ask, but he didn't. Nor did he sit
down. He stayed where he was, pacing, watching as his father went outside to the watering trough and searched in his
pockets again for the blue bandanna. He wet it from the

trickle of water that ran constantly by gravity from a pipe at the trough, and then he brought it back into the barn.

"Sit down," he said.

"It's nothing," Adam said, reaching up to touch the place that hurt so over his eye. His hand came away bloody.

"Did you think I was not telling you the truth? Sit."

Adam sat down again, and Jacob adjusted his spectacles and found a clean corner of the bandanna. With that, he quietly began to wash the blood from Adam's face. It hurt when his father wiped the place over his eye, and he winced.

"Sit still," Jacob said gruffly. "Even as a little boy, you couldn't sit still."

"Pop, you don't have to do this."

"You are still my son!" he said sharply, and Adam let it go. It was not his place to worry about whether or not Jacob was upholding the strict rules of the *Meidung*.

"I have never known why you are like this, why you decide what you decide and never change it. Adam, Adam, it aches me to see you like this!"

"Don't hate seeing me happy, Pop," Adam said quietly.

Jacob moved away to a small cabinet on the wall, bringing back a jar of the *Zeek Schmer* he kept there. How many times had Jacob done this for him? Adam wondered, soothed his wounds with the homemade salve his mother cooked all day on the kitchen stove and put into baby food jars?

"I didn't say the truth just now," Jacob said. "I do know why you are the way you are. It's because, of all my sons, you are the one I see myself in most. It's a man's vanity to want a son to be like him, but you are the son I will lose because of it."

"I can't be what you want, Pop," Adam began, but Jacob made a hissing noise of protest to stop him.

The old man fumbled at removing the lid on the jar of ointment, and Adam took it away from him, opening it and handing it back again. Jacob gave a quiet sigh and reached into the jar, taking a bit of the salve onto his fingertips. His fingers were gnarled and weatherbeaten from a lifetime of working the land, and Adam closed his eyes as his father gently rubbed the salve into the cut. The camphor and turpentine smell of it rose between them, and with it, the memories of his childhood and all the scraped elbows and cut fingers that had come to him while he worked at Jacob's side.

He had tried hard to learn to become a man, a man who could farm the land as well as Jacob Sauder did, and feed his family, and be firm or be gentle with his children. Strange, Adam thought. He had never considered it, but perhaps it was true. He and his father were alike. He had always understood him, even during their worst arguments about Quinn. Even when Jacob had punished him, he'd never doubted that his father loved him.

He looked into Jacob's face. There were tears gathering at the corners of his father's eyes, and they suddenly brimmed over and slid unheeded down his cheeks and into his beard.

"I haven't failed you, Pop. Not the way you think," Adam began, but he didn't go on. This was the last time they would be father and son together, and they both knew it.

"Pop," he said as his father turned to go. "Pop, I'll be getting married in two weeks, on Saturday afternoon, in the meadow down there by the willows. I would like it if you and the family would come. Quinn doesn't have any family but this one. It would please us both if you could be there."

Jacob stood silently for a moment, but he made no reply. He walked out of the barn to the broken wheel he'd been working on, and he didn't look back.

It's over, Adam thought, staring after him. It's really, finally over.

And he felt nothing. Not happiness, certainly, but not sadness, either, except in a detached way, as if it were all happening to someone else. He wished he could have spared his family the upheaval and the shame, but he had always known that he belonged with Quinn, just as he had always known that it would take his leaving here for them to be together. He looked across the field toward the Tyler place. Quinn was waiting there, thinking the worst, and he had to get back to her. In the end, his father had been right. The time for talking and listening was over.

He saw David as he cut across the backyard. His brother was standing near the grape arbor where Jacob wouldn't see him, waiting for Adam to pass. But Adam wasn't hiding anything ever again. If David wanted to say something to him, he would have to come out into the open to say it.

After a moment of struggling with his conscience, David approached.

"What is it?" Adam asked him. "You want to call *me* names, too?"

"I want to see if you're hurt."

"Quinn is the one who is hurt."

"I didn't meant what I said to her. I—I'm sorry. I want you to tell her that."

"No. You tell her, David. If you want her to know that, you'll have to make the apology yourself. I won't do it for you."

"It hasn't been easy here! I have a lot of responsibilities!"

"And you have a lot of jealousy because I might have married Sarah."

David flushed crimson. They had never spoken of Adam's courtship of Sarah Stolzfus, and he expected David to deny his resentment now.

"You had no reason to say what you did to Quinn," Adam said. "I hate to think that you would hurt her so because you still think you're being stuck with my hand-me-downs."

"You told Pop all about it, I guess."

"No. I didn't tell him. This is between you and me. It has nothing to do with him, except that he didn't bring you up to call any woman, regardless of what you think of her, a whore."

"I told you I didn't mean it!"

"And I told you I'm not the one who needs to hear it!"

Adam walked on, but then he turned back. "David," he called, waiting until his brother looked up at him. "You have a good wife, the one you wanted. And she's married to the man *she* wanted. She's going to have your baby. The two of you will have a happy life together. Don't begrudge me the same chance with Quinn."

When he reached the edge of the field, he heard a chorus of voices in the house calling his name. Anna and Mary.

"Adam!" Anna called again. "Wait for us!"

His two sisters bounded out the door, but there was still the *Meidung*, and they grew embarrassed when they reached him, standing awkwardly.

"We're not afraid to talk to you," Anna finally announced, more for her own benefit than his. She was clearly afraid—they both were—and the fact that they'd come to him anyway made it all the more precious to him.

"I'm glad," he said, not trusting his voice. "I wanted to say goodbye to you."

"Are you going to marry Quinn?" Mary asked.

"Yes."

"You won't ever be back here then?"

"No." He held out his arms and hugged them both soundly. "Go on back inside now. Are Eli and Aaron here?"

"No, they went to help old Mr. Zook with his milking. His hired boy is sick."

"Then will you tell them I'll miss them?"

"I'll tell them," Anna said.

They started for the house, but Mary turned back to him. "Adam, I'm glad you and Quinn are getting married," she said in a rush before she lost her nerve.

"So am I. Go on now."

His mother was coming out the back door, and he walked toward her to save her the exertion of catching up with him. He was about to minimize the cut on his face and the dried blood on his shirt, but she didn't give him the opportunity, meeting him at the end of the stone path and hugging him tightly before he could say anything.

"Don't cry, Mom," was all he could manage.

"I don't cry for your going. You've been gone a long time—ever since Quinn left, all those years ago. I just don't want you to leave with bad feelings between you and David."

"Mom, I don't have any bad feelings. David knows what to do if he wants to make it right between us."

She leaned back to look at him, to satisfy herself that what he said was so. "Look at your face. Come inside, let me fix it."

"No, Mom, Pop's already taken care of it."

If that surprised her, she didn't show it. "Don't forget us, Adam."

"No, Mom. I won't forget."

"And you and Quinn—you be careful out there in the world."

"We'll be careful, Mom. Isn't Daniel here?"

"He's here, but he's afraid to see you, Adam. He's afraid of the shunning."

Adam looked away, out across the fields. Poor Daniel.

"I'll go and talk to him."

"No," his mother said. "Not yet. I'll tell him you wanted to. And I'll tell him that you still love him, no matter what happens."

He nodded, acquiescing to his mother's handling of the situation.

"Don't forget us!" his mother said again, but she didn't wait for him to reply. She managed a wavering smile, then she turned abruptly away, leaving him much the way Jacob had.

He looked back once as he walked on the dirt road between the cornfields, hoping to catch a glimpse of Daniel. He saw no one. He took a shortcut across the stepping stones over the creek instead of going the long way to the bridge. He had but one thought now: Quinn. His fight with David had done nothing to reassure her that he was doing what he wanted to do, and he watched the house anxiously as he approached, half expecting her to be waiting on the porch.

But she wasn't there. He was relieved to see that at least her car was parked where he'd left it.

He could smell something cooking when he reached the backyard, and she met him at the door with a wooden spoon in her hand and flour on her nose. He smiled, and the worried look she was wearing wavered.

"What are you cooking?" he asked as he stepped inside, as if nothing out of the ordinary had happened, as if he weren't standing there with his face cut and swollen and blood all over his shirt.

"Adam!" she said, throwing her arms around him. He lifted her off the floor, leaning back, savoring the feel of her against him. How good it was to hold her! His body responded instantly, and his hands slid over her to press her closer. Once again, he marveled at the miracle of it—Quinn glad to see him, Quinn lifting her mouth to his.

He moved her bodily to one of the kitchen chairs, pulled it out from the table and sat down with her in his lap. She curled against him, and he cradled her close, for in comforting her, he comforted himself.

And what a relief it was to know that, while his anger at David had been painful for her, she had understood.

"Everything's all right," he whispered to her, knowing how much she wanted to ask him and that she wouldn't.

"Is it?"

"Yes."

"Are you sure?"

Her hand clutched the front of his shirt, and he placed his hand over hers. "I'm sure. I'm sorry about what David said to you."

"You didn't fight with David any more, did you? I don't think he meant it."

"No, I didn't fight with David. I talked to Pop. I invited him and the family to the wedding."

She sat up to comment, but he pressed his fingers against her lips.

"We won't worry about whether or not they'll come. I've asked them. That's all I can do."

She gave a heavy sigh and closed her eyes. "I wish—"

He didn't let her go on, pulling her against him and holding her fast. "Don't. Don't, Quinn," he said roughly. "There's no point in wishing."

But she sat up again, reaching up to rest her hands on his shoulders, her eyes searching his face, assessing his injuries up close. "*Zeek Schmer*," she said abruptly, wrinkling her nose, and he smiled a smile he didn't quite feel.

"Pop thinks *Zeek Schmer* cures everything."

"Even wayward sons?" she asked quietly.

"Quinn . . ."

"I'm sorry, I'm sorry. I told you I'd do better, and I will."
She sighed heavily. "Adam," she whispered, leaning against
him again, "we're orphans in the storm, you and I."

"It never storms forever," he whispered back, and she
smiled.

"It can feel like forever. Oh, no!" she cried, jumping off
his lap. "The pie!"

He laughed in spite of the trials of the day. "What pie?"

"The pie I'm burning for your dinner. Corn Pie," she
said as she threw open the oven door. She showed it to him,
only slightly overbaked.

"Looks good," he said, but his mind was already on the
two weeks he was committed to work in Gettysburg.

"What enthusiasm," she commented.

His eyes met and held hers. "I'm not very hungry."

"Neither am I," she said, setting the pie down heavily on
the counter. "I just made it to have something to do while
you were gone. I knew I couldn't help you, and I didn't seem
to be able to add and subtract—well, what the heck. I
probably used sugar instead of salt, or salt instead of flour,
or something."

She still had her back to him, and he got up from the
chair, putting his arms around her and holding her tightly.
He buried his face in her neck, and she reached up to touch
his hair.

"You don't listen to me, do you?" he said. "I told you
everything's all right."

She sighed heavily and turned to him. "I'm afraid," she
said candidly, her eyes searching his.

"Don't be. The worst is done. It's only going to get better now." Did she believe him? He couldn't tell.

"I hope so," she said after a moment. "Do you want to
eat now?"

"No. I want to go to bed with you."

It wasn't the answer she'd expected. It wasn't the answer he'd intended. It was simply the truth. They were orphans in the storm, and he needed her. She said nothing, reaching around him to turn off the oven, and then taking him by the hand.

He followed her lead. Wherever she wanted to go, he would follow. Always.

"You've got flour on your nose," he told her when he kissed her on the stairs.

"You don't look so hot yourself, Sauder," she responded, making him smile. "Don't worry. I'm going to fix us both."

It had never occurred to him that one might make love in a shower, but it was his exquisite pleasure to have her show him the possibilities. To stand naked with her under the steaming hot water, to soap her fine body, to have her do the same for him. Such intimacy with another person. Such pleasure. He could die from such pleasure.

And yet he didn't want to consummate his passion there. He stepped out of the shower, pulling her with him, lifting her up to carry her to the bed. He didn't care that they were both dripping; she didn't care. There was only the need, only the body that ached with desire, only the knowledge that his love for her was returned. With the full force of his passion, he plunged into her, and she responded, met each thrust, until they both lay spent and sated and no longer so alone.

I didn't know, he thought. *I didn't know it could ever be like this.*

What if Quinn had never come back here and he'd spent the rest of his life alone? Before, when they'd been lovers, the physical relationship had been exciting, primed by the danger of it and by the lustiness of youth. It had been like forbidden fruit for them both. But now, when his love for her had been tested by time and by their long separation, there was no comparison. It was beyond anything he'd ever experienced, this oneness of body and mind.

We are the same person, he thought, turning over to look at her.

She was dozing. He stared at her face, at the dark lashes that lay against her pale skin, at the curving lines of her mouth. She was so beautiful to him.

He gave a quiet sigh. He was tired, and he was restless with something he couldn't name. He listened to the wind in the maple trees outside, a warm spring breeze that dried the ground so that a man would work in the fields. A patch of sunlight fell across the bed, dappled sunlight that moved with the wind in the trees.

He drew a deep breath and slowly released it, letting his eyes close. He *could* name the restlessness in him, and there was no use to pretend otherwise. It was caused by the need to know. He leaned forward to kiss Quinn softly on the shoulder. Her skin was still damp from the shower they'd shared, still fragrant from the soap.

He reached up to touch her hair.

Quinn, he wanted to say. *Quinn, where is our son?*

But he didn't, and that was the restlessness in him. He needed so desperately to tell her that they had to find their child, and he was afraid everything with her would end if he did. She had said she didn't know where the boy was, and he'd believed her—except that that had been *before*, when she'd just come back and he'd been so wary and suspicious and he'd tried so hard to pretend that he didn't love her.

He opened his eyes to find her looking at him.

It was still there in her eyes, he thought. The fear he'd seen her first day back.

Why are you afraid, Quinn?

"Your face looks terrible," she said, and he smiled. He smiled, but she knew. He could feel it. She knew there was some wrongness between them, something they both knew existed, and something they both could identify—if they dared.

I'm afraid, too. He wanted to tell her this. But he didn't.

He sat up on the side of the bed. "I have to finish the porch," he said, rummaging through the clean clothes David had brought until he found something to put on. The rest of his everyday clothes he rolled together and stuffed into a duffel bag Quinn had put into the box for him. He felt something between one of the shirts. An envelope. He took it out and opened it. It was his birth certificate, the one his mother had kept in the big Bible on the shelf in the sitting room. He handed it to Quinn.

"I'll need this to get married. Do you think you could bring it up to Gettysburg one afternoon next week? We could go get the license and—" He broke off because of the look on her face. "What is it?" he asked quietly. "Is this too fast for you?" He tried to smile. "I'm not going to have to go tell my father he's uninvited to a wedding, am I?"

She reached for him, and he took her into his arms. She kissed him gently, careful of his injured face. "No, no. I know what I want. I want a life with you. I just—you've been so quiet. I know it's a sad time for you. I just didn't know if you still—"

"I have no regrets, Quinn. Well, one," he said candidly. "Daniel. He wouldn't talk to me today. He's afraid of the *Meidung*."

"He asked me to take you to live with me," Quinn said, and Adam smiled, feeling infinitely better suddenly. Daniel, child or not, was in tune with everything. If he didn't have Jacob's blessing, he had Daniel's.

"When did my little brother do that?"

"When I came to your grandfather's carpentry shop to talk to you. He was very worried. If I couldn't make you stay, then he wanted me to take you with me."

He kissed her softly. "I told him once that I'd known you since before we were his age. I told him you were my friend." He looked into her eyes.

Now. Tell her now you want to find our son.

She hugged him tightly. "That's right! Now. Let me feed you before Holland gets here," she said, getting up.

He let the opportunity slip by. It had hurt her so before when he'd asked. He didn't want to hurt her anymore.

"If you're going to walk around like that, I'm not going to be interested in food *or* Holland."

She smiled at him, looking young and carefree the way he remembered her. "I wish you weren't going."

"I don't want to come to you with nothing, Quinn. The money I make will help us get started."

"I know. It's just that two weeks is a long time."

"Not compared to eleven years," he said, and her smile faded, the specter of their son between them again. She looked as if she were about to say something, but she didn't, pulling a T-shirt on over her head instead.

"Come help me with the porch," he said, because he wanted to be close to her as long as he could.

She was smiling again as her head emerged from the shirt, as if his request pleased her. "Be right there."

He went downstairs, and they worked on the porch nearly an hour, finishing it in time to share the corn pie before Holland came.

This is what he wanted, he told himself. To just *be* with her. To work and to laugh. To feel the love and the warmth and the undercurrent of sexual desire running strong between them. And he told himself that there was no reason to worry.

He took several helpings of the pie, because it was as good as his mother had ever baked, and he told her so.

"She taught me to make it," Quinn said. "One summer when I was always underfoot. Holland's coming."

"Come here then," he said, holding out his arms to her. He kissed her deeply, feeling his need of her as he always did. He lowered his head to press his face against her breasts for a moment, the love he felt for her nearly a physical pain. "Want to come with me?"

"Yes!" she said emphatically, and he laughed.

He gave a resigned sigh. "Saturday afternoon, two weeks, all right? And you'll come to Gettysburg before so we can get the license?"

"My pleasure, Mr. Sauder," she said, smiling up at him.

"I'll call you," he added.

"You will?" she said, as if that possibility hadn't occurred to her.

"It's all right for me to use the telephone now, Quinn," he reminded her. He made himself let her go, swatting her on the behind and walking outside, because Holland was already on the porch. He dreaded this initial encounter with Holland. Quinn had been tactful at best; his face did look awful.

"What the hell happened to you?" Holland demanded on sight, and Adam sighed again. He took the duffel bag he'd forgotten from Quinn's hands, letting his eyes linger on hers for a moment so that she would know the things he couldn't say with Holland watching. He put his hand firmly on Holland's shoulder to steer him away from questioning Quinn and back toward the truck.

"Holland, you've been good all day today about not asking about things that are none of your business. Don't push your luck now."

"Don't push my luck?" Holland asked, grinning.

"That's right. Now get into the truck."

"I'm not to push my luck," he advised Quinn over his shoulder. "I'm to get into the truck. You didn't do this, did you, Quinn?" he asked, pointing to Adam's face. "I was married to a woman one time who was that touchy about who drove her car."

"You want to come to a wedding?" Adam asked him, interceding before she had to answer.

"Whose wedding?" Holland said suspiciously.

"Mine and Quinn's."

"Well, if she did that to you and you still want to marry her, it must be love, is all I got to say."

"Do you want to come to the wedding, or don't you?" Adam repeated, glancing at Quinn and trying not to grin.

"Hell, yes, son. Me and mine'll be there with bells on."

Chapter Thirteen

With bells on, Quinn thought. Unfortunately, it wouldn't be that kind of wedding. She had no family, and Adam's wouldn't come. But she was happy anyway. Almost.

The house was so empty. She had thought it empty before, when she'd first come back, but devoid now of Adam's presence, it was nearly unbearable. On Sunday afternoon she worked on Edison's financial reports—when she could put Adam out of her mind enough to do it—and on Monday she made herself available for the possibility of his telephone call, never straying out of earshot of the phone and breaking up the time by finishing the financial reports and admiring the repair work on the porch. Adam didn't call, but she didn't worry; telephone calls were expensive. She continued to work around the house, eating on time and even napping, all the while with the same thought echoing happily in her mind: *Adam and I are getting married.*

On Tuesday she drove into town to take Edison's reports to him. Her good mood had persisted, and she greeted his receptionist, Margaret, warmly as she entered the office. Perhaps too warmly, she decided; she could feel Margaret making the comparison between this meeting and their last.

She was ushered in immediately to see Edison, and she waited until he was nearly through looking over the files she'd brought before she mentioned anything to him.

"I was wondering if you'd be busy—"

"Want to invite me to a wedding?," he interrupted, trying to keep a straight face.

"What makes you think that?" Quinn asked, trying to give as good as she got. "And how did you know about it anyway?" she asked testily when he grinned. She couldn't surprise him with anything.

"It's out in the Amish community," Edison said. "The proverbial grapevine. Jacob Sauder's Adam is marrying English—you're the English. Saturday, two weeks, I'm told. Ah, three in the afternoon. It's to be an outside wedding out of deference to Adam's family. Oh, and Margaret and I are invited already."

"You are?"

"Mmm," Edison said, thumbing through a few more papers. He looked up at her over his reading glasses. "Unless you object?"

"Oh, no," she assured him. "Do I get to know who invited you?"

"The bridegroom himself. Talked to him this morning. Margaret and I are handling the reception. Close your mouth, Quinn, before a fly flies in."

"You talked to Adam?"

"Honey, now you know when the Amish get married, the bridegroom handles the invitations. This is going to be one bang-up wedding. I'm looking forward to it. Margaret, too.

You got anything in particular in the way of food you want served?''

"What? No," she said, a bit bewildered.

"Good. Margaret and I were hoping you'd just let us run wild."

"Well, don't run too wild. I don't want to have to sell what's left of the farm to pay for a wedding reception."

He grinned. "You won't. It's all taken care of."

"What do you mean it's all taken care of?"

"Never mind what I mean. Now, I've got to get to court. Anything else I can do for you?"

"No, no," Quinn said, still bewildered.

"Good! Go buy your wedding dress or something."

She didn't buy a dress. She went to buy groceries, finding along the way that the wedding guests also included two hardware salesmen, a veterinarian and the entire staff of the Amish Country visitors' center. The latter invitation troubled her a bit; she didn't want to get married surrounded by tour buses.

She came home to find Margaret waiting on the porch— with six ladies from the Mennonite Church who did Pennsylvania Dutch catering as a service project for the church missions fund.

"They want to do the cooking here, Quinn," Margaret explained as Quinn unlocked the back door.

"Margaret, I don't even know how many are coming."

"That's all right. Adam said to plan for about a hundred."

"A hundred!"

"That's what he said. Do you mind if we see what dishes you have?"

"I don't even know a hundred people," Quinn said under her breath. And she knew she didn't have enough dishes.

But she stayed out of the way while Margaret and the Mennonite ladies worked that out. The kitchen was large, and that pleased them—that and the fact that Quinn didn't have much in the way of furniture.

"Plenty of room for the tables," they assured her.

They gave Quinn a menu for her approval: roast chicken with bread, herb-and-giblet stuffing, mashed potatoes with gravy, cold ham, celery in sweet-and-sour sauce, coleslaw, canned peaches, bread and butter, pickles—three kinds— strawberry jam, apple pie, cherry pie, whipped cream, chocolate cake, mints.

"Do you think that will be enough, Quinn?" one of the women asked her in all seriousness.

"Yes," Quinn assured her. Particularly since she'd envisioned ten guests at most. "Margaret," she whispered, taking her aside, "how much is this going to cost?"

"It's already paid for."

"By whom?"

"Your husband to be."

"He doesn't have any money."

"Well, he had enough for this. Anything else, ladies?"

Margaret left with her cooks, and Quinn paced around the kitchen, not seeing the men on the back porch until they knocked. They were not Old Order Amish—she could tell that by their hats—but they were still Amish. Beachy or Church Amish, she thought.

"Yes?"

"This is the house where Adam Sauder will marry Quinn Tyler?" one of them asked.

"Yes," she said, looking around the group.

The speaker took off his hat. "We come to give our gift for the wedding."

"I don't understand."

"We have the glass panes. We will put them in the windows now."

With that, he withdrew, leaving Quinn full of questions with no one to ask.

The telephone rang, and she went to answer it.

"I miss you," a beloved voice said in her ear, and her heart leaped.

"I miss *you* Adam, you won't believe—"

"Quinn, I need you to come to town—now—to the courthouse."

"They're fixing the windows—I didn't get their names—it's a wedding present—the courthouse? What courthouse?"

"This one. I got a ride here. Can you hurry?"

She hurried, remembering to ask the name of each of the men working on the windows so she could tell Adam, and remembering, when she was already backing out of the drive, that she had to have the birth certificates. She hurried back to get them, leaving the motor running and dashing through the yard, nearly bowling over one of the men who picked that moment to step down from the ladder.

"Oh, Mr. Zook, I'm sorry! Did I hurt you? I have to go get the marriage license—no, I have to get the birth certificates so I can go get the marriage license."

"*Snickelfritz!*" he said sternly to admonish her, but then he laughed, and she laughed with him. That was precisely what she felt like—a rowdy little kid.

She hurried as well as she could in a town full of tour buses. Adam was waiting on the courthouse steps, pacing anxiously. She ran the last few steps to him, wanting to throw her arms around him and hug the stuffing out of him, and knowing she couldn't do it. No public displays of affection. It was only officially that Adam was no longer Amish.

He looked so handsome to her. His face looked better, he was still wearing Amish clothes—a blue shirt and black trousers—and he was all business. He had no greeting for her other than a short nod, and he barely looked at her as they went inside. But when he opened the courthouse door for her, he said, "I love you, Quinn." He said it so quietly that no passerby could have heard it, and even she wasn't sure.

Until she looked into his eyes.

No one was ahead of them, and it took only a few minutes to fill out the forms and pay the fee, in spite of the obvious curiosity of the clerk. Clearly, while they might see the Amish come in for a license, they were not accustomed to "mixed marriages." She wanted to take Adam's arm as they walked out together into the bright sunlight, but she refrained. She knew the rules of proper behavior. But Adam's fingertips lightly brushed hers as he gave her the envelope with the license to keep.

"My ride is here," he said, looking over the top of her head. "He's helping me with the carpentry at the B & B. He's a good helper." He reached up as if he were going to touch her cheek, but then didn't. She could feel the warmth of his hand on her face as if he had.

"Can't you stay?" she asked hopefully. "I could take you back."

"No. I have to get some things I need for the job. He won't know what I want."

She gave a soft sigh. He was looking at her mouth.

"Well, I have to go." He walked off a few steps. "Quinn?" he said, turning back to her.

"What?" she murmured, letting his beautiful eyes probe hers. It was torture being this close to him and not being allowed to touch him.

"I can't wait to be your husband."

Her heart soared.

It was only later, when he called from Gettysburg, that she remembered she hadn't asked him about the expected hundred people at their wedding, or how they were going to afford it.

His answer was simple. "I have some money put by. I want to marry you the best I can, Quinn."

She didn't need a hundred wedding guests, but she understood his need to do the best he could. He didn't want anyone thinking that there was anything clandestine or shameful about his "marrying English."

"How's the work going?" she asked him, sensing something in his voice that made her want to get into her car right then and go find him.

"Good. The wife of Holland's nephew bought all the books at an estate sale—a whole library. It's going to take a lot of bookcases for them." He sighed. "The guests at the B & B get in the way. They think I'm part of the tourist attraction, like the battlefield. What do you call it? Living history. It surprises them that I don't know about the two armies and the generals and Pickett's charge."

She waited for him to go on, but he didn't.

"Where are you now? At the B & B?" she asked.

"Burger King."

"Burger King?" she repeated, her voice incredulous enough to make him laugh.

"It's something you don't know about me, Quinn. I have a bad weakness for french fries."

"I knew that about you," she assured him, and he laughed again. But something was wrong. "Adam, what is it?"

"Tell me—" He broke off, and she could hear a car or truck going by.

"Adam?" she said when the silence that followed lengthened.

"Tell me if you love me, Quinn. I need to hear it."

* * *

The wedding gifts continued to arrive, from people who knew her father, from people Adam had done carpentry work for, and perhaps from people who were simply curious to see the woman who had set the Amish community on its ear—twice. Late Friday afternoon she was interrupted at her computer work by the UPS man with a huge box from Philadelphia.

It was from Jake and the staff at the accounting department—a microwave oven and a note saying they'd all be there for the wedding. She kept walking around the box, smiling. Adam. It wasn't only his friends that he'd invited; he'd taken care to invite hers, as well.

Late Saturday afternoon she had a visit from Daniel. She saw him crossing the fields, and she waited until he came up onto the porch, letting him knock loudly because she thought that little boys would probably like to do that—knock on a door loudly.

"Yes?" she said solemnly, as if he were a stranger to her. He looked up at her. "Daniel Sauder," she said, pretending to recognize him, and they both smiled.

"I came to see you, Quinn Tyler," he told her.

"So I see. I'm glad you did. Come in, please." She held the door open wide for him, and only then did she notice that he had something in his hand, something wrapped up in brown paper and tied with string.

"Come into the kitchen," she said, leading the way. "I need somebody to help me eat some chocolate chip cookies and drink some milk."

"I can do that," he said, and she smiled.

He took off his hat and sat down at the table, watching her as she got out the cookies and poured two glasses of milk.

"Adam isn't here," she told him, in case that was the reason he'd come, or if not, in case he was still afraid of the *Meidung*.

He took a bite of cookie. "He's in Gettysburg."

"That's right," Quinn said, eating a cookie of her own. "I forgot about the grapevine."

He sighed. "I don't know about any grapes. This is a good cookie," he advised her.

"I'm glad you like it." She pushed the plate in his direction. "Have another."

He took one, and he handed her the small parcel he was holding.

"What's this?"

"A marriage gift," he said with his mouth full. "Will you unwrap it now?" he asked solemnly.

"Yes, if you don't mind."

"Now I want you to see it. I made it," he told her as she began to pull off the string. "Eli helped me cut it out. And Anna helped me paint. Aaron said it was the wrong thing for a present. But I said you liked them—"

She had the paper off.

"—and you need one."

She held Daniel's gift in her hands. "It's beautiful," she said, swallowing hard. She cleared her throat. "It's—it's the most beautiful thing I've ever seen."

"You like cows, Quinn Tyler, ain't? Cows like this, standing in the flowers."

"Very much." She took a deep breath to steady her voice. "It was so clever of you to make me one, especially when I—" she didn't want Daniel to think he'd made her cry "—need one the way I do."

He looked at her and nodded, then smiled. "One more cookie?"

She returned his smile, thinking how innocent and dear he was. Like Adam had been at his age. Like all Amish children.

"Take all of them," she told him, and his smile broadened into a grin.

"This is a good kind of cookie," he said again, filling both hands. "I have to go now. Will you put my hat on me, Quinn Tyler?"

"My pleasure." She picked up his hat and set it firmly on his head. She opened the door for him, as well. Then she went back to the kitchen table, sat down and picked up the wooden figure of a cow standing knee-deep in flowers.

There was a knock at the door almost immediately.

"Quinn Tyler," Daniel said when she opened the door again. "I forgot this telling." He was still eating cookies, and his mouth was full.

"What telling, Daniel?"

He swallowed hard. "Pop is coming to see you."

Oh, Lord, Quinn thought then and a hundred times a day afterward. And she began to look for him constantly, expecting every sound to herald the arrival of Jacob Sauder. But he didn't come. She had thought that she wouldn't mention it to Adam when he called, but she did. Almost immediately.

"Your father is coming to see me."

Adam said nothing.

"Adam? Did you hear me?"

"I heard you."

"Then *say* something."

"Better you than me?" he offered, teasing her.

"Adam, this is serious! What could he want?" She didn't mean to sound so distressed, but a visit with Jacob Sauder was nothing if not distressing.

"I don't know, Quinn. You'll just have to wait and see."

But Jacob was in no hurry. He waited until the early morning of the day of the wedding, when Quinn was trying to deal with the Mennonite ladies cooking and moving furniture all over the house and with Adam's sudden telephone announcement at the crack of dawn that he wasn't coming from Gettysburg until after noon. Basically, she was ready. She had her dress, a simple pastel-pink cotton dress with a dropped waist and a white lace collar. And she had a minister to perform the ceremony—Edison's brother, whom Adam already knew somehow. And several men had come, apparently at Adam's instruction, to mow the grass in the meadow. And Lord knows, she would have enough food for the reception, even if all hundred people came.

But she wasn't prepared for Jacob Sauder's visit, and she was just beginning to let herself hope that Daniel had been mistaken, or that Jacob had changed his mind, when she saw him come up on the back porch.

Oh, Lord.

She competed with one of the Mennonite women to open the door, but she didn't ask him inside. The kitchen was full of women cooking, and it was her wedding day. She didn't want her feelings hurt if he shared David's attitude toward entering her house. Bracing herself, she went out onto the porch to talk to him.

"Your father was a good neighbor," he said without prelude. "And your mother, when we had our trouble with the school board, was a good teacher in our school and careful of our ways. I have a marriage gift for you if you will accept it."

A marriage gift? Quinn thought, wondering if she'd heard right. Jacob Sauder wanted to give her a marriage gift? She suddenly realized he was waiting.

"Yes, of course," she said quickly, but Jacob had nothing with him. Except the carpenter's helper sitting on the top step, the one Adam had carried when he worked on the kitchen, the one that had belonged to Adam's grandfather. He abruptly bent over to pick it up and thrust it into her hands, as if it had to be done before he changed his mind.

"This gift is for *you*, Quinn Tyler," Jacob admonished her. "You understnad that? Not for anyone else."

"Mine?" she said. She looked down at it. It was heavy with carpenter's tools, and it was all she could do to hold it. She looked up into Jacob's eyes, suddenly understanding. Jacob was trying not to break the rules of the *Meidung*.

She cleared her throat and hoisted the toolbox up a bit to get a better grip on it. "Thank you, Jacob. For *my* gift. This is exactly what I wanted." She stared into his eyes, and she had never been more truthful. She had no use for carpenter's tools—Adam did—but she had great use for the gesture that meant that Jacob Sauder, even if unable to condone Adam's decision, at least understood.

To her surprise, he almost smiled.

"Jacob," she said when he turned to go. "I know Adam asked you to come to the wedding. It's at three this afternoon in the meadow there, close to the willows. If you can't come, it would mean a lot to us both if you could just be close by. You wouldn't have to stand with us if it's too... wrong for you."

He refused to acknowledge her invitation. "You take care of those tools, Quinn Tyler" was all he said. He walked back across the yard toward his own place.

Edison called shortly before nine to tell her that Jake had arrived and that the two of them had some things to do before they came out. She thought the announcement a bit odd, but she had no time to worry about it.

At one, she made a last inspection tour of the house, It needed painting. It needed repairs. But it had a semi-new porch, new windowpanes, and two thriving rows of tomato plants and a four-in-one apple tree, and she was proud of it.

Margaret brought flowers for the living room and pots of red geraniums for the front walk.

"You've been very kind," Quinn told her as she directed the last-minute setting up of tables.

"It's been my pleasure, Quinn," she said. "I know what you're going through. Of course, with me, it was the other way around."

"I don't understand."

"I thought Edison might have told you. I married English."

Quinn looked at her in surprise. She'd had no idea Margaret had been Amish.

"Old Order," she said. "Like Adam."

"Did it work, your English marriage?"

Margaret smiled. "It worked. It wasn't easy, but then, no marriage is."

"You don't regret it, then?" Quinn realized suddenly how desperately she wanted to hear her answer.

"Sometimes," Margaret said candidly. "I don't regret marrying Thomas. Things that are worth having come at a price, Quinn. And he's worth the price I had to pay. But I miss the simplicity of the Amish life. Living close to nature and letting the world take care of itself with no help from me. It was so...easy then. Would it rain or wouldn't it? Would the peach crop be good or wouldn't it? That's all I worried about."

"How did you meet Thomas?"

"Oh, he had a summer job with the vet. The cows got sick. And then I was running our roadside vegetable stand. That boy bought enough tomatoes to kill him."

They both laughed.

"Do you want to know what I really think?" Margaret asked. "From personal experience and from poring over the paperwork on all those divorce cases of Edison's?"

"Tell me."

"I think it doesn't matter how mismatched you are when it comes to money or religion or education or race or age or anything else you can think of—as long as you've got one thing. And it's not love, either. You can be as alike on the surface as two peas in a pod, but if you don't have the same philosophy of life, the love won't last. If you don't feel the same about the way you live in the world, and about the way you deal with the people in it and with each other, it counts for nothing. Thomas and I were kindred spirits. And so are you and Adam."

Quinn thought about this for a moment. "Margaret," she said finally, "thanks." And she didn't mean just for the flowers and the Mennonite ladies.

"You're welcome, Quinn. You've got some time before the wedding. Go on upstairs, take a nap, get ready in peace. I'll man the door and take care of things down here."

"If anybody comes," Quinn said.

"They'll come."

"I don't even have a bridegroom yet."

"Now he, I know, will be here."

Quinn went upstairs, dragging the carpenter's helper with her and stopping on the landing to look at the preparations below. The old house really did look fine, and the aroma of roast chicken and baking bread that wafted upstairs was heavenly.

I'm getting married today! she thought, smiling to herself.

She looked at her watch. She had plenty of time. She took a leisurely shower and laid out her dress, but she didn't put it on. She dried her hair and wrapped herself in her robe and lay down for a moment, not expecting to fall asleep, but she woke up with Adam sitting on the side of the bed.

"Hello," she said sleepily, holding her arms out to him. "I haven't slept through my wedding day, have I?"

He smiled and lay down beside her, pulling her close to him and holding her tightly. "Almost."

"I'm so glad to see you," she whispered as his mouth found hers. His kiss was urgent from their two-week separation, but no more urgent than her response. He tasted so good, felt so good. And the soft sound he made as their lips met made her knees weak and her belly warm. He kissed her eyes and her neck, and when he found the delicate spot behind her ear, she gave a soft sigh of rising desire. His hand slid over her, finding its way inside her robe to a lace-covered breast and squeezing just enough to make her arch toward him.

"I'm glad to see *you*," he said as his mouth nibbled hers.

"Oh, Quinn." He kissed her, hard this time, throwing his leg over hers. She could feel him, his maleness, hard and aroused, against her thigh.

But then he suddenly stopped, pressing his face between her breasts, his breathing heavy and ragged. "I have to stop," he said. "Or I won't be able to."

She ran her fingers into his hair, loving the crisp, clean feel of it. "I don't want you to stop."

He lifted his head to look at her, smiling broadly. "I'm not delaying our wedding for anything. Not even this." He sat up, pulling her up with him.

"Hurry. It's almost time. Let me help you get dressed."

She was ready except for putting on her dress, and she let him bring it to her, slip it on over her head and pull it down over her hips.

"You look beautiful."

"So do you," she suddenly realized. "Where have you been?" He was wearing "English" clothes—dress pants, a blue shirt and a maroon tie. He'd even had a haircut—no, more than simply a haircut. His hair was layered, styled, perfect for him, a haircut that didn't look like a haircut.

She'd always thought him handsome. Now, incredibly, he was even more so.

"Everywhere. Jake and Edison took charge," he said, smiling again, obviously pleased that she approved. "I didn't want you to be ashamed of me."

She reached for him and hugged him hard. "Don't say that!" She leaned back to look into his eyes. "Don't ever say that."

"This is your last chance to change your mind," he reminded her.

"Yours, too."

"I married you a long time ago, Quinn."

She went into his arms again, feeling his strength and his love. She'd always felt married to him, too. Today was merely the formality.

"I want you to see something," she said, pointing to the place by the windows where the carpenter's helper sat.

He walked over to it, reaching out to touch the top of the handle. "This is mine," he said, looking back at her.

"No, actually it's mine. Jacob brought it this morning. He was very stern, except once when he almost smiled, and he was very definite. All those tools are for me."

"And what did you say?"

"I said they were just what I wanted."

Adam smiled, and he reached out to touch the carpenter's helper again. "They're all here, and a few more besides. Everything I need to make a living for us. I can't believe he did it."

"And Daniel brought a gift."

"Daniel? Let me see." He was obviously pleased, and Quinn had a brief qualm about showing it to him. It would surely call to mind what had happened to the other wooden figure, and she wanted nothing to spoil their wedding day. But she went to the dresser to get it, bringing it lovingly back to him. She watched as Adam inspected it closely, turning it over and over in his hands. He looked up at her. "He did a good job, didn't he?" He looked down at the cow again and took a deep breath. "They're doing the best they can, Quinn. I don't ask any more than that. Well," he said, looking up at her. "Are you ready?"

"Ready," she assured him.

He put Daniel's cow carefully on the dresser again and kissed her one last time. He took her hand as they went down the stairs, and the few people who remained in the house gave them a round of applause as they appeared. There were faces she recognized, and faces she didn't, but they all wished her and Adam well. She glanced around for Jake, but she didn't see him anywhere.

Edison came out of the kitchen eating a pickle. "Boy, these are good. Adam, you want one?"

"No, I'd rather get married," Adam said, making the onlookers laugh.

"Well, we got that covered, too. Quinn, honey, you are a beautiful bride!" He kissed her on the cheek and hugged her soundly. "My brother, the Reverend, is around here some-place. Ah, there he is!"

"Quinn, Adam, the hour is at hand," the Reverend Clark announced. To Quinn's mind, he was a tall, skinny version of Edison—comfortable and kindly and ready to get this show on the road. Still clinging to Adam's hand, Quinn let Edison lead the way. She caught his eye as they stepped out onto the front porch, and he smiled reassuringly. If he knew anything about whether Jacob and the rest of the Sauders would attend, it didn't show.

Please, she thought as he followed Edison down the porch steps and began the walk toward the meadow. *Please.*

The day was hot and hazy, with blue-tinged clouds that promised a thunderstorm by evening. A slight breeze rustled the leaves and the loose folds of Quinn's pink dress.

Adam squeezed her hand as they walked, and she looked up at him.

"They may not be here, Quinn. Stop worrying," he said.

"I'm not worrying."

"Yes, you are."

"Yes, I am," she agreed, and he laughed.

"Are you happy with this?"

"Very happy with it," she answered, knowing he meant the numerous guests who sat in the shade in kitchen and folding yard chairs ahead of them, and the array of food being prepared in the kitchen. Margaret had been out here, too, with her pots of flowers, more huge red and pink and white geraniums.

"It was the only gift I could think of to give you—a good wedding."

She smiled up at him. "It's wonderful, Adam."

"Wait here," Edison said when they reached the edge of the meadow. "Brother is going to stand up there with the flowers, then he'll nod at you, and you walk up there to him. Got it?"

"I think we can handle that," Adam said.

"I don't know," Edison said. "I've seen couples so nervous they couldn't handle the time of day. I don't take any chances. Besides which, if we don't do it right, Margaret will kill me."

Quinn smiled, but she was looking over the guests. Holland Wakefield and the wife who didn't mind his driving her car were there, and some Amish from the more liberal sects. But not the Old Order Sauders. She could see Jake and three of her former co-workers sitting in the third row of mismatched chairs. All of them waved. Quinn gave them a discreet wave in return, but her mind was elsewhere.

"It's not going to ruin the day if Pop doesn't come, Quinn," Adam said quietly. "It's their loss if they stay away."

She nodded her agreement. She did agree, but, oh, she hurt for him.

The Reverend Clark had reached the array of potted geraniums, and he turned to face the guests. He nodded to Quinn and Adam, then raised both hands for the congregation to stand. Adam tucked her hand into the bend of his elbow, and together they walked forward.

They walked slowly, Adam sometimes stopping to shake someone's hand. Quinn felt surrounded by the good wishes of the people who had come. Jake winked as she passed, and Mr. Zook, who had helped replace the windowpanes, and his wife, were there with their brood of towheaded children of assorted size and gender sitting on the grass at their feet. Three girls, five boys, Quinn counted. He, too, shook Adam's hand.

When they reached the Reverend Clark, he smiled, then indicated that the guests were to be seated.

"We are gathered here today," he began, speaking comfortably to the guests without a book or written notes, "to share with Adam and Quinn the occasion of their marriage. We offer them now, as signified by our presence, our friendship and our support as we witness their pledge, before God, of their love and their commitment to each other." He paused as a calico cat and her kittens strolled into the assembly.

"Daniel's," Adam whispered, smiling. The cat rubbed against his legs, then moved on.

"Now if the two of you will join right hands. Adam, do you—"

The Reverend broke off again, and Quinn looked around. The murmuring among the guests was too insistent to be caused by a mother cat.

Coming quietly through the cornfield behind them she could see the tall form of Jacob Sauder. Lena followed, holding Daniel's hand. And then Aaron and Eli, and Anna and Mary. And finally, David and Sarah. Edison was already producing chairs for them, making another front row, and Quinn clung to Adam's hand. She stood dazed, feeling the tears sting the back of her eyes. They'd come. They'd really come!

"No crying," Adam whispered, and she struggled hard to contain it, giving him a tremulous smile.

"Adam Sauder," the Reverend Clark began again when everyone was seated. "Do you take Quinn Tyler to be your wedded wife?"

"I do," Adam said, looking into Quinn's eyes, his voice strong. She looked so beautiful to him, and he was so proud to be standing with her at his side.

"Do you promise her, before God and this gathering of family and friends, that you will never depart from her, that you will care for her and cherish her, in sickness and in health, in good times and in bad, and that you will be her good and constant friend and her husband until God will again separate you from each other?"

I love you, Quinn.

"I do."

"And Quinn Tyler. Do you take Adam Sauder to be your wedded husband . . ."

She continued to look deeply into Adam's eyes as she answered, letting nothing come between them. They might well have been alone as she made the same promises to him.

My good and constant friend and my husband, she thought. That was precisely what he was. *Adam, I love you. I love you with all my heart.*

"May God be with you and help you together through all your days. I now pronounce you husband and wife."

There was a soft sigh among the guests and yet another round of applause, led this time by Holland Wakefield. Quinn smiled up at Adam, knowing that kissing the bride was inappropriate for him but seeing the desire to do so burning in his eyes. Together, they turned to face the wedding guests, both of them beaming. They were immediately surrounded with congratulatory hugs and kisses and handshakes.

"Speak to my family, Quinn," Adam whispered urgently into her ear. "Tell them they must stay for the wedding dinner. Tell them I'll respect the *Meidung*—they won't be asked to sit down at the same table with me, and I won't speak to them."

Quinn made her way through the crowd to the Sauders, intercepting them as they were about to go.

"Jacob," she called, wanting to catch him by the sleeve to keep him from leaving but not daring to do so. He waited, but his impatience with whatever she might say was already clearly visible. She plunged on anyway, feeling David's eyes on her. "Jacob, you—all of you—are the only family I have." She looked quickly at each of them. "You've been very kind to Adam and me today, but I want to ask even more of you. I ask you to stay for the wedding dinner. Adam says he will respect the *Meidung*—you need have no worry on that account. Please, Jacob," she said, glancing again at Lena. Lena said nothing, but both women looked toward Jacob, waiting. He glanced at his wife and then back at Quinn.

He made a small noise of exasperation. "I trust Adam to keep his word in this. To respect that we are bound by the *Meidung*. And I can't fight *two* pairs of eyes. We will stay."

"Thank you, Jacob."

"Quinn! Quinn!" Daniel said, catching her by the hand. She bent down so that he could whisper into her ear.

"I thought you'd wear the shiny purple dress, Quinn," he told her, obviously disappointed.

"Don't you remember? It's for parties."

He gave a sigh of exasperation, and she ruffled his hair.

"Be sure to eat everything you want," she whispered.

"Can I look for the spider?"

"If you leave him out there where he belongs." She laughed. "Daniel," she called when he was about to dash off. She bent down again to speak to him. "Adam says you did a wonderful job making the cow."

He gave her a shy smile that reminded her of Adam.

She walked back to Adam's side, collaring Edison on the way. "You have to be my substitute father," she whispered to him. "You have to seat the Sauders at the table and not break the *Meidung.*"

"You got it. Damn, Quinn." He glanced in Jacob's direction. "He's a tough old bird. I never thought you'd get him this far."

Neither did I, Quinn thought.

"They're staying," Quinn said quietly to Adam, and she could feel his relief. Together they walked to the house. He held out his arm for her to take, pressing her hand firmly but discreetly against his side. She could feel his warmth through his shirt, and the memory of his hard, muscular body—without the shirt—immediately came to mind.

She looked up at him, and he grinned.

"Better not look at me like that, Mrs. Sauder, or we won't get through this dinner."

She chuckled. "I don't think the Mennonite ladies would let us *not* eat, after they've cooked all morning. But what did you have in mind?"

"You'll see."

"Oh, good," she whispered, and he pressed her hand more firmly against his side.

Tables had been set up in a U shape in the living room, Amish fashion, with the far corner, the *Eck,* reserved for the bride and groom, where they could see and be seen by everyone who came in. There were more tables in the kitchen and one in the front hall. Quinn could see Edison respectfully seating the Sauders there. It struck her how well

Adam had planned this wedding for her, as if he were taking the best of the Amish version of the ceremony and giving it to her. She looked up and down the tables. There were candy dishes and small glass plates and pitchers and goblets, all filled with sweets or mints, and all meant to be served to the guests and the containers kept as gifts for her and Adam. There was even a kerosene lamp, tied with a pink ribbon, the chimney filled with M & M chocolates. And so many cakes! She leaned forward to read one of the fancily decorated ones: *Best Wishes Adam and Quinn*.

"David is coming to speak to you," Adam said to her as they took their places in the corner. She looked at him in alarm. Adam nodded in the direction of the hallway, and David was indeed making his way through the crowd of people who were trying to find seating.

"Quinn—" *Tyler*, David almost said when he reached her. "Quinn," he said, starting again. "I should not have said the rude things I said to you. I ask you to forgive my angry words." He glanced at Adam, and he seemed unaware of the people around them who were overtly listening.

"I've known you since we were children, David. You're Adam's brother. I don't want there to be any bad feelings between us."

He nodded and then, almost as an afterthought, offered her his hand. She shook it firmly and she thought for a moment he was going to speak to Adam in spite of the *Meidung*. But he turned away, going back to his place at the table in the hall.

She looked at Adam, who was watching his brother's retreating back.

"Did you ask him to do that?" she said.

He shook his head. "He apologized to me. I only told him I wasn't the one who needed his apology."

She reached out to touch his hand, and the wedding dinner proceeded flawlessly, thanks to the skill of the Mennonite ladies and those of Adam's friends who volunteered to keep the dishes washed and the places set as the guests waited their turns at the tables. The food lived up to its delicious aroma, and Quinn found it wonderful to be able to sit with Adam amid all the laughter and celebration.

Jake was in the second group of guests to be fed, and he made a point of coming to say goodbye and shaking Adam's hand. "Quinn," he said, turning to her. "Be happy."

"I will, Jake. Thank you for coming."

He suddenly bent across the table and gave her a quick kiss on the forehead. "And you treat her right," he admonished Adam.

"You don't have to worry about that, Jake," Adam said.

Jake gave an uncharacteristically awkward shrug and a lopsided grin. "Well, Philadelphia awaits." Then he turned and left, managing to saunter out with an attitude that was pure devil-may-care Jake Burroughs.

"He's a good man," Adam said as he watched him go.

"He said the same about you." She looked into his eyes and smiled.

"Come on," he said, standing and pulling her up with him. "Let's see if we can't make these people eat faster."

They moved among the guests, visiting together and separately, but always aware of the other's whereabouts. The Sauders ate and left quietly, with Lena turning back at the last moment to give Quinn a quick, tearful hug.

"You be happy, you and Adam," she whispered fiercely. For Adam, she had only a brave, long look. She had defied the *Meidung* in speaking to him before. She wouldn't do it again.

More people and more food and more visiting followed, until abruptly, when it was well after sundown, the wedding celebration was over. Everything was as it was before, the big tables gone, the furniture back in place. The only difference was that Quinn was no longer alone—not in this house she'd been born in, or in her life. She was pleasantly tired, and she could feel Adam's eyes on her as she moved about the kitchen.

But there was nothing more to do to it, and, when she turned to him, he was waiting.

"My wife," he whispered, sliding his arms around her and burying his face in her neck. "My wife."

She leaned back to look at him, and he kissed her gently on each eyelid, then her forehead, then her cheeks. And when his mouth sought hers, her lips parted, giving access to his sweetly probing tongue.

Her hands slid into his hair, and she pressed her body against his. *Adam.*

He broke away, needing to see her eyes, needing to see if the fear was still there.

It was.

"Quinn," he said desperately, lifting her up off the floor. He carried her upstairs and into the bedroom—their bedroom now—laying her gently in the middle of the bed. He stood up to take off his clothes, the still-strange English clothes he'd bought with Jake Burroughs's help today.

Quinn lay quietly, watching him as he knelt on the side of the bed and reached for the buttons on her dress. His fingers were trembling, and she helped him undo the row, helping him pull the dress up over her head.

He tossed it carelessly aside. His fingers caressed her smooth, warm skin and slid under the straps of her bra to bring them off her shoulders. He found the clasp—he was no longer bewildered by such fastenings—and when her breasts spilled forth from their lacy confinement, he thought he might die from the sheer pleasure of seeing her. She was so beautiful! It seemed to him that he always forgot just how incredibly beautiful she was.

He bent his head to take a taut nipple into his mouth, first one and then the other, loving the soft sounds she made as he teased her with his warm breath, then tasted her, then teased again with lips and teeth.

His suckling, sometimes gentle, sometimes not, made her whimper with desire. Her hands moved over him, as if she were savoring the feel of his body.

He moved away from her long enough to discard his briefs, coming back to her to take away her silk panties. His hands stroked the length of the silk stockings she wore, then his fingers hooked in the tops to free them of their garters and slide them down.

"Beautiful," he murmured in appreciation, giving each stocking a careless sling, and she smiled, not knowing if he meant her or the silk. He kissed her thighs, her belly, and all the while his hands knowingly caressed and caressed.

She could feel it, the love in his touch, love that had lasted all this time, love for her.

And then he was lying on top of her, his body covering hers. She reveled in the feel of him, of his weight pressing her down, of his maleness, hard and aroused between them, of the warm strength of his arms sliding over her as he reached up to cradle her face in his hands.

"I love you, Quinn," he whispered, his eyes holding hers.

"I love you," she answered without hesitation. "I've always loved you. I always will."

He shifted his position so that he could come inside her. Her eyes fluttered in response to the pleasure he elicited when he gently pushed forward.

"Look at me," he whispered urgently, and she opened her eyes. He thrust deeper. "Why are you so afraid, Quinn?" And deeper still. "*Why*, Quinn—oh!"

She heard the question clearly, but she was beyond answering. He filled her completely, and he felt so good, so good! She loved him past all reason. He was her husband,

and tonight she wanted him to give her another child—not one to take the place of the boy they had lost, but because they had loved each other so long, a child would make that love complete.

I'm not afraid, she meant to tell him, but even in her need of him at that moment, she knew it wasn't true. The knowing made her cling to him all the harder. She needed something of him, to have and to keep no matter what. She loved him. And he had to feel that love. Now. Now!

If he knows how much I love him, he'll understand.

But logic born of passion and need was not logic at all. Coherence fled from her grasp, leaving nothing but exquisite pleasure.

They lay together, arms and legs entwined, the lamp still softly burning. The evening thunderstorm Quinn expected had arrived, and she watched the flashes of lightning from time to time. She listened to the distant roll of the thunder and to the pattering of the rain against the windows. And she listened to the steady beating of Adam's heart.

He wasn't asleep. She could feel his wakefulness as if it were a tangible, living thing in the room with them. And still she said nothing.

"It's not just you who is afraid," he said after a long time.

She didn't answer him, and he gave a sharp sigh.

"This, Quinn, is where you say, 'What are you afraid of, Adam?' Then I'd tell you I'm afraid of whatever it is in your eyes that makes you always look at me the way you do. I'd tell you that I was afraid enough *not* to ask you anything else about it until we were married, because, whatever it is, I think it can tear us apart."

She abruptly sat up, and he grabbed her to keep her from getting out of bed.

"Quinn! Now. You have to tell me now."

He had a firm grasp on her wrist, and she stared back at him, finally reaching up to touch his face.

My good and constant friend.

She could tell him this. She had to tell him this. She took a deep breath. "All right," she said quietly. "I'm afraid that you want to find our son, especially now that we're married." She could tell from the look in his eyes that that was exactly what he had been hoping.

"And?" he prompted when she didn't go on.

"And we can't do that."

"Why not? There's always a chance we—"

"There's no chance, Adam."

She moved away from him, and this time he let her go. But she was trapped again. She had no place to go. She knew from bitter experience that being apart from him—even eleven years apart—was no solution. Still, if she was going to have to do this, she wasn't going to look into his eyes.

She stood up, switching the lamp off and plunging them into darkness. She moved to the window, feeling a rain-damp breeze on her skin as the curtains billowed outward. She stood naked for a moment, with her back to him, but then she fumbled on the foot of the bed for her robe, slinging it on and going back to the window. She stood looking out at nothing, her hands clasped together so that she wouldn't wring them like some distraught heroine in a silent movie.

"Quinn," Adam said. "Will you come here?" He held out his hand to her, but she didn't go.

"Is that why you wanted the marriage?" she asked him quietly. "So you could find your son?"

She turned around to face him, his features a blur in the dark.

"No," he said pointedly. "I wanted to get married because I love you. And you know it."

"Well, love me or not, we can't have our child."

He sat up on the side of the bed. "Why not?"

She stared at him.

"Answer me!" he shouted.

"I told you before. It's done. It can't be undone."

"You don't want to even try," he said. It was more an accusation than a question. "You don't want him."

"Yes, I want him! Every day of my life I want him! I want him more than anything on this earth! But it can't happen."

"Quinn—Quinn, maybe we can find him.

"No. We can't. I didn't loan him out, Adam. It's legal. It's permanent. He's been with his family for ten years."

But he wasn't listening to her. He had worked it all out in his mind, and he wasn't listening. He was Amish still; he was a loving, caring man. His son unaccounted for was more than he could bear. He wouldn't bear it. She knew that.

"I think we can get the information we need from Edison," he said.

"I don't have to get the information from Edison."

"Why not?" he persisted.

She took a deep, ragged breath. *This is where you undo it all.*

"Because I know where he is."

The room was deadly quiet, suspended in the silence of his incredulity. She was glad that she couldn't see his face. Crazily, she was aware of the sounds around her, of the rhythm of his breathing and the soft whisper of rain.

"You know," he repeated dully. "And when were you going to tell me, Quinn?"

She said nothing. She wanted to back away, not from him, but from the pain she had given him. She forced herself to stand still.

"I don't think I was," she said finally, realizing suddenly that it was true.

"Why not?"

She shook her head. "I don't know. Because it hurts too much. Because it was so...final. I was afraid—" She closed her eyes for a moment. "I didn't want to hurt you."

"And what is this now? Do you think I'm not hurt? It doesn't hurt me to have you lie to me, to have you not want us to be a family if we can? Quinn, sometimes children are returned to their real parents. Even I know that."

"Not this time!"

"Because you don't want it?"

"Because we have no choice."

He stood up from the edge of the bed, angrily looking for his pants and jerking them on. He was a million miles away from her.

"Adam," she said, and he turned his head to look at her.

"I don't believe you, Quinn. I don't believe there's no chance. And I don't understand why don't you want him. What if he needs us? What if he's mistreated?"

"He isn't mistreated, Adam."

"You can't know that. All this time you knew where he was. You had a good job in Philadelphia. You made a lot of money. How could you *not* try to get him back when you were able to take care of him? Why didn't you get him, Quinn?"

Because of you! she almost said. *Because of you!* She had only wanted him to be happy, both he and their son, and not by chance, but by design. *Her* design.

She suddenly couldn't bear any more. She walked toward the door, and he swiftly crossed the room, taking her by both arms before she reached it. "This is your house. If anyone will go, it will be me. Why are you afraid to talk to me about this?" He made her look at him.

"I told you—"

"It's what you *don't* tell me that's the problem between us! Is something wrong with him? Is he dead?"

"No, Adam, no—" She faltered.

"Tell me! Do I have to get on my knees?"

But he didn't wait to hear. He was angry with her, but not angry enough to take away his fear of knowing, his fear that it was all coming undone around him. He had to think, and he had to get away from her to do it. He slammed past her out the door.

"Adam!" she called after him, but she didn't follow. "Adam."

Dear God.

She kept expecting to hear a door slam downstairs, but there was nothing. She had to talk to him. Now. They had gone too far to just leave it.

She went down the stairs in the dark. He was sitting at the bottom of them. She stood for a moment, unsure of what to do, then she sat down beside him. His arms were resting on his knees, his head bowed, and he looked up at her.

She wiped furiously at her eyes. She was going to tell him and be done with it. And she wouldn't begin with how alone and afraid she'd been then; that had been only a part of it. That he already knew, or could guess.

She took a deep breath, trying to keep her voice steady. "When I decided to... let the baby be adopted, Edison found people for me, people who wanted a child, but none of them seemed right. I had to be sure, Adam. I had to know he'd have a good life. I wasn't getting anywhere. I kept sending Edison back to them with more and more questions. But the more questions I asked, the more dissatisfied I became. The more they told me, the less I knew.

"And then he brought me the information on one last couple. The man was thirty. The woman was twenty-six. She wrote me a letter—I still have it. There was no chance that they could have a child of their own, ever. I knew if I chose this couple, I could do something for our son that couldn't be done any other way, something you and I couldn't do for him, even if we'd married. And I could be sure that he'd be all right."

And you would be safe, too.

She didn't say that. He hadn't been safe. He'd said it himself: he'd been in hell.

"I gave our baby to them. Knowing that he's with that couple is what's gotten me through all the years since. I haven't interfered in his life—we can't interfere now—because it would be too cruel. He's happy, Adam."

"Quinn, you can't know that."

"I do know it. I know firsthand what his life is like, and so do you. We don't ever have to worry that he isn't someone special in his parents' lives. Adam . . . he's Amish."

She waited, wanting so badly to reach for him, to at least touch his hand. But she didn't, and she knew the exact moment when he realized the full impact of what she had told him. Their son was lost to them forever, even more so than if she had put him out among the "English." If they truly loved him, they could never know him, and no one knew that any better than they. Their son was being brought up Amish, and he would be well loved, and he would be innocent. He would know nothing of "worldly" things. How could a little Amish boy be told that his mother was not his mother, and that his real mother was "English"? Or that his real father, even for the best of reasons, had been excommunicated from the Amish faith?

Adam stared at her; she could feel his eyes in the darkness, feel the question he didn't ask.

"I knew what I was doing," she said quietly, and he believed her. She was another part of himself, and he understood immediately. Eleven years ago she had deliberately removed all hope, all temptation, of their ever being a family, not just because she was alone and without money, but for him.

Why didn't you ask me, Quinn? he wanted to cry out, but he said nothing. He already knew the answer: *What she had done, she had done for me.* The only thing she could salvage in all of it had been his Amishness. She knew he never would have stayed away from her if she'd kept their child, and she had put their son in the very best place she could.

He took a ragged breath. "How—?" he began, but his voice broke.

"Edison must have realized what it would take to set my mind at rest. He went to the bishops. He knew about us, and he told them about the baby. The baby was your child, too, already Amish enough for them not to want to let him go to anyone else. So they had a lot of meetings. I don't know if they bent the rules or not, but they gave Edison the name of the couple who had no children. They told him they would approve the adoption if I agreed."

"The boy's...here."

"In the state, yes. But not here. I couldn't bear that, and I didn't think you would be able to if you knew. I said I knew where he was. I know he's in the state, but I don't know which community. I don't know his last name. I'm...afraid to know those things. Sometimes his mother still writes me letters. She sends them to Edison. She's...very kind. She understands that I—" She swallowed, then swallowed again to keep from crying. "She tells me what he's like, what he can do now. He's in the fifth grade, and he likes animals. All kinds. And he likes to grow things. He's had his own garden since he was eight. He likes cookies, and he doesn't like math. I think he must be very much like Daniel."

She was crying openly now, and she got up, turning abruptly and going back upstairs. Adam let her go, when there was nothing he wanted but to keep her near.

But his mind was reeling. His son was Amish! How incredible it seemed to him, and yet how logical somehow that

Quinn would have done this thing. He had always worried about the harm that might come to the boy out in the world, just as he had worried about Quinn when she was in Philadelphia. He had been taught to be wary, and he couldn't change that part of his upbringing. But their son, for all intents and purposes, was safe.

Adam had known that the boy was likely beyond their reach. He was not so naive as to think that he and Quinn could undo the "English" adoption laws without good reason. But he had never been able to put aside the fear that there might *be* a good reason if their son was living somewhere among those rude people who intruded constantly in their tour buses.

He thought suddenly of his father, of how heavy Jacob's hand must have been in all this, and yet he felt no bitterness. Jacob was Jacob, the true believer, and both he and Jacob Sauder would know the painful absence of their first sons. But he knew, too, how much kindlier Jacob would think of Quinn once he knew that it was *she* who had contributed to the all-important Amish cycle of 'keeping the faith,' generation unto generation. Regardless of the *Meidung*, he would tell him. And if Quinn felt the need of Jacob and Lena's forgiveness, then she would have it, without reservation.

He got up from the bottom step and climbed the stairs slowly. Quinn was sitting in the dark by the front windows, staring out toward the Sauder house. She looked around sharply as he came into the room, and it was still there between them, her fear of his finally knowing what had happened to their son.

But Quinn was strong, and he could feel her bracing herself for this final confrontation. She said nothing as he came nearer.

"You will have to trust me more than this," he said quietly, and he heard her soft, ragged intake of breath. "You will have to trust me to know how you feel . . . how you felt then. Can you do that?"

"I think it's too much—" she began, her voice quavering.

"Don't!" he said sharply. "Don't do it again, Quinn. Don't decide for me. I understand, Quinn. Did you think that I couldn't?"

"I thought—knew—you'd have to go through the same things I went through to accept that we can't see him—not now, not ever. If I'd let him go to an English family, when he was old enough, maybe he could have been told about us, but I—"

She suddenly bowed her head, and he was acutely aware of her sadness, of her sense of aloneness, of all the things he himself had felt so many times in the past. He reached out to gently stroke her hair, then touched the side of her face, feeling the dampness of her tears.

"I'm so sorry, Quinn," he whispered. "I'm so sorry!"

She looked up at him. "No, no, there's nothing for you to be sorry about. I love you, Adam."

And *he* loved *her*. They still had that, their love for each other. It was alive and strong, but it would need great care if it was to survive this. He reached for her then, overcoming her brief resistance, her disbelief that he would want her close. "Put your arms around me," he said. "No one can comfort me but you."

She held him fiercely, and he took a deep breath. It was so hard, hard for them both, not to have regrets.

But regrets were useless. He and Quinn had come through a long and unhappy time, but they had each other.

"I would do anything for you, Quinn, and you would do anything for me. That's the way it is with us," he said.

"I— Do you understand that I wanted him to be like you? Oh, God, Adam, Adam—I knew what I was doing! He's gone, and I'm to blame!"

"Quinn, don't cry anymore. Don't—I love you. It's going to be all right."

But they cried together, there in each other's arms.

He kept thinking about something she had said when she first came back.

"It's the price I had to pay."

Perhaps it was true, he thought. And they had both paid it—for being young and foolish, for loving too much. But it was not so bitter as it could have been. For the first time since Quinn had left all those years ago, that dark emptiness in him was gone. Their son *would* have a good life, a life he himself would have chosen for him if he could. And they would have a good life, too. They were two halves of one whole, and neither would ever be alone again.

He gently kissed her lips, tasting her tears and his own.

"Don't cry," he whispered again. "We're going to be all right." And he believed it with all his heart. They would go on, stronger, surer—together.

* * * * *

Bibliography

Other reading:

Hostetler, John A., *Amish Society*. Baltimore, Maryland: Johns Hopkins Press, 1963

Good, Phyllis Pellman and Rachel Thomas Pellman, *From Amish and Mennonite Kitchens*. Intercourse, Pennsylvania: Good Books, 1984

Pellman, Rachel Thomas and Kenneth Pellman, *The World of Amish Quilts*. Intercourse, Pennsylvania: Good Books, 1984

McGrath, William R., *Amish Folk Remedies for Plain and Fancy Ailments*. Freeport, Ohio: Freeport Press, Inc., 1985

Seitz, Ruth Hoover and Blair Seitz, *Amish Country*. New York, New York: Crescent Books, 1987

Television Programming:

The Amish—Not To Be Modern. Produced by Victoria Larimore and Michael Taylor. PBS and The Arts and Entertainment Network

American Tongues. A videotape by Andrew Kolker and Louis Alvarez. The Center for New American Media. The Arts and Entertainment Network

If *YOU* enjoyed this book,
your daughter may enjoy

Keepsake

Romances from

CROSSWINDS

Keepsake is a series of tender, funny, down-to-earth romances for younger teens.

The simple boy-meets-girl romances have lively and believable characters, lots of action and romantic situations with which teens can identify.

Available now wherever books are sold.

ADULT-I

Silhouette Desire ®

CHILDREN OF DESTINY

A trilogy by Ann Major

Three power-packed tales of irresistible passion
and undeniable fate created by Ann Major to
wrap your heart in a legacy of love.

PASSION'S CHILD — September

Years ago, Nick Browning nearly destroyed
Amy's life, but now that the child of his
passion—the child of her heart—was in danger,
Nick was the only one she could trust....

DESTINY'S CHILD — October

Cattle baron Jeb Jackson thought he owned
everything and everyone on his ranch, but fiery
Megan MacKay's destiny was to prove him wrong!

NIGHT CHILD — November

When little Julia Jackson was kidnapped, young
Kirk MacKay blamed himself. Twenty years later,
he found her...and discovered that love could
shine through even the darkest of nights.

To order any of Ann Major's thrilling Children of Destiny, send your name, address and zip or postal code, along with a check or money order for $2.50 for
each book ordered, plus 75¢ postage and handling, payable to Silhouette Reader
Service to:

In Canada	In U.S.A.
P.O. Box 609	901 Fuhrmann Blvd.
Fort Erie, Ontario	Box 1396
L2A 5X3	Buffalo, NY 14269-1396

Please specify book title with your order.

SD 457

Available now

Silhouette Classics

You asked for them, and now they're here, in a delightful collection. The best books from the past—the ones you loved and the ones you missed—specially selected for you from Silhouette Special Edition and Silhouette Intimate Moments novels.

Every month, join us for two exquisite love stories from your favorite authors, guaranteed to enchant romance readers everywhere.

You'll savor every page of these *Classic* novels, all of them written by such bestselling authors as:

**Kristin James • Nora Roberts • Parris Afton Bonds
Brooke Hastings • Linda Howard • Linda Shaw
Diana Palmer • Dixie Browning • Stephanie James**

Silhouette Classics
Don't miss the best this time around!

SCLG-1R

Silhouette Special Edition

COMING NEXT MONTH

#493 PROOF POSITIVE—Tracy Sinclair
Tough divorce lawyer Kylie O'Connor privately yearned for a happy marriage and bouncing babies. But cynical Adam Ridgeway wasn't offering either, and Kylie's secret couldn't keep for long....

#494 NAVY WIFE—Debbie Macomber
Navy officer Rush Callaghan placed duty above all else. His ship was his home, the sea his true love. Could vulnerable Lindy Kyle prove herself the perfect first mate?

#495 IN HONOR'S SHADOW—Lisa Jackson
Years had passed since young Brenna coveted her sister's boyfriend. But despite recently widowed Warren's advances, Brenna feared some things never changed, and she'd forever be in Honor's shadow.

#496 HEALING SYMPATHY—Gina Ferris
Ex-cop Quinn Gallagher didn't need anyone. Yet sympathetic Laura Sutherland saw suffering in his eyes—and her heart ached. She'd risk rejection if her love could heal his pain.

#497 DIAMOND MOODS—Maggi Charles
Marta thought she was over Josh Smith. But now the twinkling of another man's diamond on her finger seemed mocking...when the fire in her soul burned for Josh alone.

#498 A CHARMED LIFE—Anne Lacey
Sunburned and snakebitten, reckless Ross Stanton needed a physician's care. Cautious Dr. Tessa Fitzgerald was appalled by the death-defying rogue, but while reprimanding Ross, she began feeling lovesick herself!

AVAILABLE THIS MONTH:

Silhouette Intimate Moments

JOIN BESTSELLING AUTHOR EMILIE RICHARDS AND SET YOUR COURSE FOR NEW ZEALAND

This month Silhouette Intimate Moments brings you what no other romance line has—Book Two of Emilie Richards's exciting mini-series Tales of the Pacific. In SMOKE SCREEN Paige Duvall leaves Hawaii behind and journeys to New Zealand, where she unravels the secret of her past and meets Adam Tomoana, the man who holds the key to her future.

In future months look for the other volumes in this exciting series: RAINBOW FIRE (February 1989) and OUT OF THE ASHES (May 1989). They'll be coming your way only from Silhouette Intimate Moments.

If you missed Book One of Tales of the Pacific, FROM GLOWING EMBERS (IM #249), you can order it by sending your name, address and zip or postal code, along with a check or money order for $2.75 for each book ordered, plus 75¢ postage and handling, payable to Silhouette Reader Service to:

In Canada	In U.S.A.
P.O. Box 609	901 Fuhrmann Blvd.
Fort Erie, Ontario	P.O. Box 1396
L2A 5X3	Buffalo, NY 14269-1396

Please specify book title with your order.

IM261